MIDNIGHT CAVALIER

traveling love's mysterious pathways

Tony Kane

CONTENTS

1

The warmth of his hand shocked Janet Fellows at first. "It's just from dancing." She told herself, fighting back the idea that he could be attracted to her. A little self-consciously she lifted her face and looked into the bright blue eyes of Oliver Block. The twinkle within them and the small smirk twitching at the corners of his mouth delighted her. A sigh fought hard to escape from her lips. Janet suppressed it; afraid it would reflect the fact that her heart was pounding hard inside her chest.

The twenty-four-year-old school teacher from Harmony, Ohio was transfixed on the young man dancing with her. She had never been the object of attention before, and it sent a warm, exciting glow throughout her body. How could she, the old maid of Harmony, and one of the oldest dancers in the room be the prize this man was seeking? She debated with herself, but he was dancing with her. He had asked her not one of the younger women. It just had to be Litchfield, Janet told herself. It just had to be the place.

There was something in the air. She had felt it the second she had stepped off the red two-tiered coach in Litchfield Center. The atmosphere was statically alive with excitement and sexual electricity. Spring had sprung in this part of western Connecticut. It had not even started when she had left from her home in northern Ohio. The reality of being so far from her home, and being surrounded by the giddy laughter of other young ladies making the same journey, had only heightened the emotional upswing she felt as she disembarked that first day.

At six foot, dark haired Oliver Block had been the tallest among the handsome young men serving as a welcoming committee from the Tapping Reeve Law School. He had smiled at her then as well, tipped his brown felt short top hat and even offered his arm to help her navigate the coach steps. Janet Fellow's heart had fluttered that day as well. Now a week later she stood among the shy students at Sarah Pierce's Litchfield Female Academy waiting to be asked to dance.

Oliver propositioned her with a nod and a glance toward the dance floor. "Was it proper?" She asked herself and looked into the eyes of the other young ladies waiting their turn to dance.

There were several who were envious, and their eyes showed red. Some of the young ladies' faces showed disappointed with the idea that they were not the chosen ones, or that she, the old maid, might be prettier than them. A few even maintained that standoffish façade Academy students held toward the ex-soldier from Sharon, Connecticut.

Only one of the young ladies standing in the group seemed happy for Janet. That was Abigail Stuart. The sixteen-year-old from South Carolina was also one of Janet's roommates at the Academy. She smiled over at the older student and nodded encouragement. She understood what it was like for Janet to come out of her shell as a matron teacher.

In Harmony, any social interaction with men was frown upon, and could lead to dismissal. Janet had seen it happened. Janet looked again at Oliver Block and knew if she walked out with him rumors would fly.

* * * * *

In barely a week's time at the nationally acclaimed female preparatory school, she had been informed all about the young men studying law just down the street at Tapping Reeve's Law

School.

Oliver Block was the topic of several conversations. "Stay away from him," was the warning she had received from the upperclassmen when she had mentioned his name that first day. "He flirts with all of us." They had warned. "He's not the type of man you ever want your name related to." There, the hint of what might be meant by his attention was left unsaid. The twenty-four-year-old Janet was a little confused but assumed it meant that he was only looking for the type of women who did not wish to be married.

She had learned in confidence from the same ladies who now had scornful looks on their faces that Oliver had been in the army. His appearance at Tapping Reeve's Law School was the "payment" for his withdrawing attention from a young lady of a well to do New York family. And the other students both male and female had an unenvied fear of him. No one trusted him with their secrets, feeling that he would easily share his knowledge for a few pieces of gold. Reputation was everything in 1820, and Oliver Block's reputation was dark. It would cast a shadow on all who stood near him.

James Baldwin Mathers, the name of another member of the welcoming committee was bantered about as well and almost as often. "Now there is a person you should align yourself with." The senior students assured her. "His family is very wealthy and respected in Maryland. He's going to be a top lawyer or governor someday."

James Baldwin Mathers had been assigned to carry Janet's baggage to the academy, and so had the opportunity to exchange friendly conversation with her that first day and since. It was customary for the female students to participate in a daily singing procession along the shared Common, also known as the Green, of Litchfield Center. They also took numerous promenades with classmates and even male escorts. A faint glimmer of attraction had appeared in James' voice each time they had greeted each other when passing in the center of Litchfield. But James had remained on the opposite side of the dance floor when he arrived at the tea today.

That thought played in her head, as Janet looked into the eyes of Oliver Block again. The request to dance came once more to those sensual twinkling blue eyes.

"Don't!" Her mind called to her feet as Oliver began to lead her away from the other young ladies waiting to dance. "Don't dance with him; your reputation will be forever ruined!" Her eyes scanned over Oliver's squared shoulders to the face of James Baldwin Mathers. Their eyes met, and a hint of shock filled his hazel eyes, or was it revulsion? Janet could not tell.

"By why had he not asked her?" her heart questioned. "If he was as friendly minded as he had proposed over the past week, why had he not crossed the dance floor just once in the past half hour?"

"I'll show him." Janet's ego thought. "If I dance with Mr. Block just once, maybe it will cause James to squirm. Maybe he will be shocked into asking me to dance."

Oliver's hand lightly tugged, pulling her toward the dance floor. "Only six months," a new small voice called to her from her heart. "Only six months and you'll be back in Harmony." She looked at the young man holding her hand, his blue eyes piercing into her soul. His smile warmed her. "Six months and no one will ever ask you to dance again." The voice came from her heart.

"But you're reputation?" Her head questioned. "You have to think." It was the voice of her mother, a conscious she had tried to remove from her head when she first arrived in Litchfield. She had only six months to enjoy this life and then it was back to Harmony and spinsterhood. The thoughts of her future life pained her. Janet took a deep breath remembering the small farming community in northern Ohio. She had only six months to live and discover the joys of life that all other women understood. She was not going to pass up the opportunities Litchfield was going to provide.

"This is your first assignment," her heart sounded like a teacher, "Jealousy." She again glanced over Oliver Block's shoulder catching James' eyes. Janet smiled at her mischief. "Why had the young man not asked you? Maybe he's shy or afraid. This dance will let you know." Janet licked her lips in anticipation of what she was not certain, but in anticipation of something.

After all the inner debate was over, she remembered that it was her first dance at Sarah Pierce's Female Academy. She was tired of waiting. In almost a half hour of proper ladylike patient waiting, she had not been asked by anyone to dance. She decided not to pass up this opportunity.

Boldly she accepted Oliver's invitation. Maintaining eye contact with James, she walked with Oliver toward the assembled dancers congregating in the center of the room. She also felt the eyes of several of the young ladies behind her stabbing her with contempt and envy. "If they're going to talk, I might as well enjoy the sin." She told herself. "After all, they already consider you an old maid. Let them gossip."

"But Oliver Block?" her mind questioned. "He's so mischievous." She could not finish the thought as Oliver stopped walking and turned toward her, pausing for the music to begin.

Janet looked down at the high polished floor, waxed and shined so that it glowed in the sunlight coming in through the ceiling to floor windows of the room. It was actually two rooms, divided by sliding walls that could be opened to allow for a large dancing surface. The woodwork was simple but still spoke of the wealth of the owners of the home, the Tallmadges of Connecticut. Janet was so impressed with her surroundings that her sensations were overwhelmed. She had never seen, felt, smelled or heard such wonders. She simply could not take it all in. So she decided just to focus on her dancing partner.

A dark blue wool suit coat with tails that extend down to his mid-calves covered Oliver's frame well. His shoulders were square, but Janet could tell he did not have any padding in his shoulders, unlike other dancers there that evening. The weight of the coat must have added to the heat he was feeling from the exercise of the dance. He had already danced twice with other women at the Academy. It had also been a warm April day outside and even hotter inside the first floor room. Janet caught a hint of cologne on Oliver, sweet cologne that was to mask the musk of horses and perspiration so commonly experienced when next to a man of the time.

Oliver's frock coat framed a white silken double-breasted vest that Janet Fellows knew had come from France on the last packet ship. This garment was left half unbuttoned so that it opened at the top to review a light blue ruffled shirt, also fresh from France. The white neckerchief knotted at his throat gave him an air of rakishness. Janet shook with delight knowing that the other ladies were staring at her, his latest dance partner. His polished knee-high black riding boots held a mirror-like sheen. They actually snapped as he walked her to their central location seconds before, but now they stood rigid waiting for the music to start. A slight hint of his white stockings peeked out between the top of the boots and the buckle of his matching blue pants.

Fashion was everything to the students at the two schools in Litchfield. It dictated social status and acceptance.

As Janet took in this fine figure of a man, she could sense Oliver's own eyes scanning her. They traced down the red ruffled ribbon line she had sewn the night before on the top of her only formal light white linen dress. The ribbon ran from her puffy right shoulder around her open bodice back to her puffy left shoulder. It was a flag of independence, something she would never have been allowed to wear in Harmony; the Puritan heritage from the town's original Connecticut settlers was still adamant. A matching ruffled kerchief strategically placed between them discreetly hid her firm pink breasts. It was the latest fashion from France; the other students had assured her. As was the fact that now only light cotton undergarments, a chemise and a soft cotton corset laced up the back, were worn underneath formal dresses instead of the rigid stay framed corset she had to wear in Ohio. Without these substantial supporting garments, she almost felt naked. But the freedom of movement and breathing was tremendous to her, making her feel more content with her womanhood. Her breasts suddenly thrust into public view did not embarrass her, but instead filled her with pride because of their shape that flattered the rest of her figure.

She felt Oliver's eyes rest for a moment on that covering kerchief, and the heat he had sparked inside her, roared right into the very center of her breast. To be held tight in his arms became her desire. To kiss, just once that provocative mouth, now stretched into a full smile, became her obsession. Only once before, had she been kissed. She recalled and again licked her lips, this time, more to heighten the memory than in anticipation. That kiss had come when she was an adolescent, a scared, surprised adolescent.

"Why are you remembering that?" She asked herself and looked to the ground, afraid that her eyes showed her thoughts. A burning came to her cheeks as she blushed remembering the tender, nearly frighten, kiss a soldier had tickled across her lips so long ago. Breathing deep, she regained control of her thoughts and looked again at Oliver. His lips formed an impish smile, and she could not help but wonder what taste would come with a kiss.

"God," she prayed. "Why do you tempt me so?" She wanted to rub the burning from her cheeks for she knew they were redder than they should have been. The whole gathering would know she was thinking naughty thoughts, but just then, the fiddler struck up the tune; <u>Sunday Promenade</u> and the dancers began to circle the floor. The music allowed her to focus on the dance, not her partner, and for a moment, her mind was free enough to marvel at how she had come to be in the Tallmadge's home the center of attention of two young, handsome men.

Janet Fellows had come to the small hamlet of Litchfield, Connecticut from Harmony, Ohio to study at Sarah Pierce's Litchfield Female Academy. The town of Harmony had offered her the tuition in barter for her continuation as the teacher in the local one-room school. She had a six-month leave of absence, basically in exchange for the remainder of her life.

The twenty-four-year-old schoolteacher had long ago accepted the fact that she was to be unmarried her whole life. Not a single man in the Harmony area had ventured a smile at her let alone a kind greeting beyond politeness. But here at the Academy's mandatory tea parties and social dances, she could and would draw the attention of several handsome men. The delightful thought teased her as the dance slowly progressed across the hardwood floor, well accustomed to such weekly entertainments.

The dancing pair turned the corner of the promenade march and skipped danced back down the long line of previous lead couples. As they danced down the middle of the male and female lines, Oliver was required to take both of Janet's hands in his. Once again the warmth of his touch shook her with desire. Her breast barely contained within the bodice of the light summer dress, bounced with each step. Janet could feel Oliver's eyes fixed on her cleavage. A smile burned on her face, not just because of the joy in her heart at dancing. It was wonderful to be the focus of a young man's desire. Her heart skipped to that thought and the rhythm of the music.

"Oh, the things I'll write tonight." She thought of her diary, and closed her eyes, allowing her desires to spin pictures in her head.

Sarah Pierce's Female Academy in Litchfield was one of the country's most prestigious schools for young ladies. It was established in the western Connecticut town in the late 1700's at about the same time that Tapping Reeve established his law school in the same community. This school was the nation's first law school and soon gathered the finest young men in the country to its door. Where there were young men and women, love was soon to follow. Litchfield soon became the cradle from which many of the nation's leading families were born.

Reaching the end of the parted line, Oliver had to release his hold on Janet's hands. The dancers stepped back opening the lane for the next couple skipping down the lane and side-stepped toward the front of the dance.

Janet's heart momentary panicked. "What if the music stopped? What if the dance ended too soon, and Oliver did not take her hand again?" But her mind knew the truth; the couple still had to corner off with three other couples, and then promenade again down the line until they were the head couple at least once. The panic subsided, as she met Oliver's eyes again. They reflected back his attention to her face. She blushed.

"How did all this happen?" She questioned herself. "How did you become so lucky?"

* * * * *

Janet had been born in Harmony, Ohio. She was the sixth of eight children. Her parents had migrated to the fire lands after the British had burned their home in New London, Connecticut during the Revolutionary War. Ohio at the time had been part of the Connecticut land grants and many from the Nutmeg state had moved to the frontier looking for easier farming and prosperity. Janet's parents were prosperous enough to provide her five brothers with homes and farms, but the girls had no dowries. Her two sisters had found poor farmers to share their lives with, but for her, that basic pleasure was denied.

Instead, her ability as a scholar was soon the talk of the town. Barely out of grammar school herself, Janet replaced her own teacher, who had become pregnant but unmarried. Fifteen-year-old Janet watched as the rural community drove her seventeen-year-old former teacher and friend Luella Bates out of town in disgrace.

Town folks had witnessed Luella spending time with a member of the 1812 War army that had marched through northern Ohio on its way to remove the western lands of Indians and British soldiers. This group would be the same army that would invade Canada under General William Harrison. Members had also served under Harrison at the battle of Tippecanoe just a year before.

A burning hatred filled Janet at the treatment of the young teacher. It was not because of the teacher's behavior. The young men in uniform had also infatuated Janet. But instead, the hatred rooted itself in her heart toward the prejudice of the founding fathers. Many of them had been the fathers of bastard children conceived well before they had married their wives. It was common on the frontier at this time to hear the old saying "the first baby can come at any time. The rest take nine months."

Harmony being what it was, a small farming community, it was not a Mecca for handsome young men. Once the teacher, Janet found few men willing to court her for fear of her intelligence. So Janet devoted herself to her school, and her pupils. Now at twenty-four, the community felt it should honor her for all her years of devotion. They unanimously agreed to send her to Litchfield Female Academy. Many townspeople noted that though Janet matured quickly, she did lack a formal education that would help the community youngsters in the long run. The school in Litchfield had a superior reputation and its location in the town founders' home state sealed the deal.

* * * * *

Three other couples joined with Oliver and Janet and formed a square as the dance continued. First, the opposite couples bowed and promenaded together in a small circle, and then the diagonal couples repeated the same steps. Finally, all four of the couples circled their little square. Each time that Oliver's body came near, Janet's heart stopped and the obsession he had started with his first touch, tickled her breasts.

When he held her waist and arm as they promenaded around the small circle of their group, she had allowed her eyes to close. The strength of his arm around her and the tenderness of his touch blindly leading her twisted a desire in her stomach, and a rush of heat filled her body. Never had anyone touched her like that. She almost melted to the floor longing that the small dance within the dance would not end.

But once again the fiddler struck up the opening chords of the song. The couples stepped back into two lines their hands extended over the middle their fingers barely touching. Turning to the head of the dance floor, they dropped their hands and again promenaded down the long line until the new head couple turned the corner to skip down the lane formed by the dancers.

Janet ventured a peek out of the corner of her eye at the calves of Oliver covered by his black boots. She did notice that his thigh muscles were well defined underneath his tight blue suit pants, symbolizing his prowess as a horseman. A fever wave crossed over her face, as she blushed at the thought of them riding more than a horse.

"My God, Janet," her mind scolded her, "You are being so wicked tonight." She diverted her eyes quickly back to the dancer in front of her as they progressed down the line. The woman was dressed similarly to Janet in a light high waist dress; hers was green, with enlarged or stuffed shoulders. Janet also knew that the dancer would have had a high white front or poke bonnet waiting for her to put on after the dance to cover her hair bun. The bonnet was something Janet did not like, and she was relieved when others also removed their bonnets to dance. She was accustomed to wearing her hair loose, or pulled back, without a bonnet.

Reaching the corner, she bowed to her partner took his two hands, and skipped danced up the middle. Once again his blue eyes twinkled at her, and she fought back another sigh. She closed her eyes forgetting all the people around her and concentrated on the warm touch of Oliver's hands. Her heart beat with the rhythm of the music and her thoughts channeled in on the dance steps that Oliver was so gently leading her through.

* * * * *

Using her hand fan, Janet fanned her face once more to help cool down after the dance. Her heart was still all a flustered. She could not help but look in his direction. "You are acting like a little lovesick teenager," the teacher scolded herself. "Stop that; others will see you," she told herself. But the joy at being in the same room as Oliver Black was just too powerful for her logical mind to overrule.

The dance had not lasted all night as she had hoped so many times during its duration. The fiddle music reached an ending and her partner had unfortunately left her on the side of the room yet again, with the other academy students. Oliver then crossed back to the gentleman's side where he was once more surveying the young ladies in attendance.

The blue eyes of the handsome law student from Connecticut looked over to her a second time. His smile sailed across the room and touched her heart. A burning tickle raced across Janet's face, and she knew she was blushing. A giggle behind her told her that some of the other students at the female academy had noticed her infatuation.

Forcing her eyes to look away, she studied the hard wood floor of the large room. The tea was in the Tallmadge home of Litchfield. The family was one of the wealthiest in the community. They had gained their money through a China trading company that imported and exported around the world. Their fame, however, came from their service in the Revolutionary War. It was a Litchfield Tallmadge who escorted Major Andre to his death. It had been a Litchfield Tallmadge who was with Washington at Trenton, Valley Forge, and Yorktown. It was also a Litchfield Tallmadge who helped the new nation support itself in the years after the war.

Their home, located just off the Green, was a monster of a mansion even in 1820. It contained all the latest modern connivances. One of the most impressive features, however, was the large dining room that could be made even grander by the opening of sliding walls that separated it from the front parlor. This expanded space was the site of the tea and dance.

Janet eyed the floor for a mere few seconds before finding her glance focused again on Oliver Block. This time, his face was turned from her, and his wavy brown hair met her vision. It was neatly trimmed, squared to the nap of his neck, and her fingers called out to run through his locks. The thought sent another flutter to her heart. A warm sensation followed that crawled throughout her body and came to rest in her breast.

She sighed again, fighting hard not show her emotions. But inside she knew all the other girls were looking right at her.

"Miss Fellows," a deep voice came awkwardly slow to her ears. "May I have the privilege?" Janet turned to the sound and found James Baldwin Mathers standing next to her. His hazel eyes begged forgiveness, while his friendly smile enticed her.

"It worked," she told herself. A shiver of triumph shook her. "Jealousy was an incredible weapon in the war of love." She had known that dancing with Oliver Black would cause the other to claim a similar prize. Now he stood there his hand outstretched, palm up in anticipation of her acceptance.

James was a handsome man. His brown hair and green eyes complemented his square-jawed face. Like Oliver he also had a dark suit coat on without padded shoulders, his was black not blue, with tails that played at his mid-calves. It was the style of the early 1800s. His vest also parted at the mid-chest area revealing a white shirt with fewer ruffles, but a like blue neckerchief showed a little vanity. He also had a pair of riding boots, but they stopped below the knee, showing more stocking. They were not as polished, and Janet wondered if they were for show, more than actual riding. She knew that Oliver was a well-respected horseman, but that label never graced James in any of her conversations about Mr. Mathers.

James' matching breaches, like Oliver's, were tight and showed off his well-developed leg muscles. His were more slender than Oliver's, and Janet was fascinated. A sensual thought raced through her mind, and a coy smile crossed her face, which she quickly rubbed off.

"What if I said no?" The idea rocketed through Janet bringing another smile to her face. James misunderstood that smile and nodded to her.

"Thank you, Miss Fellows." He stepped closer and Janet did not have the heart to say no. They walked to the center of the room, just as she had done minutes before with Oliver. Once more she looked past her partner to the faces of the other female students. This time instead of disgust or contempt on their faces, there was only envy.

* * * * *

"Well you made a nice gesture," James Baldwin Mathers looked into her eyes later that afternoon. "No one else would have allowed that man to be their dance partner for more than one dance." The two were sharing tea at the end table of the gathering. The tables had been situated across from the dance floor after the fiddler had finished nearly two hours of providing dances. The ladies of Mrs. Pierce's school then became the hostesses of tea. Once all the tables had been set, and tea and delights served to the men, the ladies were allowed to join the tables. James had requested that she sit next to him, beating Oliver's invitation by a few seconds only.

The look in James' piercing green eyes did not hint at his true feelings. Janet could not tell if James was sarcastic or merely reprimanding. "He has a reputation for," James bit his tongue in thought, "for finding young ladies who share more than polite conversation." Janet blushed. "Forgive me," James was equally embarrassed. "But one should always know your position and that of your noble foe." He addressed himself as if he was already a member of the legal bar.

Janet looked up from the floor where her eyes had modestly fallen.

"I guess it is your frontier manners that showed." He forced a smile on his face, which his green eyes contradicted. "I'm sure out there they do not have as structured a society as we maintain here." He looked over at the tea setting. "Do you hold any social teas even?" His question came with the genuine inquisition.

"No, we're too busy killing Indians, to correctly set up a bone china tea service." She almost barked out. But instead, she answered that her community was like an early New England town, where the farmlands isolated neighbors. "Special occasions and Sunday church gatherings, however, were as lively as any tea here." She held James' eye to stress the point that she was not as rustic as he apparently thought.

"I meant no disrespect." Embarrassed he quickly looked down to the ground. "I was just aware that you are new here, and the rumor mill is very active." He looked back at her. "Already I can hear the gossip birds singing about the long conversation we are having now. Their songs could easily twist it into a proposal of marriage." He sipped his tea, to regain control of his tongue. "Forgive me if I speak out of turn or inappropriately. But I have been the victim already of a false accusation." He looked over his shoulder as if to check that no one was eavesdropping. "There is a group of young ladies who come here only to become brides. I fear that your behavior at this social could have the other ladies place you into the category." He paused, like a good lawyer, allowing the statement to register in Janet's heart. Finishing his tea he carefully placed the cup on the saucer, so that it did not click. "I am only interested in your reputation currently. Without prejudice, allow me to be your conscience, your social guide while you adjust to this community." He locked his hazel eyes on to Janet's. "There are so many who would venture to stab you in the back while smiling to your face. Beware." He turned away and helped himself to an apple Danish that the students had prepared at the female academy.

Janet took the opportunity to check the teapot. Noting that it was empty, she excused herself and walked to the kitchen. For the first time since she arrived at Litchfield, the excitement vanished. A nagging fear crept into her; similar to the one she felt whenever the town leaders in Harmony observed her classroom.

******

2

Closing her brown eyes, Janet paused as she walked up Litchfield's North Street from the Tallmadge Manson to the white-washed academy building. The warm sun was just beginning to settle in the west, causing the heat of the spring day to die slowly. But the warmth of Oliver's hand in hers played again in her memory. The strange sensation of fear that had come over her near the end of the tea vanished with the memory. A smile etched on her face that hurt the corners of her mouth. She shook her head in delight. Her bonnet almost shook independently, and she stopped to tighten the lace ribbon bow under her chin that held it to her head.

Why this man's attention played so solidly on her heart's strings, she did not know. But he did, and she enjoyed every second of the particular song. There was something about him, something that she could not quite put her finger on. "I think you're just excited about being here." Her mind tried to rationalize the sensations for her. "Oliver could be almost anyone, and you would feel the same way." The cynical voice spoke from years of disappointment and loneliness.

Then the memory of James' hand holding her hand came to her mind. His dance had been a short formal waltz and involved more direct contact. James' touch had been hesitant at first but soon relaxed, as the dance demanded more of his concentration. Their eyes danced with each other as much as did their bodies. Janet noticed as they glided around the floor that his glance rarely left her face. It was pleasant being inside his embrace, one arm around her waist and the other cupping her lead hand. His steps were light to the music, and they skated around the floor with little effort. She fell completely under his command, something that she had not done before.

Now walking home in the evening light, she could still feel the touch of James' hand on her back. The thought caused her breast to tingle with desire. "Maybe that voice is right," she said to herself. "Maybe I'm just excited to be here, and anyone would cause this reaction."

Janet adjusted the knitted yellow wool shawl she had wrapped around her shoulders secretly craving that it was the arms of either Oliver or James wrapped around her. And she began to compare one to the other.

James was so majestic, so proper, but it was Oliver's touch that sent chills through her. His eyes had reflected a maturity that James was missing. He apparently had experienced things that neither James nor Janet could imagine. His manner was relaxed all the time, as if he was in complete control, and rivaled her command of the situation. His words came smooth and meaningful. His attention was on her, and what she wanted to say, unlike James, who appeared to be more self-centered in his conversation.

"But remember he was the one who warned you about Oliver's reputation." That voice in her head spoke. "He was the one who volunteered to protect you against the rumors that will undoubtedly fly."

"Yes, but Oliver was the one who seemed to be reading your mind." A little voice from her heart spoke for the first time. "He was the one whose stare stopped me." Again a smile hurt the corners of her mouth, and she tried to wipe it away. It would not be good for anyone to see the look she knew was on her face. "He was the one you really want to kiss. You just want to feel his whole body. To find out if it is as warm as his hands." She placed the palm of her hand against her cheek, pretending it was Oliver's open palm warm and tender against her face. She shook realizing that she was allowing herself to travel into a fantasy world. The world in which she might meet Ivanhoe, the book she had just finished reading or some other cavalier of her own creation.

"Stop that Janet," the voice in her head stated. "You are falling under an incantation that cannot be reversed without a lot of pain." She knew full well what would happen to her heart if she allowed the men of the law school to venture inside. Over the years she had maintained a secret locked inside of that organ, a secret love. The fact that no one in Harmony had attempted to break into her heart, had only allowed her secret desire to nest undisturbed, unconquered. It now was firmly fortified within, serving as a measure to compare any possible lover against. And Janet knew no one alive could measure up to that mythological figure in her heart.

"But Oliver is intriguing?" She thought and shook again. "He would come close. A horseman, a soldier, a confident companion, everything you wanted, when you were young." She shook her head in despair. "When you were young, not now," she repeated.

* * * * *

"Janet? Are you alright?" Abigail Stuart asked as she came alongside the schoolteacher. A strong smell of lavender met Janet's nose, and she instantly knew who was standing next to her. The younger girl was the daughter of a merchant in Charlestown, South Carolina. She had been sent to the Litchfield Female Academy because her aunt and her older sister had also attended the school. Her perfume water was the talk of the other students, for the youngster always worn it heavy. She sprinkled it not only on her body but also into her brush so that her hair smelled.

"I'm fine Abigail." Janet opened her eyes and nodded. "I was just lost in a memory." The younger student smiled, not sure what to say. She was only sixteen. Her figure, however, spoke of a maturity that was beyond the average sixteen-year-old. She wore a white cotton dress similar in cut to Janet's. It folded tightly from the top of the corset to her waistline, which was just below her ample breasts. The dress pleated out creating a curve to her figure that highlighted her hips. This design, made her figure more pleasing for men to view. Enlarged shoulders also added to the effect, and Janet noticed that Abigail received a lot of attention by the law students during the dance. Like Janet, Abigail's young firm round cleavage was also exposed in an open front, covered discreetly with a white-laced handkerchief, just as her mother had shown her to do down south. It had been Abigail's idea to place the red ribbon across Janet's front, to highlight her bodice, since her dress had a green lace ribbon sewn on in South Carolina. The two of them had spent the night sewing Janet's dress.

"I was just concerned because you-all had stopped here for so long." Abigail continued to explain when there was no need. "I have heard that some women after a dance are affected by a fever which can downright be powerful enough to kill you."

"I have a fever," Janet mused to herself. "But it's not one that'll kill me." The faces of Oliver and James flashed through her head and her smile burn her blushing cheeks. She looked into Abigail's green eyes and said out loud. "No fever, just a flush."

"I know," Abigail's eyes grew wide with excitement. "I feel it too. All those handsome young men were just fighting over us to dance with them." A small southern accent came through her animated words. "Lord I nearly swooned from all that attention." She waved a small hand fan over her face, to hide the blush that was on her cheeks. Abigail was very attractive. Her strawberry hair matched well with her green eyes. The small patches of crimson on her high cheekbones whenever she blushed hinted at innocence that any male would love to conquer.

"We were certainly the center of attention tonight." Janet flashed her eyes with delight.

"Well, at least you-all were." Abigail modestly added.

"Don't underestimate your impact." Janet continued, not willing to let a fellow woman downgrade herself in front of her. "I saw you charming a number of those law students." Red flashed across Abigail's face again. 'You don't have to be ashamed of your natural beauty. Your hair, your eyes both work like flames to a moth." Janet leaned into Abigail's ear as she took her right hand in hers. "And we know who the moths are." There was a lustful hoarseness to Janet's voice that surprised both women.

They giggled and holding each other's hands in friendship continued to walk the dirt pathway alongside the wide road toward the Academy. They both shared a room in the basement of the school with three other students. All five of them were new arrivals, but Janet was the oldest by far. They ranged in age from ten to twenty-four. The room consisted of one rope support bed, two pine four drawer dressers, a high back oak chair, small oak table and a pine nightstand to hold the washbasin and pitcher. This arrangement made it necessary for the five to become close friends or enemies swiftly. The five were lucky to find that they could tolerate each other and the week had passed quickly. Janet became the unofficial room mother because of her age.

"I thought that I was going to be the oldest," Abigail suddenly said, as if she had been reading Janet's mind. "I mean among the students." She looked over at the older student. "No disrespect. But I'm nearly an old maid in Charlestown." She smiled, bringing a glint to her hazel eyes. "What are you-all called in Ohio?"

"A matron teacher," Janet retorted, "and I'm proud of it." They shared a smile that eased any possible tension or hurt feelings between them. Janet had come to like Abigail almost instantly.

Abigail had a mouth that would just blurt out without thought when she was excited or when she tried to save face. Her slips of the tongue caused more embarrassment sometimes than Abigail's original statements. But her innocence was always present in her eyes, and you knew she did not mean any harm, no matter how insulting her words had been.

After a week of the acquaintance, Abigail vaguely reminded Janet of Luella Bates and her responsibility for the teacher's dismissal. This recognition of her former friend in Abigail was the first time in years that Janet had allowed herself to recall the long lost friend and the soldiers who came to Harmony in late 1812. The bitterness inside of her swelled as she knew things she still could not admit to being true concerning what happened to Luella. Looking over at the innocent Abigail shortly before the dance Janet vowed not to let anything similar happen to this girl from South Carolina.

"My aunt was thirteen when she came here, and my sister was fourteen." Abigail continued to babble on like other teenagers Janet had taught in school. The girl was not even looking at Janet but was instead looking down the road as she walked and talked. "I was kept by my mother at home. I think she just did not want to admit she was getting old. I was the baby in the family." She stopped and watched a flock of crows soared over their heads in the darkening sky. "It's amazing how many birds there are here." Janet followed Abigail's glance and agreed. The birds let out a cry that drowned out anything else Abigail might have added to her history.

When the crow caw had stopped, Janet ventured a question. "Why are you here?" Abigail stopped and looked her in the eye.

"Why to get a husband dear." She smiled that same girlish smile that had been flashing throughout the dance. "You see my father gambles a bit, and the need for additional cash has left certain other long-term items neglected." A tear started to come to Abigail's green eyes, but she brushed it away. "One can't have a state senator or even a senator's son without a dowry." She fought tears again. "And of course one can't live with a husband who is anything less than a senator if you're a Stuart of South Carolina." She looked away from Janet and breathed deep. "My sister is the proud wife of Samuel Calhoun of South Carolina. His cousin is John C. Calhoun the senator from our state. I'm sure you-all heard of him."

Janet had indeed. His name was one of the most well known in the country. Many of the leading men in Harmony felt that he would one day be president. Currently, he was among a group of leading senators and governmental officials known as the second generation. This group included Daniel Webster and John Quincy Adams.

"My sister met her husband while he was here studying law just like his cousin John C." Abigail continued.

Janet knew it was true. John C. Calhoun had been a student at the Tapping Reeve Law School. He was one of the many southern gentlemen who ventured to Litchfield, Connecticut to study law. Most of these Southern men returned with a family connection to the North.

"The Calhoun family is going to be one of the top families in the South if you listen to that Samuel talk. But he has a silver tongue, just what a good politician needs." She smiled again, the tears gone from her eyes. "Being so lucky with his first wager, my Daddy bet the house on me." She laughed out loud. "I can already hear my father using that line if I happen to marry a man who rises to the House of Representatives."

"Do you want to marry?" The words left Janet's lips without her thinking. She had accepted her fate for so long she did not even think about marriage.

"Of course silly what else is there for a respectable woman?" The words hung in the air like a slap in the face. Suddenly Abigail realized what she had just said. Her eyes nearly popped out of her head, as her hands covered her mouth in shock. "I'm so sorry," she stuttered and then turned her head away, the tears erupting. Without waiting, the sixteen-year-old ran off down the road.

Janet stood there for a minute watching the youngster run away. In her mind, the words formed that would answer Abigail's question about what else there was for a respectable woman. "Become an old maid." Tears blurred Janet's view. "Become an old maid." The words hammered into her heart opening an old wound. The pain of her future lonesomeness was very raw, despite the fact she had accepted the fact for so many years.

Wiping the tears away with a scented handkerchief, she recalled again the comradeship of the two men with whom she had danced. Their spirits were still so active in her heart, so viral. They continued to reach to her across the town, touching her desires yet again and tickling her heart into believing the words might not become reality. "Six months," Janet spoke to herself, "Six months and then." She did not finish the thought out loud.

* * * * *

Meanwhile heading south from the Tallmadge Mansion was James Baldwin Mathers. His pace was slow and reflective as he angled his dark felt hat just so on his head. His mind, at the exact same moment, was filled with the smile of Janet Fellows. His head still spun with the music of the dance, and the swirl of the waltz he had partnered with Janet. "She is just the right size." He pictured holding her again. "She's just the right height."

He had first seen her on the top step of the Albany coach. Her brown eyes had triggered an instant attraction, but then Oliver Block had moved in with his arm and escorting smile. James stopped his walk home from the dance and looked around the common area of the small Connecticut town. No one was within earshot. "I hate Oliver." James said out loud.

"Seconds after arriving, those poor girls were bombarded by the charms of that louse." James growled to himself. Once again he looked around the Common. Litchfield was typical of New England villages. The green common area had become surrounded by the market and professional buildings needed for the village people.

It reminded him also of the Common he had seen in Williamsburg, Virginia while he was a student at William and Mary College. The capital of Virginia had a large common area that the Governor's house faced. Other elegant homes of Williamsburg's wealthier families hugged the side of the green. James mused how the surrounding structures defined the New Englanders and Southerner's attitude toward money.

Litchfield in 1820 held a county courthouse and simple clapboard Congregational Meetinghouse right off the Common. Several merchants and tradesmen had built shops around the green area, but few houses and none of the wealthiest families lied directly off the Common. Four wide dirt roads also ventured forth from the Common, these headed in the four cardinal directions, north, south, east, and west. Their names derived from these compass points. This Common was the stopping place of coaches from all the four winds, allowing anyone to travel to Litchfield and its two excellent schools.

Nearly a year before, James had come up the South Road from the port in New Haven to begin his studies with Tapping Reeve. Other students had been there to greet his coach, as he had been present to greet Janet's coach as it stopped right in the middle of the large grassy area. Now, however, on this spring evening, only the buildings that framed the area were his companions. The sun was just below the horizon of the western group of buildings leaving shadows on the grassing plain before him. James traced the pattern of their rooftops with his eyes still fuming over Oliver Block.

"The bastard danced with her." He whispered afraid that the buildings would not keep that confidence. "He danced with her five times." He looked at his open hand to symbolize the number five on his fingers. Then shaking his head in disgust, he clinched his fists a number of times.

"Well, I'll not look the other way this time." James told the shadows. They knew the truth about his character and that of Oliver Block. They had seen the two over the past year of study: James' efforts to fulfill all the expectations of him set by his father, and Oliver's efforts to crumble these achievements. Though James could not prove it, he was sure that Oliver was behind the false accusations leveled against him.

Anger flared as James recalled the rumor that he was paying for other students' lecture notes. In Tapping Reeve's school, students were expected to listen to both Reeve and his assistant Judge James Gould lecture on the legal process in America. These lectures had to be transcribed by the students as they sat there. Often it was suggested that a professional scribe be brought into the room to capture the lectures for prosperity, but the two legal teachers refused permission. If you did not make a lecture, then it was impossible for you to obtain the notes unless you paid a fellow student. This frown on action is exactly what James' enemies at the school rumored. To gain a reputation for not caring enough to attend class was dreadful, and a black spot that James would not be able to overcome in the small world of Maryland law.

James Baldwin Mathers had come to the Connecticut law school after graduating top in his class from William and Mary in Virginia. His name was already well known among the people of Fredrick, Maryland where he lived. His father had been a state representative from the western district. His grandfather had served with distinction not only in the state senate but also as a member of the Senate under the Articles of Confederation.

His uncles and great-uncles had all served in the Armies of the Revolution and the War of 1812. He could not allow anything to darken the name of Mathers.

"If I had just the inkling of proof," James assured himself. "I would have challenged him." He quickly slapped the back of his right hand against his left's palm, as if he was striking the face of Oliver Block. James again looked around him. The law students frowned on talking of duels. Aaron Burr, the man who had killed the nationally respected Alexander Hamilton in a duel, was Tapping Reeve's brother-in-law. Dueling or even talking about dueling was avoided around the head of the school. The country still did not approve of Aaron Burr's shot.

But the southern gentleman inside of James Baldwin Mathers could not contain himself. "If only." He growled again the lion's voice coming from inside a kitten. "If only I could prove it, I'd have my satisfaction with Mr. Block on the field of honor."

Winds came up and cooled the heat that was building within the young man from Maryland. He resumed his walk toward the Oliver Wolcott home in which he boarded, with of all students, Mr. Block. He had seen firsthand the scars on the ex-soldier's chest as well as knew the skill the older man had with a sword and musket.

"But this time," James pleaded with himself. "This time, you will find the courage." There in the coming evening of late April, James Baldwin Mathers admitted to himself the truth. He was scared not of Block or any other student in Reeve's law school but instead of women. He found it the hardest thing to find words that flowed from his lips, instead of crossed-examined. For years he had concerned himself with proper behavior, manners, and appearance, but had forgotten any study of small talk and gaiety.

That was the center of his rivalry with Oliver Block. The Connecticut native was adept at talking, charming and dancing. He carried with him an aurora of adventure and mystery. What did

James have?

"Class." James answered his own question. "I have class, breeding, and education." He hunted his brain for a method of gaining the attention of Janet Fellows. He wanted her attention, if for no other reason than to be one better than Oliver Block. James would have to erase the dances Janet and Oliver had shared from her memory and replace them with something centered on him so that she would be totally focused on James Baldwin Mathers. He smiled at his hope and then asked. "Replace them with what?"

Poetry, the word hung in his mind for a second, poetry. Like many southern men of the time, he considered himself a "Renaissance Man" skilled in several of the fine arts. In his case writing poetry was one of his arts. "That's it," he smiled to himself. "Some small ditty that reflected Janet's brown eyes," he said out loud and again pictured the young woman in his arms as he danced with her that afternoon. His hands quivered with excitement at the memory. He had held her, face to face, while Oliver only managed to do group dances. "I know what color her eyes are! I wonder if Oliver does?" He rubbed his hands together in excitement. The warmth caused by the friction eased some of the shakings he was experiencing. "I held her." He closed his eyes and allowed his mind to drift back in time.

Once more he steadied her frame as they glided around the floor to the waltz. Her deep brown eyes stared at him, reflecting the smile he had on his face. Smoothly, effortlessly he escorted her to the music. The softness of her dress and the heat of her body came to his backhand. Through the linen fabric, he had felt her warmth. He had felt her breath, and matched it with his own breathing. Joined in just this one activity, James had floated in a dream world of possibilities.

"Oh to write this down, now," he spoke softly to himself. "What to say, the words will have to capture that flow of the music and the lightness of her steps, but more importantly, it must represent the uncertainty that we both felt in each other's arms." He quickened his pace, hoping to reach his room while the ideas were fresh in his mind.

Excellent penmanship was a pride of James. And his poetry work would be the finest manuscript he could muster. He had dabbled with a few themes when he first sat down to compose, but the idea of his eyes linked to Janet's from across the dance floor had sparked the most artistic flair. Sitting for a few minutes in silence at his writing table, he pictured Janet, not only at the dance but the first time he had seen her. Her large brown eyes blazed into his thoughts, and he shook with an unexpected longing.

His pondering drew deeper into his memories of Janet. After taking her to the academy that first day, he had noticed her several times as the girls of the school made their daily promenade around the Litchfield Common. It was at this parade that students from the law school were permitted to talk to their Litchfield Female Academy peers. Of course one had to have a proper introduction and chaperon, this James succeeded in obtaining when Tapping Reeve himself, presented James to Janet on the second day of her stay. James always made sure his actions were well within the social norms. And he found himself exchanging greetings with the new Ohio student several times in the week she had been at the school.

All of these meetings now played in his poetic head, stirring feelings together like a witch's brew. The caldron was his heart, an innocent heart suddenly bombarded with shivers of passionate lust and delight. His right hand visibly shook, and a trembling raced through him. He found himself pushing his heart further and further into an abyss of his own creation.

Like a good artist he was falling in love so that he could experience the sensations first hand, only then would he be able to suffer them, envision them and detail them in words. He allowed Janet's brown eyes to grow in his head, becoming like a cool summer pond waiting for him to dive in. The image kept drawing him deeper and deeper into the fantasy, until he lost all idea, all consciousness that he was causing the artistic falling, and his pure heart slipped in the undertow.

The poetic words came then, flowing forth unchecked from his mind through the quill pen onto the paper. Black ink splattered off the tip of the pen onto his white linen shirt, but he did not care, he was well within his muse, as a writer of the time had often said. James alliterated off of the poem's title.

From Across the Room

Faint allusions

Filter through

Filling hopeful

Fanciful dreams

For eternity.

From across the room

I watch you.

James reread the poem, and his heart beat harder in his chest. "Could it be," he questioned himself. "Could it be that you have found someone that you are truly interested in?" The question hung in his head, but his heart skipped as an excited, filled shiver surrounded him.

Janet's tender red lips appeared in his mind's eye. He had taken the time to notice how full her lips were and imagined kissing them. Their sweet wet appeal caused him to unconsciously lick his own lips in anticipation of that first kiss.

Closing his eyes he floated into a daydream of Janet in his arms. Her hot breathe tickling his neck as he held her close for a long embrace. Then stepping back, his eye roamed over her luscious body, seeing once again the curve of her well-formed breast hidden by the red handkerchief. A passion in his groin made itself known, and he soared into a world he had not known existed in his life, his naive heart leading the way.

Her voice came to his ear once more. Her intelligence rivaled many of his fellow law students, and her bashful tone delighted his heart causing a smile to burn on his face.

Once more he took up his quill pen and dipped it in the India ink.

I have seen you.

He wrote as a new title completely under the spell of his virgin heart.

I have seen you for days - weeks - months
From across the room.
I have watched you for days - weeks - months
From across the universe.

But it was when I started talking, talking, talking to you
That I started falling, falling, falling in love with you.

I had considered you for days - weeks - months
From across the room.
I had noticed you for days - weeks - months
From across the universe.

But it was when I started talking, talking, talking to you
That I started falling, falling, falling in love with you.

Conversing with you.

Sharing wit with you

Debating with you

Opened mind to mind - soul to soul,

Creating perceptions

Bridging thoughts

Marrying hearts.

I had kissed you for days - weeks - months

From across the room.

I had embraced you for days - weeks - months

From across the universe.

But it was when I started talking, talking, talking to you.

That I started falling, falling, falling in love with you.

Putting the pen down, his eyes roamed the paper. The words startled him at first. Was he really feeling that emotion so prevalent in poetry, or had he simply found the word that would make the writing meaning full? His heart skipped a beat and he knew. His body shook again with excitement.

Then sadness covered him. He had never been able to approach other women. He had never been one to express his feelings in the open. James Baldwin Mathers was the perfect hermit. He was an oyster closed around that precious jewel called love.

"Janet," his voice filled his small attic room, "Janet." Tears blurred his eyes for a moment, the emotions so high, waiting to burst from within him. Words failed him, and he doubted his resolve to share the two poems he had written.

"Maybe it's too soon." He justified his new stance. "Maybe I'm just a blind writer, seeing things that are not there." He thought of Janet again and recalled her smiling at him. Her dark brown eyes twinkled with pleasure as they danced together. Her left hand tenderly squeezed back in answer to his own squeeze of disbelief that he was holding her on the dance floor. She seemed to realize that he was just as much a novice as she appeared.

The poems words echoed again in his head. Goose bumps raced across his body as he admitted what his mind wanted his heart to beat out loud. He was falling in love. "I had watched you for days - weeks - months from across the universe." The words clearly stated what he was feeling. He had met Janet Fellow only one week earlier, but he had known her for all his life.

******

3

The bright spring moonlight danced through the window creating eerie shadows in Oliver Block's attic room. Because of the abundance of natural light Oliver reached over and snuffed out the candle he maintained for illumination. The moon beams bounced off of the slanted exposed framing of the roof's trust system helping to create these unique shadows. Dust from the old wooden frame members filtered through the air adding a hazy appearance. Looking at it Oliver slipped gently into a dream world.

Her radiant smile reached out of his mind and triggered an unfulfilled longing he had lived with for too many years. In his mind, he reached out and touched her silky smiling cheek as he had done for so many years. Then he shared a soft tender kiss on her sweet lips. Coaxing with his lips, he explored her wet welcoming mouth, as only a well-seasoned lover knows how. She tipped her head back and kissed with her full lips, hard and firm.

Oliver sitting in the Litchfield attic could still taste that long ago kiss on his dry lips.

Breathing deep, he brought himself back to reality. He was on the turn rope bed he rented, dressed in just his shirt and breaches. The framework of the roof surrounded him. The bark of the tree remained on some of the beams, as well as the natural roundness. By looking in the unfinished attic, one could clearly see the original classic post and beam construction. Only later in time, as the Litchfield area became more prosperous, did the owners of this house modify and add to the original central chimney designed home.

"Corporal," The voice of Lieutenant Michael Premont the Third called down from his brain. "We need to have the tent spotless." A knowing smile came to the officer's face. "There will be company here tonight! Yes, sir, Oliver, it is a company more important than any general." The excitement in his eyes still shined years later in the mind of Oliver as he remembered that night from Litchfield. Oliver focused again on the roof over his head. The night was the worst time for him.

This central chimney design was common among the houses in Litchfield; he focused all his attention on the framework overhead. So it was, for most of the houses, Oliver had visited in his year in Litchfield. These original structures were modified, however, as wealth came to the small community in western Connecticut. As with clothing fashion, the residents tried to remain up to date with their architectural designs. The Tallmadge mansion was a prime example, with its enlargeable room, and high windows it showed off the owners desire to scream to the world that America was growing strong and talented. The fact that both Sarah Pierce's and Tapping Reeve's schools were in this small town added more viewers to the showcase constructed by the Tallmadges and others.

Oliver's mind slipped again, and he could not help but think of his own family's farm in Sharon. It too had originally been a small dwelling that grew with the family, much like the house he was staying in, in Litchfield. But he did not think that his parents ever put on airs like some of the students and residents in Litchfield. He knew that his soul would not let him be a fraud. He was merely a horse trainer who happened to be allowed to attend law school. That could be why he was outside of the student's society and confidence. He did not belong there, but it did not bother him. He was there not for himself but others, others that couldn't be there.

*****

Oliver shook his head of the memories he knew would be coming back. They always did when he thought about the others. They were not sad memories, but instead happy-go-lucky memories. But because of who was in them, depression would follow. No one from the visions was left. Instead, Oliver tried to focus his attention on other matters, any question that would keep his mind busy and filled.

Now he looked at the shadows as he lay in bed. His current thoughts provided a wall, blocking his memories. He did not even want to see that haunting sweet smile that had haunted his thoughts for the past eight years. Instead, he forced himself to think of only the present.

Oliver noted to himself that he was one of the luckiest law students. He had managed to arrange a bed in the ex-home of Connecticut Governor Oliver Wolcott Junior, the house was currently owned by the governor's brother Frederick, but was still called the old Governor's house. This house was the same home that Governor Wolcott's father, of the same name, had owned. Here the future signer of the Declaration of Independence had helped plan out the state's revolution against King George III. In the backyard of this large white house in Litchfield, a large brass statue of King George dragged down from its pedestal in New York City, had been melted down into bullets for the cause.

The best part of this location was that the small brown single room law school was almost across the street from the Wolcott house. The home was also the scene of several important socials and teas not only with the young ladies from the Female Academy but also with members of the Connecticut political and financial world.

The current Governor Wolcott and his brother Fredrick had made their money through investments in woolen mills. Oliver Junior had also served as Secretary of the Treasury for President Jefferson. As Secretary, he had supported Eli Whitney's scheme of making firearms with interchangeable parts. The concept proved successful not only in the firearms industry but also in several mills that the two brothers owned.

Oliver's effort to brush aside the past was working. He continued to lay on his bed located next to the chimney for warmth, looking at the shadows, recalling the day. It was his nature to reflect on just the current day and all that had happened, as he struggled to rest for the night. Sometimes sleep would not come while he was indoors, and he reverted to his service days seeking solitude with the horses of the Governor's stable, still maintained at the old family's home, since the younger Governor Wolcott's residence was just down South Street from his father's house. As part of his rental agreement, he took care of the horses along with the Governor's groom Benjamin Arts. Arts often found Oliver in the stables at all hours of the day. There were nights when he even slept in the stables. This night was not one of them, though his mind was too worked up for resting because the experience he had at the latest dance.

"Janet Fellows," the name crept across his lips as filled the air with its musical sound. An excitement enveloped him that he had not known before. Its cause was Janet Fellows, the school-teacher from Harmony, Ohio.

The five foot two auburn-haired woman had danced with him five times, a record for the man from Sharon. Most of Mrs. Pierce's scholars had been warned against him so that they would only politely accept one dance. Janet either had not been warned or did not care. A lustful smile crossed the man's face. "Didn't care," his husky voice echoed around the eaves of the attic.

He closed his eyes and pictured the young lady in his arms

again. Her deep rich brown eyes had focused in on his instantly when he first approached her. He had been the subject of several eyes before, but Janet's had triggered a different reaction within Oliver. There was no apprehension in them; he had noticed when he suggested a dance. Instead, there was a longing, almost a pleading to remove her from the gaggle of ladies at the end of the dance floor. Janet's eyes told him that here was someone who was not afraid of him or what others were likely to think. This realization caused a smile to cross his face, even now several hours later as he lay in bed.

Living in memories of the past had dominated Oliver's life, but Janet Fellows was the here and now. His heart stirred a little at the thought that a real kiss could be the reward if he pursued her a bit. "More even might follow." He whispered to himself thinking of the red ribbons that outlined the beautiful figure of his interest.

* * * * *

Janet Fellows was not like the younger girls whom he had teased and conquered in the past year at the school. No, he shook his head confirming his thought. She was a woman who knew her mind and did not care what others considered proper. "She's just like me."

He thought for a second about the reception he had received from the established families and law students when he first arrived. No one honored an ex-soldier, especially an ex-soldier from a war hated in New England. So he developed an 'I don't care' attitude. Janet Fellows would be a perfect offset to his own personality.

Replaying the events of the dance he suddenly shook his head in disbelief. "I should have known; she would dance." He thought to himself. But instead of correctly guessing Janet's reaction, he had allowed himself to be taken by surprise when she accepted his invitation to dance. He was sure she would have turned him down because he had improperly asked her not with words, but by merely indicating his desire with a gesture of his head. That was not the socially proper thing to do. "Mrs. Pierce instructed her students in the finer arts of manners." Oliver shook his head in remembrance of other young ladies from the Female Academy he had approached. "One should always make the man beg, was a rule Mrs. Pierce taught," Oliver spoke aloud.

But this Janet Fellows was clearly different. It was a refreshing difference that Oliver found delightful. It was a difference he would like to investigate more. A desire came to his mind fit for a soldier, and he licked his lips in anticipation of a long passionate kiss, something he knew how to do well. The lustful smile on his face increased in its intensity as he remembered that Janet had only recently arrived and might still fall under the sway of the community's social norms if allowed to be "educated," by the teachers and students of the Academy. If he could get to her first, then her education might take a different approach, a different path. The thoughts brought more visions often found playing inside a soldier's mind. He smirked and huffed.

"This was the time to strike." He whispered as if a general was planning out a campaign. "This will be her weakest moment while she is new to the school and the community." He recalled the low cut white dress that revealed a little more than Janet might have wanted. The red ruffled handkerchief drew more attention to the hidden view than it would ever cover. His tongue instinctively licked his lips in a pure sexual thought. The smell of a woman's perfume trickled seductively along the line of her cleavage flashed into his memory. Closing his eyes, he clearly recalled being allowed the delight of enjoying such a fragrance up close.

He had kissed a woman before. Well, he had kissed several women before, and the idea of Janet's lips parting their tenderness on his aroused him. There was nothing like the soft, warm touch of lips to lips, he mused. The slight wetness of a woman's lips pressed hard against your own, he thought, caused more excitement than the brisk air on an early morning horse ride.

Horses were his passion. He used them in comparisons to almost anything. His family had been breeders of horses in the northwestern part of Connecticut since before the Revolutionary War. His family was one of the original settlers in the most rural section of the state. A deed signed by King George II supported the Block's claim to their piece of Connecticut.

This family farm was more like a plantation for breeding stock than a typical New England subsistence farm. It consisted of hundreds of acres, but little of it cultivated. Most of the land remained meadows for the horses. The fertile soil of the Housatonic River Valley allowed the family to grow its needed life-sustaining crops on only a small section of their land; the rest the family used for breeding and pasture.

"Janet would make an exceptional filly to have in the stable." His voice filled the now nearly dark attic room.

"Truly," A baritone voice came back from the dark. Oliver's heart jumped. He had forgotten that his roommate was present. James Baldwin Mathers shared the attic with the Sharon native. He was descendent of Cotton Mathers from Massachusetts Bay history and a member of one of the leading families of Maryland. This connection instantly earned him a place at the old Governor's home. It also helped that the older Wolcott had been a friend of the Mathers family from the early days of the American Revolution.

"I'm sorry," Oliver spoke after regaining control of his heart. "I thought you were asleep."

"No just contemplating." James' voice came again. It was a

strange sensation, Oliver noted in his mind, having a conversation in the dark where you were totally unable to see the face of the other. Without that contact, you could not judge how to take their words. Without the ability to read their face, you did not know if they were serious or sarcastic. He moved cautiously in his next statement.

"So was I." Oliver listened, but James did not respond. "It was an excellent tea."

"Yes, indeed. I saw that you made a conquest." James's voice faltered a little at the end of the sentence causing Oliver to think before responding. He knew that the younger man did not care for his company. He could not understand why, for he had remained outside of Mathers' social circle for most of their year together. Oliver just chalked it up to the prejudice he had often found thrown at him by the wealthier class. But James' voice hinted at something beyond his usual aloofness. It was as if James was emotionally troubled.

"I would not call it that." Oliver finally spoke a caution in his voice.

"Oh come now, my friend," James took a high tone. "You manipulated her time throughout the majority of the dance."

Oliver remembered that James had spent several days before the tea in the company of Janet Fellows. He had watched as the Marylander purposely had Tapping Reeve speak for him to the young lady one day on the Common. A laugh almost escaped from Oliver's lips. He had beaten the wealthier man, and it gnawed into the Marylander's stomach that an uncouth soldier could outclass him. To Oliver, it was just a typical campaign on his part. He saw the objective and brashly charged.

"I waited for a respectable time for you to make the first move." Oliver quickly countered feeling as if James was cross-examining him. "You failed. I succeeded."

"I guess you did." Oliver heard James' body shift in the dark, and he pictured the other as having sat up in bed. "I suppose I must yield that point to you. But in the future." James' voice paused in reflection. "In the future, I might not be so willing to yield."

"So noted," Oliver responded sitting up defiantly, crispness in his voice he could not explain. It was not that he wanted to fight over a woman, but it was pleasurable to know that he had inflicted a few dents in James' outer social crust. "So noted James," Oliver whispered with a smile. He looked back out the single window of the attic at the moon. He knew that James could see his silhouette against the light while he still could not see James. "I'll be aware of your intentions now. Thank you for the candid conversation." There was not strain in their formality. It was the usual tone of conversation between the two. From the first day they had moved in together, they had not been friends, simply fellow students or even more exact fellow business associates. This conversation was the first time that James Mathers had confided his feelings about anything beyond a legal point to Oliver Block.

Block sat there in the moonlight thinking about the topic of their conversation. For a moment, it made wanting Janet Fellows even sweeter.

* * * * *

Janet woke up in a sweat and shot up into a sitting position. The other four girls in the bed did not move beyond an annoyed rollover. Janet placed her right hand on her breast and felt her heart pounding inside. The dream had been so real so vivid. Breathing in several deep breaths, she tried to calm herself once more. A funny tickling played in her ears, and she rubbed then to help relieve the feeling. Finally, she lay back down and closed her eyes, but the vision was still there.

It was a knight in shining armor. Well, not a knight, more of a tall, lanky cavalier on a chestnut mare, that was riding away from her. His light blue woolen coat framed his square shoulders in the sun. These were shoulders upon which, she longed to rest her head. The flowing white plume attached to the top of his black leather helmet bounced with each stride of the vanishing horse. His matching black riding boots stopped at the knees where a pair of white riding breeches extended up his shins to the edge of the blue coat. This knight was the ideal man, the perfect Dragoon who had ridden with the northern Ohio Militia traveling through Harmony when she was an adolescent. She had seen him, even talked to him quickly, but never actually knew him. However, his vision had haunted her for years in the form of this dream. She remembered having it more often when she was much younger, but it had occurred less often as her hopes of being married faded.

This vision was what every male would be measure against in her heart. This ideal man was what James and Oliver would have to square off against and wrestle if she allowed them to enter her heart.

Janet opened her eyes knowing that it was useless to try to sleep. The vision would be there, and so would the heat inside of her heart, that the dance had started. "It was the dance," she whispered to herself. "It caused him to ride again in my mind."

Slowly she eased her chemise-clad body out of the rope turned bed. Being the oldest she had claimed the far left side of the bed as hers. The younger girls did not argue with her. The youngest students looked at her as if she was their mother, and snuggled against Janet when she slept. The thought that she could be a mother figure was disturbing, as much as the dream had been.

The wooden floorboards of the shared room were cold under her feet. The sensation helped Janet clear her mind. Cautiously, silently she made her way to the door of the chamber. Her evening coarse wool robe hung on a wooden peg next to the door. The girls all hung their clothes there in case they needed to make a trip to the necessary. It was late enough in the spring that the weather permitted midnight visits to the outhouse located in the rear yard of the academy building. During the winter, the chamber pot would have been the friend of the young ladies.

The solid wood door creaked softly on its hinges, and Janet eased her body through the smallest possible opening. A long dark hallway led the way to the staircase to the first floor and the heavy back door. Other doors lined the hallway. These led to other rooms let by the Academy to its students. A matron teacher slept in the room nearest the staircase. It was her job to maintain the respectability of the school and its students. That meant only females were allowed in the hallway. It was a job that the teacher performed by shooting students evil stares. Janet just shook her head as she quietly passed the teacher's room door that was slightly ajar. She was almost as old as the teacher herself and did not fear the looks. She was accustomed to using such looks in her own classroom.

Bright stars and a lazy moon meet her eyes, as she emerged from the back door of the school and stood for a moment on the uncovered porch. The big dipper and Draco the Dragon twinkled down from the heavens, reminding her of her life in Ohio. The skies were very dark there so that stars seemed to jump out of the black background. So it was in Litchfield.

The call of nature was not as urgent as she had first thought, and Janet stood in the middle of the night looking up at the stars. Pondering why she had accepted the gift of the town fathers, she traced with her eyes, the outlines of several of the constellations. They had paid her tuition and travel cost, with the agreement that she would return to Harmony to teach for the rest of her life in their debt.

For a moment she recalled as a youth how she had wanted to

paint. But that was not a noble occupation for a woman. The door only opened to either marriage or teaching. Her eyes, however, still saw things as if they were on canvas. Now in the rear of the Mrs. Pierces' Female Academy, Janet could not help but see the great Greek heroes and gods outlined by the stars playing in the heavens.

A slight breeze came up and shook the trees around her. She looked at the branches just beginning to be covered by leaves. They seemed to be reaching for the stars, like fingers of some monster's hand trying to grab a unique Christmas diamond from the silky black purse of the sky. She mused at her own imagination and recalled the dream that had caused her to venture outside.

His kiss was wet and powerful, throwing a fog of dizziness over her head. It tasted of coffee. Fresh campfire brewed coffee, like the type she had smelled when visiting the soldiers of the northern Ohio militia. Viselike arms enveloped her in an embrace that squeezed the breath from her with a passion. She breathed in slowly refilling her lungs and felt her breast rub against his white uniform shirt, held in place by silver engraved buttons.

Janet was dressed only in her chemise in her fantasy. Her breasts were free of their confining rigid corset. Free to be excited by the cool wind, or the tempting desire of a hand, even a mythological hand, touching them, fondling them.

A hand slowly undid each silver button bit by bit revealing a small patch of curly brown hair on his chest. The same hand then reached over and caressed her neck. Affectionately it massaged behind her left ear. Her face tipped up, and they kissed again, just as passionate, just as haunting. Their lips played with each other, carefully coaxing and caresses softly becoming one with each other.

Then ever so tenderly, their lips parted and his tongue explored her mouth. It licked her own tongue and twisted around it as if it was dancing with her to some sensual minuet.

The dizziness spun her head into a falling sensation, like when you are on that edge between dreaming and waking. But Janet did not fear crashing into the ground from this falling. Instead, she floated in ecstasy, allowing whatever would happen, to happen.

Her own tongue then ventured forth into his mouth. Cautiously at first, it tasted his tongue and then caressed it ever so gently. Another deep breath flowed from her, causing her to shudder with further dizziness.

"This is all a dream," she said, over and over. "But it feels so real." It shivered her body with goose bumps and brought her heart to life. Pounding filled her ears, as the sensation of their tongues touching continued to tickle in her brain. His firm arms enwrapped her with an embrace as tight as she could squeeze herself. And she eased her body into a position that would enjoy his feel even more. The smell of burning campfire wood and coffee filled her head as if all this was an actual memory, not just a fantasy. But she knew it was a fantasy; it could be nothing more than a fantasy.

* * * * *

The hand massaging the back of her neck slipped down her spine. His fingertips raised a flood of goose bumps throughout her body. The warmth of his touch reached inside of her, tickling a warm response deep inside her. Her breast pressed hard against her thin linen chemise, and as always in the dream, she realized that she was not fully dressed. How that had happened, did not matter for by then Janet was convinced she could not go back. The spinning in her head, the fog in her heart all pointed to a desire to have this illusion, this perfect man. Inside she knew that no one would ever kiss her like that in Harmony, Ohio. No one would ever hold her like that in her whole life. But the fantasy continued despite the knowledge that it was just a dream.

His lips departed from hers and traced the line of her neck with soft light kisses. She turned her head allowing his lips a full kiss on the side of her neck. Her lover complied and added a little nuzzling to his kisses. An intense tickling sensation rocketed from her neck straight to her stomach. Her nipples perked up against the linen material. His lips sucked again on her neck, and she sighed continuing to fall into the fog of dizziness.

Suddenly his teeth nibbled a tender little bit of her neck. "God," her voice escaped in a moan. "God," she repeated as he nibbled again. This time, her breast called out to be caressed, and she felt his tongue slowly descend her neck toward the waiting breasts.

Her hands traveled up over his muscular back, manifestly evident beneath his loose uniform shirt. She ran her fingers through the ends of his hair. His soft, long hair careened through her interlacing fingers. She put a small pressure on the back of his head pressing his lips harder against her neck and then against her breasts.

Excitement vibrated through her, and her left breast tingled as if cupped by his right hand. His fingers carefully pulled in the folds of her chemise raising it inch by inch up her legs. Coolness on her bare legs signaled exposure to the night. His hand then crawled over the chemise touching her skin itself. "Yes," she murmured. "Yes." His fingers cup her cheeks and then scratches gently all the way up the middle of her back. Their lips meet again, and she can't help but taste the coffee once more.

Oh, what a dream, she tells herself, and allows it to continue.

The cavalier's fingers leave her back, and trace down the straps of the undergarment. Slipping alongside her breast his hands, barely touch her skin, tickling the tiny hairs that cover her body until they rested on her hot, sore nipples.

"God," she cannot stop from exclaiming as first her left then her right nipple was lightly kissed, fondled and then pinched. "Lick them." She hears a disjointed lust filled voice call out from her mouth.

The straps of her chemise slipped off her shoulders, and her breast erupted from their confinement.

Warm, wet lips encircled one nipple at a time, sucking, licking, till they swelled with desire. Her head fell back on her neck, unable to support its weight under the passion that was roaring throughout her body, sent from her breast.

"Oh God," Janet's disjointed voice comes once more as his tongue twirled around her right nipple, "Oh God!" Her heart warns not to open her eyes. It comprehends that the fantasy would abruptly end with that simple action. But every time, whether there in Litchfield that spring night or when she was a fifteen-year-old, her eyes would open at that moment and the cavalier disappears.

Janet snapped out of her dream suddenly wide awake, finding one of her hands caressing her own breast, and another tenderly rubbing her stomach. Her eyes quickly scanned the backyard of the Academy; embarrassed, afraid that someone might have seen her. No movement, her eyes report to her brain. No one was there to watch or to kiss, she reassured herself, half sadden that it had only been a dream. Standing up from the rear porch step she had unconsciously sat down on, she fights back a depressed tear. "Old Maid," her words echo in her head.

And then ever so faintly she smelled a hint of coffee and the musk of horses as if she was back in the militia's camp of her youth. Closing her eyes again, she watched as the soldiers of her adolescent memory marched away. And the Dragoons of the regular army, riding so straight and proud on their chestnut steeds dazzled again in the shiny sun of Ohio.

"It was the dancing." Her voice spoke in the dark of the Academy's backyard. "There is no other reason for that dream to come back." Janet let out a long slow breath bringing her back to reality and Litchfield. Oliver's and James' faces flashed yet again in her mind, and an excited shiver shook her. "No," she told herself. "You are destined to be that girl in your fantasy no matter how many young men want to dance with you." Tears came to her eyes, and she stood begrudgingly accepting the truth.

*****

4

She could feel his craving, penetrating eyes on her as she sat there in the designated dark wood pew at the Litchfield Congregational Church. The pews were worn dark and smooth by the many years of church attendance not just by the students but the by the whole community. New England church attendance was nearly mandatory even in 1820. From the Puritan blue laws to the Great Awakening, attendance was engraved in the behavior of New Englanders. Even with the modern culture brought to Litchfield by the two school's diverse students, the tradition of Sunday services was never missed.

The students of the Litchfield Female Academy always attended the church service Sunday morning as a group. They traveled down North Street in a procession, singing and chanting all the way. Each student wore a white formal gown with a sprig of wildflowers in the bun of their hair and a simple white linen bonnet. Unlike the bonnets the girls wore to the dance the evening before, these bonnets did not have the high fronts but instead fell softly over their hair. The formal gown covered the light cotton slip like undergarments and soft corsets that were the fashion.

The bolder of the girls did not wear their corsets, knowing that the high-necked dresses would not reveal the absence of the undergarment. Instead, these girls enhanced their figures by running an extra fold of material down the front of their dress and pulling it underneath each breast. This enhancement was then pulled back and tied with a bow on their back, just under their shoulder blades. The puffed up shoulders on the dress made them look like angels with wings. This extra frontal fold acted as support for the more developed ladies and hinted at future figures for those not as matured. Janet was one of these bolder students, as was Abigail.

The day was hot, and sunny, typical of late spring instead of April; a Connecticut student informed Janet. But it was also noted that New England weather was never the same day-to-day, let alone year-to-year. The beautiful weather drew many of the residents of Litchfield to the Common before church services. All the eyes of the town had been on the girls as they marched in step down the sunny street, around the community green area and into the church.

Embarrassment, and confidence filtered through the girls, well at least through Janet as she promenaded down North Street around the Common and into church. "It will be like promotion night, before the town elders" Janet told herself as the march began. "They are just there that night to make sure students leaned. But this is different." Her voice trailed off as she realized it was her body, her mannerisms the parade spectators would be watching. She had never experienced such a fragment example of voyeurism in her life. "Except maybe when the soldiers watched us walking pass their camp."

The sting of the smile on her face, at the memory of her youth caused Janet to quickly cover her face. "Not now," she cautioned her memories. "Don't come to life now." The memory hung there in her head, however, ready to consume her mind, when suddenly, Janet found herself marching forward with Abigail at her side.

Looking up, she saw the endless column of white dresses, stretching down the road. "Little girls," her mind spoke, slamming the door closed on her midnight cavalier. "Most of them are just little girls." She looked at Abigail, and then down at her ownself. "We're the most mature. All eyes will be on us." A smile of pure delight radiated from her face.

"The law students will be looking at us today," Abigail whispered. "They can't help but be looking at us. We're the prettiest of the group."

"You're correct," Janet gleamed back without moving her face to see Abigail. "They can't help but notice us." Pride filled the Ohio woman, and she physically held her head higher, extending out her figure more. "If this is a parade for attention," she spoke to herself. "Then they will have a clear view of me."

But that attention was not as nerve-racking as what Janet felt now sitting inside the church. She knew that his eyes were on her; glued as if she was the savior, about whom the minister was preaching.

She knew because she had looked up from the leather bound hymnal once and caught James Baldwin Mathers' hazel eyes. A slight smile fought to blossom into a full laugh on her face. Self-consciousness now loomed in her body. "Was her hair perfect?" her heart spoke with uncertainty. "Yes of course it was, you and Abigail made sure before placing your bonnet on."

"Did the dress with its high cut bodice provide a pleasing display?" The next doubt was voiced within "Yes, maybe not as well filled at Abigail's dress, but much more pleasing than the younger girl's apparel."

"Were her cheeks rosy not blanched?" Janet touched her right cheek for the hundredth time since first feeling his eyes examining her. Her cheek was not warm. It was not showing her uneasy embarrassment.

All these thoughts and much more raced through her as the eyes continued to scrutinize her from a pew across the central aisle from her. James sat among a group of other law students, she guessed because of the age of the men around him. But his attention was clearly not to anyone near him or the service. She could feel those sharp hazel eyes, reaching out like adoring hands, trying to caress her body from across the church.

She allowed the fantasy to weave into her mind and tingled her heart a just little. Like the cavalier in her dream the night before, James could be the one holding her. Janet looked his way, and their eyes caught again. He was not discrete at all.

She smiled, and he smiled back. His square jaw did not look so rigid when he smile, a hint of teeth behind his full-lipped mouth added to the smooth effect. His curly brown hair was neatly trimmed to frame his face. It was a handsome face that contained a hint of a brown beard. His eyebrows joined through a thin line of hair above the bridge of his Roman nose. His mouth was slightly parted as he smiled, and then resumed a closed posture in an attempt to pretend he was listening to the minister. But he never took his eyes away from her face.

He was captivated, Janet told herself, and she had done nothing. She was not sure if she was disappointed or excited by the fact.

A white neckerchief made a large bow under his chin and matched a pearl white shirt visible over his opened off-white vest. He had put on his best suit, she thought, like all of the law students, when they came to the church. A brown-tailed suit coat covered his shoulders and framed the rest of his visible body.

A heat crawled up from Janet's breasts as she looked again at his full sensuous mouth. Was this the mouth that she had kissed in her dream? Her stomach twisted into a knot of passion, and her nipples tickled the linen of her unsupported cotton undergarment. She allowed her mind to believe the tied fold around her breasts was his hand tenderly fondling. For a second she closed her eyes and saw the cavalier with James' face. Were these the lips that had nibbled on her neck so many times over the years in that dream?

"Oh, wouldn't you love to find out." She whispered.

"What?" Abigail Stuart whispered back, and Janet looked over at her neighbor. Her white dress hid her long slender neck.

"That's a shame," Janet thought to herself. "Her neck was one of Abigail's most attractive features." She paused in thought not mentioning the other features that would attract men's eyes. But the week's sewing could not hide her figure, and Janet was almost ready to believe that James' stare was more intended for the younger student. But then she remembered he had not danced with Abigail the night before, it had been Oliver who danced with the younger student.

"Nothing," Janet answered adding a dismissing flip of her hand.

A sharp crisp "shush" came from the students' assigned matron teacher situated seven bodies further down the pew. Unlike the students, the teacher was dressed in a dark dress, of an earlier fashion period with a rigid corset, cut low across her breast line. The two students blushed. Abigail pretended to drop her hand fan so that she had to lean closer to Janet.

"You-all need to stop thinking of men, and concentrate on your salvation." There was a glint in her eyes as she looked at Janet, and the Ohio native almost burst out laughing. "And tell that Mr. Mathers that his eyes are extremely distraction to one trying to read the good book."

The southern girl had told Janet before the service that she was a Southern Baptist of the pagan branch. She did not know why the girls had to attend the two-hour long service when it was such a perfect day for horseback riding and picnicking.

Now sitting on the hard wooden pew, a dull pain crawling up her lower back, Janet agreed with becoming a pagan like Abigail. The cool of April had switched almost overnight into a hot summer like day. But Janet was stuck inside a crowded church sweating in a long formal gown, listening to a monotone minister talking about the reformation.

Janet looked again over at James, and their searching eyes met once more.

He had straightened up in his posture at her glance. His shoulders were back, revealing a well-developed chest. Like the farm boys she had seen while growing up and had taught, James Baldwin Mathers was no stranger to the ax and the woodpile. It was an everyday chore for the males in the early 1800s to split a cord of wood a day, just for cooking purposes. Wood was in constant need, and so there was never a day without some chopping or splitting. Iron like arms and squared shoulders were the results of the consistent exercise, and Janet just loved it.

She allowed her mind to drift off as the monotone church service continued. Her mind's eye envisioned James' bare chest. There would be a tuff of brown hair matching that on his head centered between his strong shoulders.

Bringing her dream to life, she envisioned resting her head on that tuff. Closing her eyes she drifted into her fantasy, listening to his heart softly beating in his chest. The rhythm of his breathing would calm her, soothe away all her fears and tensions. Wrapping his arms around her, he would bring her close to the world where their warmth merged as if generated by one body. Nothing from the outside would penetrate their love nest. So she would write if she were Walter Scott. Visions of Ivanhoe also played in her head, merging with her fantasies of James.

Janet opened her eyes again; to find herself still sitting on the hard wooden pew, next to lavender scented Abigail. Her eyes darted across the room at James. This time, the hazel eyes did not meet hers, but were concentrating on another object or person in the church, this one up and away from him as if in the balcony. Janet tried to follow James' stare, but as she moved her head, she came face to face with the matron teacher's eyes. A cold, severe chill came from the teacher's black eyes, and Janet quickly looked down at her hymnal hoping to appear as if she was preparing to sing. Her hand fan opened and helped push away some of the heat rising from her body.

"Alright," she said to herself. "I was wrong about those old teacher stares." She felt ashamed at being disciplined by a woman who was near the same age as Janet. But then she was also falling back into student mode something she had not counted on when she came to the school. She felt sure she would always think as if she was a teacher. Sitting there now, she realized it wasn't that hard to become an adolescent again. It might even be fun.

* * * * *

Like a squadron of fancy dressed Dragoons on inspection parade, the girls of the Litchfield Female Academy progressed past the eyes of Oliver Block. A pure lust came to his face. Anyone of these ladies could satisfy the needs of an army, he told himself. He then shook off the idea as if it was the manure of the barn. "You have fallen into the gutter, my friend." Oliver addressed himself. "You're here to get away from that life." He could not help but recall the marching and the fighting he had seen as a young man. There it was widespread habit for a man's language and thoughts to deal with only the sexual part of love.

Janet marched passed, and his heart skipped a beat. He looked away afraid that she would see him, and know what he had been thinking. She was pure to him, a pure that the white of the dress reflected outwardly. Virginal was the term in his heart. He was not, and could never return to that image of himself. Too many things had happened in his past for him ever to forget. But then he had learned to live, and live well.

He followed the female procession into the Congregational Church. Expectation was that the law students attend weekly services. "A good lawyer, after all, should not keep company with the devil." Oliver voiced his thought. "Until you are in private practice anyway," Oliver joked.

Seeing no room in the lower pews, Oliver proceeded to the

second story of the older whitewashed church. The building was one of the first in Litchfield. As was typical of New England towns, the meeting building was quickly erected so that the Puritan founding fathers could hold sway over the population. It consisted of a large open area on the first floor that contained two sets of pews separated by a wide central aisle. The front of the structure held an altar and two doors. One of the doors led into a small minister's office the other to a coatroom. In the back, there was a small alcove just to the left of the door, which led to a staircase to the balcony.

The balcony was the slaves' quarters; Oliver could not help but reflect. He knew that the wealthy members of New England churches purchase their pews for generations. The balcony, however, was free.

It was here that the poor farmers, freedmen, and even the occasional slave listened like their masters, hoping for salvation. Today was no exception. Occupying the upper pews were the seldom spoke about dark-skinned residents of Litchfield, as well as some of the outer region farmers. Oliver felt at home up there.

Oliver was cynical and had been most of his life. He had run off when he was 14 to the army because there was no place for him on his father's farm. He was the third of five brothers but the only one with character enough to stand up to his father. The final argument came over the method he used for breaking a horse to ride. Oliver had developed a gentle hand, one based on patience and trust, while his father continued to use a heavy hand. "You must show them who the boss is," the elder Block would command. "They are stupid animals who need guidance and firmness." He would break colts in a matter of days, shooting those that would not train quickly.

Oliver, on the other hand, could turn almost any horse into a ride. He was working on a stubborn colt slowly making progress when his father decided that the animal was not worth the effort. Without conferring with his son, the older Block had the horse eliminated. In the morning when Oliver ventured to the stables to work with the colt, he found the horse waiting to be buried in the corral a bullet hole in its head. His anger caused him to storm in on his father's toilet. His father stood there, shaving lather on his face, in mere underclothing.

Oliver clearly saw his father's muscles dropping from age. The effect made him look small and human, not the large dominating man who had ruled the Sharon farm in Oliver's teenage mind. It was a sight his son would remember all his life. The two screamed at each other and exchanged blows. The older man had to pick himself up from the wooden floor of his bedroom. The time had come for Oliver to find a new home.

Taking his horsemanship, the young man found a place with the Connecticut Governor's Foot Guard. This particular unit of the state militia provided a mounted escort for the governor. Unfortunately for Oliver, his father's arms reached all the way into Hartford, and his position disappeared one day. But the experience provided enough self-assurance to Oliver, and he was soon accepted into the Fourth Regiment of the regular army as a house trainer and mounted trooper.

This last position was looked down upon by the wealthy. Oliver had discovered that fact when he came back to the state after the 1812 war. Connecticut had been so against the war that it hosted a convention designed to vote for independence from the country. The Hartford Convention proved fruitless, but the anger at the federal government's war continued with in the Nutmeg State. This anger continued throughout the four year conflict that Connecticut did not even sent its militia to help defend the federal capital when the British troops attached it. Even in New York, his service to the nation did not impress many. The scars on his chest simply reminded Oliver that heroes come and go as quickly as the wind or a good quarter horse. He no longer talked about his service.

Oliver looked down from the balcony of the meetinghouse. A sea of white dresses met his eyes. The bonnets hid the curls of Janet's dark auburn hair, but Oliver had no problem locating her among the waves of white. Studying her, he followed her glances to the left where James Baldwin Mathers sat.

Oliver shook his head and sadly snickered to himself. "So the man from the South may have won."

"He is more handsome." Oliver admitted. "And he has that spotless reputation all virgins want. But she had seemed beyond that pettiness." He watched Janet some more in her virginal white. "It is the effect the teachers wanted. That was why the male students wear dark dress in juxtaposition." The cynical smile came again to Oliver's face. "It is all a method for trapping the poor young hearts of the law students. "

He was too smart for that. He was also a few years older than most of the students at the law school. Instead, he would watch James Baldwin Mathers fall. Again looking across the room, Oliver took in the little drama between Janet and James.

A devilish grin came over his face as he caught James' eyes. There was anger on the face of the southerner, and Oliver almost burst out laughing. Instead, he lowered his glance right to Janet and mustered his best sheepish look. If James was going to feel a smidgen of jealousy, Oliver thought, I might as well shake his whole heart up. He continued to stare down at the manifold of white dresses as the congregation burst into song.

The hymn was well known, and Oliver allowed his baritone voice to lift out over the choir loft filling the church with its virility. His voice was well recognized in the small church of Litchfield, and the resonance soon reached James' ears. The Southerner, for appearances sake, quickly took his eyes off the ex-soldier and found the correct place on the sheet of music. He, in turn, lifted his voice to be heard across the church's first floor.

As the congregation began to sing the second verse of the

hymn, James' ear did not distinguish Oliver's voice from the others. He ventured a sideways look into the balcony. Mr. Block was gone. He glanced over to where the Female Academy students were all clustered together. Oliver was not there, not that anyone was allowed to sit with the young ladies during the service, but knowing Oliver, James thought of the other man's reputation, he would not put it past the Sharon native sneaking into the designated pews.

A strange trepidation came over him, and he tried not to look behind him. His heart told him that if he did, Oliver Block would be back there like the bogeyman, ready to strike. "You'll be safe if you will just keep looking in front of you," his mind called as his heart beat quicker from fright. "You'll be safe if you just keep singing with the rest of the congregation," his heart told him over and over.

* * * * *

Meanwhile, coming down the stairs to the balcony was Oliver Block. His steps were near silent, as he had learned in the army. He spied Arthur Griswold at the bottom, the last man in the doorway. The new law student had come from Willimantic in the eastern part of Connecticut to study law after he had worked his way up from the depths of the local woolen mill. He looked completely lost in his rural coarse handmade clothing causing a group of other law students to shun him. Oliver, however, knowing they shared the knocks of the world enjoyed his company.

"Arthur," he whispered just loud enough for the tall, muscular man to hear him. He was almost as tall as Oliver but was wider from his work in the mills. Though the law students shunned him, the women, especially that group of women looking for a husband, found him attractive. Oliver knew them, and that was one reason he called to him. The other looked his way. Oliver motioned with his head, and the Arthur followed outside.

The service concluded, and the young ladies of the Academy turned as one and filed out. Now came the moment most of the young girls longed for all week. It was permitted for the young men and women of Litchfield to exchange social pleasantries for the next hour. The girls from the school would gather at the foot of the Congregational Church staircase waiting for a young gentleman escort to guide them around the Common. The matron teachers would position themselves at various spots around the Common, with an eye toward the promenading couples. Mrs. Pierce meanwhile placed herself in the center of the area to exchange greetings with the older established families of the village. She was the hub of this giant coach wheel that spun around the green each and every Sunday. Invisible spokes radiated out of her to her charges and the law students hopped on for a ride of love.

Oliver Block was immediately in position with his companion Arthur the second Janet and her shadow Abigail appeared in the May sunlight. "May we?" Oliver did not even finish the question before Abigail had accepted.

The face of the sixteen-year-old showed how enthralled she was with the rakish ex-soldier and his elegant clothing. But to her surprise, Oliver was not looking at her, but instead toward Janet. He turned slightly to indicate that Arthur was to be Abigail's escort around the common. The southern girl had been trained well and knew that one could not back down from an acceptance of an invitation, no matter how dreadful it might be. So the two couples interlaced arms and began to traverse the wheel.

"You have an excellent voice," Janet ventured, aware that it was hard for her to force the words from her throat. Was it the extra pounding that her heart was doing, or the dryness in her throat that was making it hard to converse? She asked her heart but did not know the answer.

"You could hear me over the din coming from the loud mouth Baptist and Methodist students?" Oliver joked. A commonly expressed saying of that time was that the Congregationalists were pale singers to the bible-thumping Baptists and Methodists.

Janet noted to her surprise and disappointment that Oliver was completely at ease in his manner and talk. It was disappointing to the Ohio woman, to think that she would be so affected by this man's presence, but he felt nothing. Well, there was no outward sign of his feelings. Arms interlinked, they continued to circle, exchanging glances at each other every now and again.

"It is a pleasant day," Janet tried again to start a conversation, with a weak thought because no other came to her mind. Instead, all her senses were zeroing in on the touch of Oliver's arm in hers, the smell of his morning cologne masking that of the horse's musk he must have ridden earlier. There were tell-tale signs of hay and dirt on the long black riding boots he had on again. These boots once again crawled up his legs to cover the bottoms of a pair of white muslin trousers. The latest thing from Europe, she recalled, was for men to replace wearing breeches with trousers, even at formal occasions. Fortunately for the women that had not completely happen in Litchfield, for breeches tended to hug a man's calves tighter than trousers. His dark blue frock coat did not cover as much of his thighs as the one he had worn at the dance. This time, Janet could see much more of his legs. Even in trousers, they excited her.

Passion coaxed thoughts from her dream. Her lips dried and she couldn't help but lick them with her tongue. "Oh to be licking his lips," the midnight thoughts spoke to her. His firm crossed over grip on her right hand proclaimed an inner strength that rocked her. She looked at his blue eyes and was transported into a fantasy world - the world of her midnight dream. She could see his lips moving in response to her question, but did not care for the words. Instead, she pictured the kiss, the coffee-flavored kiss that had haunted her since she was fifteen.

Once more her tongue licked her craving dry lips. She almost closed her eyes, hoping that Oliver could read her thoughts. "Please," she ventured in her mind, "please stop, spin me into your arms and kiss me! Just once, just one kiss before I have to go back." The idea of Harmony and teaching snapped her thoughts back to the words coming from his sensual mouth.

"Yes, I believe that the weather has finally turned." He concluded an answer to her statement. They passed a group of churchgoers; among them was James Baldwin Mathers. His face was red with anger, and his eyes met Oliver's as they came near. "There's James," Oliver spoke to Janet but did not take his eyes off the southerner. "I believe that he is a bit jealous of my holding your arm." There was a smirk in his voice, which Janet could not help but notice. "I believe that he would like to be here in my place, and most likely is considering ways of killing me right now." With that, he turned to face Janet. The woman looked into the ex-soldier's gleaming blue eyes. They paused for a second in their stroll, almost getting hit by the couple behind them.

Janet's face flushed with a cherry red around her cheeks. Her mouth opened to protest the comment, but no words came out. Oliver's stare so struck her dumb that even thoughts could not form in her head. Her breathing paused along with her heart.

"I am sure he feels that way." The law student stated, and returned to strolling. Janet could not help but follow. "You must have seen his green tint last evening as you danced with me." Oliver shook his head as if sorry for the other man. "It is a pity he's so young," Oliver paused as if in thought. "I don't mean in age, I mean in knowledge." He looked again at the side of Janet's face. "You are too much of a woman for him." Oliver noticed another flush of crimson on her cheeks. "He still sees the world as noble and worthy. I think he even believes in the poets' words concerning mankind and love."

"You don't?" Janet finally found her voice. Oliver had struck a chord of cynicism that she felt. Sadness from deep inside came across his blue eyes. It was sadness that Janet did not want to see, but she could not bring herself to look away. It longed to escape through his eyes, escape from its prison in his heart and mind, where it festered. His eyes turned cold, hollow and scary. Oliver's pain physically moved Janet. She almost wept at the knowledge she had hit a hidden cord of remorse.

Oliver sighed heavily before answering. "I have seen death. I have held that molded paste of earth called a man after the spirit has fled." There was a hurt anger in his voice. "Nothing matures you faster than having to bury friends with the question why them and not me, never answered." His voice grew distant, and Janet knew she had lost Oliver to the world of battle memories.

"I live now with their memory here in my heart, and in my head. I see the future they never will have, and I cry." The words came unchecked. For the first time in his life, Oliver found himself able to express the emotions so coiled inside of him for years. "When I see others salute the flag, I picture them, my friends. Not dead, but as they were, laughing, joking around the campfire."

He paused and looked at Janet's upturned face. There was a hint of a tear in her eyes and his heart stopped. A shiver raced over him, causing the hair on the back of his head to stand on end. "Oh God," he whispered to himself. There was a welling up of emotions in his chest he had never felt before. His heart started again with a jolt, and his breath came out loud and hard. Never before had he allowed his words to flow so unguarded. The cries of the battlefield left him for a moment as he dove into Janet's brown eyes for comfort.

Her eager eyes blanketed him with an understanding and pity

he had never known. She welcomed him without a word or gesture beyond her tearing eyes.

Memories, long stored found the sunlight of Litchfield as they continued to walk. Oliver told of his years with the army. Silently Janet walked beside him, listening, stroking his hand when she heard tears in his voice and squeezing it when he found it hard to continue.

Finally, he stopped aware that the circuit walk was coming to a close. "You need to be aware that I cannot offer you what James will provide. I am the second son so to say. James will be the master of his father's estate. I, on the other hand, have but my experiences and a small bank account." He caught Janet's eyes again. This time, there were no tears, but a disappointment.

"I'm not here to get a husband." She spoke a conviction making the words crisp. "I have contracted an agreement with my town to return to teaching after six months here. I do not know how either of you could have thought otherwise. I did not lead anyone on. I simply danced."

"Well, forgive me," liver smiled, humor returned to his manner. "That will come as a surprise to our friend James. He was bold enough to address me on his feelings concerning you, practically calling me out to duel." A laugh escaped from the ex-soldier. "The child does not know." He drew a little distant again, and Janet felt troubled. Something on his face once more hinted at death. "You need to speak to him then. He will never believe me. He has it in his head that I dislike him, and spread rumors. I really do not care about him beyond his attention to you. And that is all I will say on the matter." He looked away and slowly began to remove his arm from hers.

"No," her heart called out loud, "don't let go!" Oliver paused and met her eyes.

"You haven't told me," she said, holding his attention, "About the rumors." Oliver looked deep into her eyes, as if he was trying to read her mind a quiver crossed his face. "I mean your own rumors."

He smiled the rakish smile he had given her at the dance the evening before. "Yes you should know. Nothing, nothing is real you do not see yourself. I served with a gentleman from New York City, who had a sister. His father treated me as a son. She died." The blues eyes clouded over. "A broken-hearted man found in me hope for the future he had lost." Oliver shook his head. "That is all there is to my rumor."

"Were you in love?"

Oliver looked away as a couple passed them still on their stroll. "If I loved her, I didn't know it then. I have only loved someone once but that was as a child in a distant place from here. That was before the battles, before this life of fulfilling my friends' dreams."

"Thank you." Janet's voice spoke from deep within herself. Her heart's emotion giving it wholeness she had never heard before. "Thank you for all that you have shared. It must not have been easy." Their fingers touched as their eyes scanned each other's face. The warmth of the sun was cold compared to the passion that came from her and flowed through her hands to him. "Please call me friend. I will always listen. Always help you." Again her eyes watered.

Oliver bit his lip; shocked at the effect he had brought to her. "You know that James and I are leaving here soon?" She shook her head. "Well our studies here are almost done. This Friday we'll be having a mock trial if you are interested in watching. It is one of the last requirements we have. I must argue a case against him."

Janet nodded and Oliver bowed. Tapping the brim of his black top hat, he turned and walked away.

*****

5

The sick, forlorn look on James' face caused Janet to burst out in a short laugh. She caught sight of the law student as she turned toward Abigail after Oliver had left. The sun had brightened that day after a morning of rain showers, making it so pleasant to walk, so pleasant to be outside. A sweet fragrance of newly opened flowers filled the air, and a slight breeze held the sudden heat in check. Janet was just basking in the glow or was it a glow that was coming from her. Oliver's eyes, troubled as they were, had triggered an inner flow of emotions Janet did not fight.

Looking back at the next couple, she noticed James trying to catch her eye. Frustration and jealousy brought out wet eyes and melancholy to James' square face. "Lovesick," Janet said fighting hard to control her laughter. She rubbed the smile from her face as Abigail and Arthur Griswold approached still arm in arm.

"Has your escort left you?" The blond young man from Connecticut questioned as he reached earshot. His hair was shoulder length and fell unhampered out from under his broad brim low cut farmer's felt hat. He certainly did not put on any of the English dandy airs that Beau Brummell represented, that was James' style, nor did he have the military bearing that Oliver maintained. But there was something appealing about him, something that came across in his naturalism and his relaxed personality. It was honesty that Janet had not sense with many of the other law students. It reminded her of her home in Harmony, a solid farming community rooted to the earth, not concerned with the world events thousands of miles away.

"Has your escort left you?" Arthur asked again, unsure if Janet had heard him the first time. Janet nodded, yes. "Well, then you are welcome to join us." Arthur offered and looked over at the young lady on his arm. The red head nodded a delighted smile well entrenched on her face. Abigail did not seem as annoyed as she had when the stroll had begun.

"Maybe this would be the man she came looking for," Janet whispered to herself, eyeing the law student from head to foot. She took in the outfit he wore. It was nowhere near as exquisitely made as those of Mathers or Oliver. No, this man did not have the money behind him that other students flaunted. He may have had the drive to be Abigail's mate, but Janet dismissed the idea, for she knew her roommate was looking for a future political leader, not just a lawyer.

"Abigail certainly did not want someone who had worked for a living," the cynical side of Janet spoke in her ear. Janet remained silent, however, something that she had learned to do over the years of dealing with the founding fathers of Harmony.

"Thank you," Janet stepped toward Arthur's extended left arm when the sound of a footfall stopped her.

"No, I will escort her." James' voice showed evidence of having hurried there, "If Miss Fellows does not mind." He panted between words. Janet turned and faced him. A blush covered his face from the excursion and spring heat. His hair appeared disarranged, and his brown frock coat failed to sit right on his shoulders. James straightened himself up to his full height, adjusted his jacket and extended his hand to Janet. His eyes reached out to her, desperately seeking, desperately hoping she would accept his invitation to walk together.

An amused smile came across Janet's face. "He is actually jealous," she told herself. All that Oliver had revealed was correct.

A fresh warming glow came over her that wrapped around her like a comforting embrace. What a miracle. She thought. Just a few short weeks ago no one had ever looked that way at her. Now she had James love struck, and Oliver was confiding in her. Janet extended her left arm so that James would come alongside. The power was all hers! She looked at the side of James' face and wondered was this really what she wanted?

"Thank you," James whispered as he took her arm and started to promenade around the Common area circle. A hint of perspiration covered the hand he laid on her bare arm. She could also see a few beads of sweat from under the brim of his correctly placed brown top hat. "I was afraid that I would not have a chance to talk with you today." He spoke, his words coming quickly, as if he was out of breath. His eyes remained looking straight ahead as if he was focusing on a forward spot during an oral presentation. "I have many things I would like to say." His voice hesitated a little. Janet's heart thumped.

"Here it comes!" The emotional part of Janet's heart screamed in delight. "Here come those words you've only heard in dreams." She took a deep breath, unsure what else to do. "Will it just be said then without looking at me?" She questioned. "Or is he going to turn me to face him, place his hand on his heart and proclaim his feelings for the whole world to know?" The voice from her heart began to sound like a teenager, one of the teenagers she was currently in school with, or worst, like the maidens in the novels she had been reading recently.

"Stop that." The mature side of Janet spoke up. "You can't expect life to be little melodramas." But it was too late to call back her emotional side. It was far too late. That side of her had been pent-up too long.

All those years in Ohio, all those years teaching children, and living an old maid's life, was now being set on its ear. She could not believe it. Her heart jumped a beat in excitement, and a wave of heat passed over her. Janet fanned her face to hide the reddening she knew was coming to it. Her heart listened ready, even willing to be held even if it was just for a second, by this young man.

Instead, her brain took over, and she switched the topic. "I see that you're taking on a beard." Her voice rose at the end of her statement to make it sound like a question.

James' face showed surprise at the question, but his mouth continued unhesitant. "I thought it was the time that I step into the role I will have to play upon leaving here." His voice sounded more clinical than she had hoped. "I feel that a mature man has a beard. It is an outward symbol of his manhood. It also served as an instant statement to his ability. Think about the men you have known and see if it is not true. A man with a trim, neat beard tells the world around him that he is a determined, organized person. While one with a bushy mass on his face tells the world that he is flaunting his manhood, but does not have control over it."

"And what about clean shaved men?" She teased with her question.

"They are lost in the idea that they still are young boys." Janet held back a laugh. Clean shaved Oliver Block seemed far from a young boy, so did the Secretary of State John Quincy Adams or a dozen other clean-shaven men she had met. But she did not want to debate the issue. Instead, she remained silent, contented to listen to the law student continue his diatribe on beards and other facial hair. Just when Janet's mature side felt satisfied that James had placed behind him the issue of his feelings, James turned the conversation back with the same urgency in his voice he had when they began to stroll together.

"I know that I should not talk like this openly to you." The law student stared forward again, ill at easy. "But I feel that if I don't say something, I'm going to miss the opportunity." He finally looked over to her. Janet could feel his eyes scan her from head to toe. The same intensity those hazel eyes had examined her with during the church service, reached out and caressed her now.

Self-consciousness mixed with a hint of desire filled the young lady from Ohio. It was great being the center of attention, she thought. It felt better than she had expected or experienced. It shook her with a shiver of passion. At that moment, the fantasy she dreamed in the church about resting her head on James's chest resurfaced in her mind. Unconsciously she drew his arm closer to her, and allowed her mind to drift into that dream world. The white dress felt even tighter than she had imagined it could. Her breast wanted to bust out with desire, but they were well confined. Still, they longed to be free, to be in his hands feeling his kiss.

"I have been thinking of you." His voice hesitated again as if choked in his throat.

Janet smiled to herself. She knew how that felt, being too tongue-tied to get a word out, but it was strange that she did not feel that way around James, only Oliver. Maybe that was a sign, she thought. A sign, Janet questioned, but for whom, Oliver or James?

"I don't mean to offend. I just wanted you to know that you have been in my thoughts recently. Well more like my only thought." He paused in his steps and physically turned her face to his with his hand. For the briefest of seconds, she thought James was going to kiss her. Her eyes closed and she tilted her chin waiting for the touch of lips.

Oh, the touch of a man's lips like in her dreams that was what she wanted. Her heart called out. All the emotions from her midnight vision swelled within her again. Right there, right then, on the Green in Litchfield, she wanted to feel James Baldwin Mathers' lips on hers. From the back of her mind, the taste of that coffee kiss screamed forth.

But the kiss did not come. She opened her eyes and saw a

scared puzzled look on James' face. He did not know what to do, she told herself. "He's just as lost as I am." She thought.

She smiled up at him and then became aware that the matron teacher was also looking at them through her dark colored poke bonnet. Its high front clearly showed which way she was looking, and she was looking right at the couple.

"We should be walking otherwise they'll separate us." She indicated with her eyes, for James to look at the now approaching teacher. James followed her glance and nodded. He turned back to the right and continued to walk. The chaperone returned to her post.

"Before I came here I was at William and Mary College in Virginia." He spoke again, looking forward. "I studied my Latin and Greek till I was the top student. My father expected that of me. Here I am working hard to be top again, because that is what a Mathers does, be the top. But you have caused me to put that aside. I find myself not wanting to read or study law anymore." He took a deep breath as if what he was going to say would bring about the end of the world. "Last night I could not sleep. I saw you in my dreams. Not that these dreams were bad or offensive, but instead common dreams. Dreams I know I had experienced before." His right arm slipped out of hers, and his hand fished into the inside breast pocket of his suit coat. "I took the liberty of writing my thoughts down in poetic form." He pulled out some folded sheets of paper.

The sun shined on them and shot a beam into Janet's eyes. Curiosity awoke inside Janet. "So it was not going to be an oration of love and strong emotions," her head told her. "No, it has taken the form of poetry, like Shakespeare." She smiled to herself.

Once more the sensation of delight filled her at being the center of this man's attention. "Poetry," she spoke to herself. "He's written me poems, like the great lovers of the past. He has placed on paper his love for me, to be read forever." Her heart skipped a beat and a catch came to her breathing.

"So this was what Luella felt." The thought came from deep within her heart. It was a thought Janet did not know had a voice inside of her. Her best friend's fall from grace had been quickly stored inside of her, unexplained. "This moment of delight," her heart continued its explanation. "This moment of uncontrolled heart jumping and tickling shivers was what Luella felt each time she looked at her young Lieutenant. No wonder she allowed him to take her heart, soul and life." For the first time in her life, Janet understood how powerful could be her heart, anyone's heart, when triggered by delight and desire.

"Now I'm not a Christopher Marlowe or William Blake, but I think I've done well." James hesitated as he slowly opened the leaves of paper. Janet could see that the calligraphy on them was neat with fancy curlicues. A firm steady hand had composed the poems. "Someday," James closed the paper before she really had a chance to read the words. "Someday I would love to have you read these, but today is not that day." He looked again at her face. Their eyes met, and she could see the folded pages reflected in his hazel eyes. She felt his eyes question hers about love, and she blushed. There was an emotional spark in the air that crawled over her skin in a shiver. His heart reached out and touched her with that simple little secret of his poems.

"I just need to know your position." The statement came not from a lovesick law student, but in the voice of an attorney preparing his case. "I need to be confident that I have a legitimate claim to what I am seeking."

The tone of his voice rang like a bell, a school bell inside of Janet. Her head silenced her heart and a cold crept across her. "He's looking for a claim, like a deed or bill of sale." Her brain hammered its thoughts into her heart. "He's calculating the risk. Should he jump or hang back until all chance of failure is eliminated?" The chilly sensation crawled over her arm making James's touch toxic. "His love is conditional!"

Janet abruptly stopped walking and turned to the young man. "Well James Baldwin Mathers, if you think I can tell you that today, you will be sadly mistaken. I did not seek your attention or that of anyone, and if you wish to gain it, you will have to work. I am not someone you can just throw a fancy word at and expect her to swoon. I don't think you really understand women if you believe that is what will happen."

James turned bright red with embarrassment. "I did not," he started saying and then paused to collect his thoughts. "I mean I only." Once again he hesitated flustered at the confrontation. "You misunderstand me. I was not expecting to sweep you off your feet. I was only stating my side. Please listen to me. I do not expect you to feel anything for me; only provide me with an opportunity to talk with you. To show you, tell you, and move you to feel what is inside of me."

Janet looked him in the eye and saw a fear she had not seen before. It was his heart calling out through his hazel coloring not to crush him. Her own heart called to her to sooth the fear away from James. She reached up and tenderly touched his face. He took her right hand in his and placed a soft kiss first on her fingertips and then the palm of her hand.

* * * * *

The hand tingled. Literally, it tingled all the way up to her elbow. Even an hour after the tenderness of the kiss had been parted on her fingertips, her hand still tingled. Janet found her thoughts flooded with visions that distracted her from all the other chores she was supposed to be doing. The water bucket did not get filled. Instead, she found herself looking at her hand. The stitches on her new dress hem did not line up evenly or straight. Instead, her eyes examined the center of her palm as if it had never been there before. Her hair remained not brushed out forever cramped into a bun on the back of her head, and the words of the Bible she was reading did not from sentences in her head. Instead, she caught herself touching, gently touching the spot on her hand where James's lips had joined her.

James' lips touching her fingertip was all that she could concentrate on at that moment. She felt the roughness of his newly formed beard tickled the palm of her hand again. And she could not help but close her eyes to relive the moment in her mind. His breath had been warm on her fingers that were so sensitive to any contact. His lips, firm and gentle, so gentle she barely felt them. This touch made the kiss even more erotic. It had the softness of a feather with the intimacy of a burning passion. That burning was still tingling. Janet rubbed her hand all the way to her elbow and smiled.

In this state of mind, was how Abigail found her, as she came into the shared bedroom. Sitting in the small straight back chair with the dress across her lap, Janet had the Bible open on the adjoining table, but was staring into space, a silly smile on her face. Abigail looked at her for a moment, aware that the older student was not conscious that she was no longer alone in the room. "Janet?" Abigail questioned. "Janet? Are you having a religious experience?"

Janet blinked her eyes and then looked over at Abigail; scarlet covered her face, as Janet realized the truth of the situation. Like waking from a short nap, confusion first fogged the edge of reality with the dream world. So it was that Janet stood for a moment between kissing James and recognizing Abigail. The southern girl straightened the light pale white cotton coverall that hung unattractively over her developed frame. It was a garment she wore when working around the house.

"Janet?" Abigail smiled at her friend. "I thought for a moment you had ventured into a world of no-return."

Janet's smiled grew larger, till it hurt the corners of her mouth. Was this love she asked? Was it this sweet this confusing, this all encompassing?

Abigail waved her right hand in front of Janet's eyes to try to get her to focus. "Janet?"

"Look at her," Janet's mind commanded, but it was very hard for the Ohio native to comply. Looking at Abigail would mean giving up the vision of James, and that moment on the Green when James threw away his composure and proper manners to publicly display his affections. Janet's heart did not want to give that moment up, even now an hour later.

"Janet," Abigail spoke firm once more fighting to break into the daydream. "I came to see if you would like to attend a picnic."

"Attend a picnic?" Janet heard her voice answer from somewhere in a cloud.

"Yes, Arthur Griswold has invited us to a picnic with a group of other law students. You need to come otherwise I can't go. It is not proper for a young lady to attend a picnic without other young ladies." There was an urgency to her voice that showed she was more interested in attending this picnic than she might have otherwise have said.

"When," Janet's detached voice asked.

"Within the hour," Abigail responded.

The statement of time suddenly focused Janet on Abigail completely in control of her thoughts again. "Within the hour," Janet joked, "How will we be ready?" Janet joked.

"Arthur asked me while we were walking around the Common." Abigail turned to the shared dresser and removed a light calico dress that served as a casual dress for the southern lady. She also pulled out a clean chemise and a cotton corset. "I guess I can wear this," She stated absentmindedly. "Arthur will not want to see me in the same dress from this morning." She looked over at Janet. "But you can still go in your formal gown."

Janet looked down at herself. She had not even changed since coming back from church. Her mind had been too distracted. Instead, she had turned to her chores unaware that her best dress was in danger of being ruined.

"No, I can't do that." Quickly Janet untied the bow in the center of her back and unhooked the neck hook. She walked over to the other girl. "Could you loosen my buttons?"

Abigail was midway of wriggling out of her coverall. When she had accomplished her own disrobing, she unbuttoned Janet's dress. They both then changed into comfortable causal dresses and helped each other tie their corsets and dresses; both laced in the rear. If they were going to the wilderness, they needed to be comfortable, but their attractiveness required addressing as well. Surveying each other, they brushed one another's hair and reset it in loose fitting buns. A simple white cotton bonnet finished the outfit. Once secured on their heads, they were ready for the arrival of the law students.

* * * * *

Just then a knock echoed from the room's door. Without waiting for an invitation, in walked Mrs. Pierce herself. Her eyes took in both of the girls immediately. A distance in her mature dark eyes told the girls that they were to be silent until the older woman had spoken the purpose of her visit. "Good," she spoke with a pleasant air.

Still dressed in the black dress from the church service, Mrs. Pierce did not sit or make herself comfortable in any matter. The dress showed off her neckline, still attractive despite her age. "You are both here." She lingered a moment to look again at each of the two. "I was hoping to speak to you together." She fixed her stare at Janet. "It seems that your promenade escapade has become the subject of several rumors already. I must warn you, Miss Fellows, the tongues of the community are very sharp.

From what I recall in the letter written by the Harmony Education Board, you are here to enrich your skills as a teacher. A position you have held for the past ten years, correct."

Janet nodded.

"Please tell me if I am not mistaken, but doesn't that same board expect you to return to teaching?" She raised her dark eyebrows to Janet waiting for an answer.

The Ohio woman nodded, trying not to show that the fact saddened her. The tingling disappeared in her arm with the realization that she was under contract to return to teaching. Once again all her dreams crashed to the ground in front of her. Everything that had happened between her and James was worth nothing. In six months she would be heading back to Ohio, and her classroom.

"Now Miss Fellows, if it had been anyone other than Mr. Mathers, who bestowed a kiss on your hand, I would be in my office writing a letter to the Harmony Education Board." She paused for effect. "Do I make myself understood?" Janet nodded. "Good."

Sarah Pierce turned her matron eyes toward Abigail. "We here at the Litchfield Female Academy must always remember that the world is looking at us as role models for the betterment of woman. That means we must always remember our proper place, tongues, and manners. Do I make myself clear?" The Southern woman also nodded. "Good then this picnic needs to be addressed. My students do not go off unescorted into the bushes with young gentlemen, even if they happen to be from the very best families in the nation."

"I was planning on escorting Abigail," Janet jumped into the conversation. "She had approached me after church with the invitation. I'm sorry I had not told you before. I was busy sewing a new dress." She gestured to the very garment lying across the single chair in the room. The head teacher looked over and nodded in satisfaction.

"Very well then," Mrs. Pierce looked into Janet's eyes. "Remember who you are and what position you hold in your own community. I will expect you to behave as if you were chaperoning your charges from Harmony."

Once again visions of her one room school filled Janet's mind. She was in Litchfield not to find a husband, but instead, to learn how to better educate the children of her small Ohio town. Nothing would change that, she told herself. Nothing could change that. Janet had signed a contract before leaving the township. She had guaranteed to return to the town in exchange for the tuition to the Litchfield Female Academy.

"I will do my best Mrs. Pierce," Janet answered her tone that of a matron teacher herself. "You may count on me and my discretion."

"Is Mr. Mathers among the attendees?" Mrs. Pierce questioned. Janet looked over at Abigail.

"I don't know," Abigail said. "It was Mr. Griswold who invited me. I'm not sure if he's acquainted with Mr. Mathers or not. I was introduced to Mr. Griswold through Mr. Block." Oliver's name sparked a reaction in Mrs. Pierce's eyes, and a sour face came over her.

"Well, that gentleman will need to be carefully watched." She looked again at Janet. "You spent time with him at both the dance last evening and the promenade today. What was the nature of his attention?"

"He was expressing his gratitude for the dances," Janet shot back suddenly enraged at being questioned by Mrs. Pierce as if she was herself a fourteen-year-old. Maybe it was the head teacher's style or habit because that was the age of most of her students, but Janet had enough of it now. Mr. Pierce had put Janet in her place with a subtle reminder of her hometown's contract. That was sufficient for the Ohio lady to return to the right path. She was not an adolescent, and Mrs. Pierce well knew that.

"He also had an invitation for me to attend the mock trial this week between him and Mr. Mathers. I felt that it would be a wonderful exhibit for me to see. I may be able to use such an approach in my classroom." She looked the head teacher in the eye, one professional to another. "After all, we know that education is not just reciting and recalling. It is making the connections between the learning and the practical."

Mrs. Pierce leaned back on her heals shocked and pleased by the fire in Janet's voice. There was something between teachers that binds them when it came to talking about how to deal with students. It was a private treasure that only other teachers understood.

"I'm glad you had set clear boundaries for our friend from Sharon. He is one that must be watched. Soldiers, even ex-soldiers have too many things buried within to allow them to be part of the normal society."

"Does that include Andrew Jackson and George Washington?" Janet questioned sarcastically. The first was currently a well-respected gentleman from the south whom many thought should run for President and the former was the hero of the nation.

"Well George Washington never really was a soldier," Mrs. Pierce justified the nations' Federalist acceptance of his past. "He merely served to earn our independence. His livelihood was a farmer." She looked again at Abigail. "As for the other Southerner, well we'll see if anything does come of him. He is not as acceptable in New England as others such as Clay, Calhoun and Adams all of whom were not soldiers."

Janet stood there silently staring Mrs. Pierce in the eyes. She listened to the head teacher, but only heard the voices of the founding fathers of Harmony. Mrs. Pierce spoke with the same superior tone, that same prejudice tone that had driven her friend away in disgrace from the little one room school. At that moment, Janet decided she would become close to Oliver if the man allowed her, just to spite Mrs. Pierce, the Harmony town fathers and any other of the old Federalists that happened to be left alive.

"Prejudice," the word echoed down from Janet's brain. The emotions that had been brewing in the back of her thoughts for ten years now came to a boil. Luella Bates had been a scape-goat for all the same beliefs that Mrs. Pierce was spouting now. She had been used by the founding fathers to show the rest of the women in town what would happen if they strayed beyond the men's accepted limits. Janet looked at Mrs. Pierce with con-tempt. She had come here to open her mind and eyes, but now only saw that the teacher was just as closed minded as her Ohio community.

Connecticut people, Janet tried to justify this close minded-ness, had settled Ohio. So the Federalist ideas and norms spread from New England to there.

"But Mrs. Pierce was a teacher, a molder of young minds!" The teacher inside Janet called out for an explanation. Anger seized Janet. This school was just perpetuating the status quo instead of reaching for changes. Janet recalled her father and his New England motto, why change it if it's still working.

"But who is judging if it is working?" Janet questioned her father and all people in authority. The United States was a new nation. Janet reflected on the work of Noah Webster and others. It needed new ideas to grow. She loved arguing with her father about ideas and beliefs because he was willing to listen. He was not that stump stuck in the bog still thinking it was a tree. She looked at Mrs. Pierce and was not sure if this was a stump or not.

"The Federalists were removed from power with Jefferson's election. They have remained out of power in the last two elec-tions, doesn't this show the populace has turned away from their beliefs and expectations?" Janet's voice questioned her teacher, not really meaning to speak out loud.

Mrs. Pierce huffed and then smiled wide. "Oh, it is good to have a fire in your soul." There was a luster in the head teacher's eyes. "Action this day," she said in Latin and then translated it for the benefit of Abigail. "You must be willing to question." She nodded at Janet. "But understand that others will not accept or tolerate dissension." She reached behind her and closed the bedroom door. Lowering her voice as if she feared others would hear; she spoke earnestly.

"The model of a Federalist mother is one I have quietly nurtured over the years. She must be able to run a household, prepare the children for adulthood and provide companionship for her husband. To do all of these she must not be a silly ignorant girl." She paused and looked back and forth between the two students, making eye contact with each.

"This model is more in depth than it sounds. Women, as far as I am concerned, are not just quiet household matrons. No, it is their responsibility to educate the children to seek out, question and experiment. We cannot progress if we did not re-examine our methods. But it always has to be remembered that we must be the silent partner in public." Caution filled her eyes.

"A wife's position is not to lead her husband, but instead encourage him, guide him, share with him. Until we are seen as equal beings, we must hold this silent partnership."

"But if we don't speak out," Janet spoke up a fire in her soul she had not been allowed to express except with her father. "We'll never gain that recognition of equality."

"That is true," Mrs. Pierce answered. "That is why I have this school. Soon maybe in my lifetime or maybe a little later than that, my students will be models that cannot be overlooked." Pride came to her face. "After all, all these husbands have to come home to my Federalist wives and their Federalist mothers." She almost giggled with mischievous delight. "It is a stealth way of gaining a voice. But it is the only way open today." Her dark eyes focused in on Janet. "You have the fire, but tack, my student, maybe more important at this time. What does it say in the Bible, you catch more flies with sugar than with vinegar."

Looking at the head teacher, Janet perceived a glow coming from within her. Janet realized that though Mrs. Pierce presented an outward façade, there was hiding a similar person to Janet inside the Academy founder.

The Ohio student felt ashamed that she doubted that this woman was not a real teacher. There was that same drive to analyze the world and make it better within Mrs. Pierce as there was inside Janet and all good teachers. Janet nodded to the older woman, and the two shared a look that spoke of understanding and appreciation. Mrs. Pierce then quietly left the two students to think about what she had said.

It was not long before a farmer's wagon lunged to a stop in front of the Academy. Arthur Griswold was among the law student riders, sitting in the hay piled within the walls of the wagon, waiting for the young ladies from the school to come join them for the trip to Bantam Lake.

****

6

A pair of brown and white short-haired oxen pulled the flat well-worn farm wagon, generally used for haying. The steady gait of the oxen lumbered over the rutted dirt path from the Litchfield Female Academy to Bantam Lake for about an hour before reaching the picnic site. Once there, the picnic goers slowly disembarked, making sure legs were still functioning after being tasseled about during the ride.

Good natured jests and counters filled the air from the lips of the law students. There was nothing better than an afternoon off from studying. The fact that the men were accompanied by some of the academy young ladies only enhanced the festive spirit of the outing.

Stray straw blanketed everyone's heads, covering hair, bonnets, and hats with little strands of hay. Janet did not mind, for the sweet smell of hay was one of the pleasures she enjoyed in life. It was comforting, reminding her of her family's farm in Ohio.

Numerous times she had crept out to the solitude of the barn at home to hide away in the hayloft. While there she would read or just imagine faraway places about which she had read. The hay would trap in her body heat, making a warm snuggly burrow in which she could visit the globe. Her family owned one book, the Bible, but she had been able to borrow others from friends of the family and of course her teacher Luella. The same smell now brought back visions of her youth, and of course her special dream.

"I have to stop thinking about home," she told herself. Too many things had been reminding her of Harmony, and she was beginning to feel pains of homesickness. She did not want anything to stand in her way of enjoying the few months she had here in Litchfield, let alone a case of nostalgia. She had seen the younger students that shared her room, fall under such bouts. It was heart wrenching, especially when ten-year-old MaryEllen cried non-stop the second night away from home. Janet had to hug her most of the night to comfort the young girl as she slept in fits and spurts.

Janet also knew that her midnight dream of the cavalier had been reborn because of her homesickness. It was causing her to remember things she did not want to, such as Luella Bates. Janet had fought for years to place these hurtful memories in the very back of her brain. But something about Litchfield kept stirring them up again.

Suddenly Oliver Block's stable callused hand appeared in front of her bonnet, shielded face. The law student was already on the ground looking up at the wagon. His gesture of help was accepted, and Janet took his strong hand in hers. His were "working" hands, hands that had known hardship, but still, they brought joy to Janet's heart. Once more, like at the dance, his warmth surprised her, as it crawled through her body. His smile triggered a heart flutter.

He remained in the same outfit he had worn to church, with the exception now wearing a riding coat instead of his dark frock coat. This coat was brownish in color and had offsetting red velvet collar and cuffs. It was held open by silver buttons that Janet seemed to recognize, but could not think of why they were vaguely reminiscent.

"Did you enjoy the ride?" he asked.

"Oh yes," she lied, adjusting her fawn colored high front bonnet back to its correct position on top of her head. Securing the yellow ribbon that laced into the bow under her chin with a simple tug, she added. "It was thrilling and educational." The sarcasm dripped from her words.

"I can imagine." Oliver smiled back. "I came by horseback. It is a much pleasanter way to travel." He looked toward a clump of trees where a large chestnut mare stood tied up. "I try to ride as often as possible." His eyes glittered with an excitement that Janet understood. She had heard of Oliver's love of horses. A loved engrained in him, by his family's farm and the reputation the Blocks had in the western part of the state concerning horse knowledge.

Other students had also made her aware that Oliver had fought with his father over the dishonoring of some local maiden. That same maiden had not been "ruined," but still had been whisked away from the Sharon area so that her family was not forever scared. But this was just one of several rumors she had heard about Oliver Block and his break with his family. Another had the soldier accidentally killing a servant, whether it was a male or female servant depended on the storyteller, and thus needed to flee his father's wrath. Still another story had the fact that he had served in a war that his father did not support, being the cause of the family banishment.

Janet did not know what to believe or not to believe. Looking into Oliver's complex blue eyes, however, she did not put any ungentlemanly actions beyond the ability of the Sharon gentleman. That thought teased up an electrical sexual sensation that shot through her and warmed her face.

"Do you ride?" The question came from Oliver in a genuine tone. Janet knew that it was unladylike in some social circles to mount a horse. But Janet was of the mid-west where the social norms were slightly different. She also fancied that Oliver would only want a woman who could ride. He would want someone who could be a companion on his early morning jaunts, which she had been informed the law student carried out daily despite the weather. His mounted specter haunted Litchfield Center not only for early morning rides but also at night.

"Yes." She looked at Oliver, seeing the surprise in his eyes. "Quiet well. Despite what many Easterners believe, women can ride horses." The smile spread on his face. "I would love to show you someday." She looked down at her comfortable dress. It would not be appropriate garb to ride a horse. "But not today, this is clearly not a riding outfit." Janet opened her arms, to give Oliver a fuller view of her dress, unconsciously hoping he would. Oliver eyed the calico dress, with its high waistline, and slightly opened bodice and nodded.

"Well allow me to escort you to the picnic area." He folded his hand around her arm, which was exposed from the elbow down. The dress had short sleeves because it was designed more as a practical piece of apparel than for entertaining. But she had selected the dress so that she would be comfortable at the picnic, not for its appearance.

They walked through a shaded tree-lined area to a clearing near the lake. Sounds of birds singing after a long winter's rest filled the air, as did the laughter of the other students. Janet stood for a moment to take it all in as Oliver discreetly continued to hold her hand.

Janet's eyes took in the sparkling blue of Bantam Lake seen just a few yards away. The sun glistened off the calm water. Green grass mixed with budding flowers filled the air with a rainbow hue.

The smell of fresh air and spring's rebirth tickled at her nose. Fragrances from flowers she knew, and some she had never seen before mixed pleasantly together in the air.

* * * * *

Pairing up or congregating in small groups the men and women of the Litchfield schools shared conversations and laughter. A happy murmur pranced in Janet's ears as she looked toward them. Their dress reflected several different opinions as to how one should relax. Many of the girls still had on long ankle length gowns, some even the ones they had worn to church earlier. A few, like her and Abigail, had dawn light semi-working dresses. All the men appeared to be wearing some trousers with dull colored vests and suit coats or riding clothes. Most of them maintained some head covering, from matching top hats to felt wide brim farmer's hats. Oliver was the exception, his hat if he had one, was nowhere to be seen.

None of this, however, registered in her mind. No, it was the feel of Oliver's fingers interlaced with hers that commanded center stage of Janet's mind. Unlike a proper handholding, palm to the back of her hand, Oliver had intertwined his fingers with hers. And she had not refused. It was in fact quite a natural feeling, entirely proper in her heart to hold his hand this way. But it was more than just holding hands; it was a converging of their wills. Suddenly all the visions of James and even of Ohio left her mind, and Janet could think of nothing other than Oliver Block. Just like at the dance, he caused a fog to cover her reality. Hopes and dreams seemed possible when she was holding his hand. There was a confidence that flowed from him into her, making everything else not matter.

She turned away from the lake and looked him in the eyes. His blue iris grew lighter in the rays of the mid-afternoon sun. His face was soft and content as he looked at her. A smile, a genuine smile of pleasure looked down on her and somewhere in the back of those blue eyes the fear she had seen before had died.

A light breeze blew his hair and sent a shiver down her spine. She lost her heart. Oliver was the man in her dream! It was clear in her mind's eye that this was the man she had been seeking since she was fifteen.

A violin struck up a tune, and the two of them looked away from each other, their hands snapping apart. Embarrassed by the tenderness they had just felt, they physically separated themselves.

The violin grew louder as the player approached. It was Arthur Griswold. His hand worked the instrument with precision, and agility, bringing a light, airy piece of music to life. The picnickers gathered around, amazed at his playing. Janet looked at their faces and could not help but be delighted herself.

She made eye contact with Abigail. The Southerner beamed with emotion. "God she's falling in love," Janet told herself, and she felt warmness in her cheeks. Did she look that way? Janet rubbed her cheeks aware that others at the gathering could be looking at her. Did she look like Abigail when she looked at Oliver? She turned aside out of embarrassment and walked away from the ex-soldier.

"It was not right," her mind scolded her, "To feel anything like love for either Oliver or James." But what was love? She had to ask. Had she ever known what love was? She knew she loved her father. He had been a rock around which the whole family had been able to rally. Her mother and siblings, she had loved them, as she was supposed to love them. They were her family.

But had she known what love was outside of her family? Her heart spoke for the first time of the deep dark secret she had been maintaining since she was fifteen. Yes. She had loved once. She had loved once so long ago that her heart had sealed it away to prevent her ever loving again. That was what the dream was; she finally confessed to herself. All these years, it was the one love she had felt.

Janet walked away from the gathering picnickers, toward a long dark pathway in the woods around the lake. In there, she told herself, she could recall the truth. She could remember, and no one would interfere, no one would know.

* * * * *

The birch and maple tree limbs gathered over the cut pathway, making a natural tunnel. She walked into the tunnel and instantly felt the heat of the day diminish. "You were fifteen," her voice whispered. "What did you know?" And she was transported back to the militia's camp and the army of Northern Ohio.

The soldiers had come to help General William Henry Harrison attack Tecumseh and the British troops who had invaded Ohio. They were young and handsome in their uniforms. They were virile and vigorous as they wrestled and sparred in mock sword fights. They were dirty and grimy as they moved heavy cannons and other material around. They were coarse and vulgar when things did not go according to plans. They were heart stopping and sexual when naked from the waist up. They were everything a young girl wanted to see and know.

Janet had traveled to the camp first on an errand for her father concerning supplies for the troops. She and her brother had ventured down with a wagon full of food that the General himself had requested when he stopped at their house which stood along the army's route of march. She had been swept away by the young men and even some of the older gentlemen officers as they quickly rode here and there in the camp following this and that shouted command.

She then returned again with Miss Luella Bates the schoolteacher. She and Luella had been friends growing up. Though Luella was almost two years older than Janet, Luella seemed the younger of the two. Her one strong suit had been in academics. No one could touch her when it came to spelling and reciting. Her voice would tremble as she read the sad parts of the Shakespearean heroines, and real tears would come when needed. She was just perfect for the town to hire as the schoolteacher.

Janet had been the adventurous one of the two. Growing up, she had been the one who talked Luella into jumping off the rock cliff into the swimming pond. She had been the one who talked Luella into sneaking out and trying the hard cider her dad hid in the rafters of the barn for aging. She had also been the one who talked her into venturing out to the army camp.

The camp itself was located in a large field just south of the center of Harmony. This area provided the troops with an open space large enough for them to pitch white muslin tents, while also providing a supply of firewood from the adjacent wooded area. Smoke from the troops various campfires filled the air each day, converging into a giant cloud that hovered over the field and the lower half of Harmony's main street. The smell of this smoke reached the students sitting in the one room un-painted schoolhouse also located in the center of the town.

Janet's first camp visit had filled her with a desire to visit more and more. Luella provided her with the perfect chaperone for a trip to the encampment without her brothers or any other male adult. A few words from her and the schoolteacher appeared just as fascinated by the activities of the soldiers. Shortly after school one day, they were strolling down the dirt path from the common to the camp.

Luella's curly brown hair was a hit among the young soldier the two girls talked to as they walked along the border of the military compound. Many soldiers extended invitations to come for coffee or dinner; some of these invitations were in earnest others as mere approaches for other favors. Luella warned Janet of the advances of the soldiers but the fifteen-year-old did not believe anyone so handsome or exciting could cause trouble.

Luella finally consented to enter the camp with Janet only after a tall statuesque young officer of the Dragoons rode up to the camp's boundary. His height was impressive, forcing Janet to tip her head upward, almost backwards to see his face. As she did she took in his immaculate uniform.

Midnight black leather riding boots framed his muscular legs from stirrups to above his knee. Their polish showed no signs of wear, indicating the officer, or his aid, spent time focused on the man's appearance. Janet's eyes scanned and rescanned the boots afraid to progress further with her eyes. But the proper lady inside of her fell aside to the teenage desire to be in the arms of a gallant knight.

White tight spotless breeches flowed from inside the boots to the man's waist speaking to Janet of a virginal field of white snow. Janet's fifteen year old mind was captivated. She had always wanted a knight on a white steed to sweep her away. This officer was damn near her dream. The breeches left little to her imagination concerning the powerful muscles of the man's legs. She tingled in anticipation of something she did not know, her eyes ventured further up the figure.

His legs were bordered by a gold leather belt upon which his silver sword hung efficiently ornamental. A canvas of rich dark blue wool encased his solid full chest. This canvas, wavered with the man's breath, like a flag waving in the afternoon breeze. Janet's eyes were glued, her thoughts only on touching that chest, outlined by silver buttons, regimental buttons with eagles.

The man's face was masked halfway by the visor of his rounded leather black helmet. The gold insignia, and white chin strap all played second fiddle to the large white feather plume that fell from the top of the impressive figure. The mystery of the half hidden face, only enticed Janet to stare further, hoping to memorize the face.

His deep blue eyes shadowed by the visor scanned both girls as he paused a second upon reaching them. Janet's heart froze as his eyes showed no emotional attraction, behind his warrior's gaze. Janet was unsure if he was going to order them away, then slowly his face change from stern to delight.

Grabbing the brim of his helmet, the officer swooped off his white-plumed hat with flair. "Miss, if you would be so kind, there is some coffee waiting for conversation and a sparkling smile." He addressed Luella.

Janet looked quick to her companion. Luella had been staring just as intensely as Janet had. Her mouth slightly opened, as if trying to form words, but muted by inner turmoil. Janet knew what that turmoil was, she was feeling it herself. An action by the officer turned Janet's attention back to the man.

Dismounting by bringing his right leg over the horse's neck, the office bounced to the ground with a clink of sword metal hitting web belt metal. His extraordinary high upon the house was no less diminished when he hit the ground. He stood over six feet high, with a rich head of flowing brown locks, a smile that shined across his whole face and deep blue eyes that zeroed in on Luella

Bowing low he extended his right hand out. "I am Lieutenant Michael Premont the third of New York, at your service." His smile brightened their day, and Janet felt her own heart misbehaving.

Looking over at Luella, Janet could tell her friend was enthralled. The teacher reached for the extended hand, and the New York man kissed Luella's offered hand. Smooth and polished the officer led the two through the tent city of military life to a small fire in front of a white officer's tent.

"This is my humble abode," the man spoke. "But everything will be prim and proper." He turned from the girls and barked out, "Corporal." A gamely young boy almost as tall as the lieutenant came from behind the tent. Skinny and round face the boy looked out of place in his large blue uniform jacket with silver buttons, his helmet also masking half his face. Janet almost laughed.

"This, here, is my aid. He'll serve you two well, as a chaperone, so there will be no questions of impropriety." The officer smiled and nodded to the corporal. "Three cups," the lieutenant ordered. The boy left and returned with a silver tea service, fresh hot coffee steaming in the cups. Michael took each cup and handed it to the girls. "I must say that this is a lovely state." He looked directly at Luella, "With many incredible views." They smiled at each other. Janet felt out of place, almost forgotten. But then the officer turned his rich blue eyes to her. "And this young lady is your sister?"

"No, she is a student and friend." Luella explained. "I'm the local school teacher." The officer looked back and nodded.

"Education is the most important thing." He looked over Janet's shoulder at the sitting corporal. "I hope to send this young boy to West Point after this little disturbance with the British is done. I can see in him the making of a fine officer and gentleman." Janet looked again at the boy sitting behind her, his face slowly being shadowed by the evening sun. There did not seem anything special about him; in fact, Janet had almost forgotten that he was still there.

* * * * *

A crunch of sticks crushed under a foot brought Janet back to the dirt pathway in Litchfield. She turned around and found Abigail standing there. "They've started a fire and are roasting some chicken. Do you feel alright?" Janet nodded. "Arthur is playing again on his fiddle. He plays so heavenly." The sixteen-year-old looked back toward the picnickers. Suddenly Janet saw it. It was the same eager face and the same smile she had seen in the army camp so many years before. At that moment, a fear crept into her, fear for the safety of Abigail and her future.

Janet and Luella would visit the camp several more times, even going at night. Luella's heart was infatuated, and so was that of the lieutenant. Unfortunately, he would be one of the many that did not return alive. Tears came to Janet's eyes eight years later in Litchfield. Abigail saw them.

"Are you-all sure you're fine?"

Janet nodded again, "It was just the smoke." She smiled away the memory. "Just the smoke, but I'll overcome that." They walked back to the picnickers. Deep masculine voices filled the air with a happy song as Arthur provided accompaniment on the violin. The smell of roasting chicken mixed with the biting smoke from the wood fire. Janet sighed fighting back the old memory the smell triggered in her head.

"You're the cause." A little voice said inside her. "You're the cause." It had been there before, but she had successfully blocked it over the years. Now seeing the same smile on Abigail's face, the voice gained more power. Luella's face flashed in her memory. "Your friend was driven from the town, lost." The voice stated.

"Janet?" Oliver's voice snapped her back to reality. "Would you like some wine?" He held a glass in one hand and a bottle of port in the other. She had noticed several others were enjoying the fruit of the vine. Some wine was the customary drink with evening meals or light picnics; she heard Mrs. Pierce's lecture on etiquette. Wine, however, made her ill at ease. The bitter aftertaste of alcohol was not enjoyable to Janet. Instead, she preferred tea or even water. This time, however, she held out her hand.

Oliver passed over the glass, and their fingers touched, just as Janet had desired.

A spark of sexual electricity jumped between their fingers, and they made eye contact. Janet wished to be lost deep inside those light blue eyes. A falling sensation came to her head as she drifted in that desire. A sip of the wine did not disrupt her journey. Instead, it heightened it.

Arthur struck up a line dance, and several couples gathered in a small clearing near the fire. Oliver escorted the willing Janet to the line after she had quickly finished her whole glass of wine. Once again his hands warmed her hands and her heart. His eyes beamed with pleasure. A warming came to her face and then her breast.

They stepped out as the notes of the music guided them toward the front of the line. His hands in hers, his body balanced and steady even on the uneven ruff of the field, she was filled with a feeling of security. This time the head couple twirled down the pathway of other danced from the head to the foot of the gathering. Each spin brought Janet's face closer and closer to Oliver's chest. The silver buttons of his riding coat loomed in her eyes, their eagles nearly impress themselves into her cheek, and Janet wished they would.

Closing her eyes, she felt the breath of the man surround her with a desire to be held this close forever. There could be nothing more fulfilling as living well within this embrace. There could be nothing as rewarding as being able to share this moment, this dance for the rest of her life.

Suddenly she tripped over a root of a tree in the pathway. Oliver's hands seized her, held her on her feet drawing her into his chest. The wool of his coat scratched her face, but the bounding of his heart reached out and touched her own heart. Pure contentment covered Janet in a shroud and she relaxed into the capable hands of Oliver Block. She was captivated by his strength and agility. Time fogged in Janet's mind, as she found her idea man, the midnight cavalier slowly shifting into Oliver.

"You're falling," her head spoke to her heart. "You are allowing things to happen that can only fade away, why?"

"I need this," her heart cried back. "I need to be loved, to be held by a real man at least once in my life." The music crept into her head drowning out its fears and concerns. Janet allowed her heart to sing the tone, Arthur played, as if he was Cupid and the fiddle was his bow.

All reserve fell as Janet found every possible moment to be held by Oliver's strong embrace. Every spin, every promenade down the line, lasted forever in her mind. Social norms disappeared in Oliver's arms. She cared nothing for the eyes of others watching or their opinions about Oliver. They were jealous. Nothing but time itself could have invaded her passion.

Unfortunately the line dance ended, and the couples returned to their wine and conversation.

The chicken continued to cook. The smoky aroma triggered memories in Janet's mind now also flooded with visions of Oliver. All of these images welded together into a world of foggy boundaries between reality and dreams. More wine slipped past her lips as she danced more dances. The falling sensation spun and spun in Janet's mind; until she was sure she was harbored deep within Oliver's clear blue eyes.

His arm slipped around her waist, and she did not reject it. A tight supporting arm, one that could hold her for eternity, she mused. And she closed her eyes to the rest of the world, allowing the dreams to come.

"Janet?" She felt a breeze on her face. "Janet?" Oliver's baritone voice echoed through a fogginess she had never known before. "Janet, I'm going to have you sit here." She felt him place her on a hard surface. "I think you might have had a little too much wine." He whispered in her ear as if it was a secret he wanted her to keep. She opened her eyes and saw his face shadowed by the sun. There was a quiet, serene look that she knew she had seen before.

Suddenly the sky over his head spun violently, and she fought hard to right herself. Staggering, she knew she was going to fall, but there was an arm, his strong muscular arm holding her effortlessly. Then ever so gently he placed her back against a tree. "Sit here a minute; the fresh air will help." Heat filled her face, and she felt the perspiration break out over her body. Oliver fanned her again with his right hand. "Things will come back into focus soon." He smiled, but the look in his eyes was one of concern, grave concern.

Janet focused her eyes on his and smiled lopsidedly. "I guess." She stumbled over words that sounded distant to her ears, "I never." She looked again into Oliver's face and saw it, the same face from her dream, just older. Closing her eyes, she shook her head to clear it. "I never drank before." She heard her voice explain, and opened her eyes again. This time, it was Oliver Block's face, not the cavalier of her dreams.

"Well, you rest here," He looked over his shoulder. "I don't think anyone else noticed. They're all too busy dancing or sword fighting." His voice trailed off as he looked away. Janet got a full view of his profile. The rugged jaw line of the soldier was as solid as the mountains she had crossed to get to Litchfield. Here was a man who had been the backbone of the nation, her drunken mind rambled off. Here was the spirit of America, her heart sang. Here was the future of the country, her mind said afraid to say what it knew. Here was a profile she had known somewhere before, somewhere back in time.

"It's just your drunken mind," she told herself. "You're just confused and over excited." She reasoned. "You have mixed all of your dreams together, and Oliver happened to be here. It's just because you were thinking about Luella."

She looked back at Oliver, and the world slowly stopped spinning. She released her hand, which had been unconsciously holding onto his arm. He looked back, and she smiled.

"Are you feeling better?"

"Less dizzy," Janet said nodding her head.

"Good." He stood and stepped back to an appropriate distance. "It will be our secret," Oliver confirmed, "my word." The statement came from Oliver's lips, but Janet's mind could hear them in a different voice a sweeter, higher voice.

* * * * *

A roar of laughter erupted from the cooking fire, and all eyes turned to it. Hatless Jon Coe of Richmond, Virginia was standing over the top of another law student sprawled on the ground his arms and legs spread open, his hat lifelessly lying a few feet away. In Jon's hand was a fencing saber designed to provide practice sport only. The blunted end of the sword rested lightly on the heart area of the prone law student. "Point," Jon triumphantly called. Arthur's music whined to a stop, as the dancers' attention turned to the swordsman. Jon then looked around the gathering. "Is there not one of you Yankees who can handle a sword?"

"Well Oliver's over there," Arthur spoke up pointing to the ex-soldier still near Janet. "He was a Dragoon. Isn't that correct?" The boy from Willimantic looked over at his friend. The ex-soldier nodded.

"Well, sir would you like to give it a try? I mean the fine art of fencing not bar room brawling which soldiers seem to know so well." Jon asked his arms spread out in invitation.

"It's true, I know how to do both well, but I do not wish to participate today." Oliver said and looked back at Janet. Their eyes met and she saw them turn a little distant. He is remembering something, she thought.

He was remembering something bad that had happened in the war.

"I promise to go slow if you feel you have forgotten your talent." Joe added sarcastically.

Oliver's face turned red with anger, and his eyes dropped in color. The force revealed on his face shook Janet. He turned back to the swordsman. "No. Not today." His voice was crisp and purposeful.

"Well some men live on reputations they do not deserve. We don't want to spoil yours in front of this assembly." Joe swept his hand around to indicate the picnickers, and a few laughed. "One should always keep up appearances even if there is no support for the framework." With that, he smiled as if to say we all know you are a liar and cheat.

Janet touched him on the sleeve and Oliver looked at her. "I hate braggarts."

"So do I." Oliver smiled and slowly walked over Jon Coe.

"The lady wishes me to place you in the wrong." He said slow and quietly, each word coming from a clenched jaw. Taking the fencing saber from the prone law student, Oliver weighted it instinctively in his hand. Then looking up into Jon's eyes Oliver smiled a cold, distant smile. Coe became visibly shaken.

"You call." Oliver said, standing his ground his body slightly at an angle to Coe. The sword hung loosely at his side, point down.

"Aren't you going to come to on guard?" Jon asked indignantly. His tone showed that he did not believe Oliver knew anything about fencing.

"You call." Oliver spoke again completely at ease, not raising his sword, not altering his eyes.

"Very well," Jon sighed not wanting to push the issue anymore, feeling that he was going to make short work of yet another foe. Turning his back, he stepped away from the ex-soldier then spun suddenly sword at the ready. "Go!"

A flash of sunlight bounced off Oliver's sword as he brought it up in perfect order countering the downward thrust with which Jon had attacked. A clink of metal hitting metal resounded. The sword bounded loosely in Jon's hand, shaken from the power of Oliver's parry. Oliver Block then swept his own blade around the sword of Coe and snapped it and Jon's arm to the right of Jon's body, giving Oliver a clear shot in on the southerner's chest. This Oliver took, and tapped the man on the chest with the tip of his sword.

"Point," Oliver called off loud and firm so that all that students gathered around knew he had scored on the Southerner. This touch was followed seconds later by one to Jon's left side. "Point," Oliver echoed his first announcement. And then even quicker than the eye could see, Oliver had stepped inside of Jon's arm's reach, smashed the sword out of harm's way and lightly landed a full saber blade cut on the center of Jon's forehead. It the sword had been real Jon's face would have been reduced by half. "Point three, my match." Oliver's breath came measured and hot on Jon's face.

The students in the clearing stood silently, as Oliver stepped back, bowed and walked back toward Janet. The Female Academy student watched as the coldness in Oliver's eyes started to warm.

"God," she whispered as Oliver came within earshot. "You don't know how much I loved watching you put him in his place." The calling on the Almighty took Oliver by surprise, but he smiled delightedly at Janet.

"You're welcome."

"Well you do know how to cheat." Jon said, unable to admit defeat. "You are supposed to stop between points." He sounded like a spoiled brat who had just lost his favorite toy to another child. Oliver looked back.

"Maybe in your play world," Oliver looked back at the 'would be' duelist, "But in battle Never." He shook his head no.

"You are not a gentleman; you're just a vile piece of work. I don't know why you are allowed to live. In Virginia, you would have been called out long ago." Oliver did not get a chance to respond further as Jon charged at him again, screaming unintelligent sounds as he came.

This time, Oliver parried the incoming sword with a downward thrust that smashed the sword from Jon's hand. Then using his left hand Oliver grabbed the southerner by the throat and pushed him hard up against the tree Janet had been sitting alongside. His fake sword found the ridge of the man's Adam's apple and rested as if it was going to slice open the trachea. "You are a villain; - I jest not." Oliver spoke under control but with an undertone of violence in his voice. "I will make it good how you dare, with what you dare, and when you dare." He squeezed the man's throat tight in his left hand. "Let me hear from you." Jon merely gurgled under the pressure on his windpipe. Oliver looked away from the boy and caught Janet's shocked eyes. Releasing his hold Oliver allowed Jon to slump to the ground holding his throat in pain. Looking around, Oliver finished loudly. "Fare you well boy; you know my mind. I will leave you now to your gossip-like humor: you break jests as braggarts do their blade, which, God be thanked, hurt not." He bowed and added to the crowd of students. "I believe that's Shakespeare's <u>Much To Do About Nothing</u>, Act five, scene one."

Oliver then threw the sword in his right hand to the ground and walked off down the same path Janet had escaped on. Janet followed waving off Abigail, who had also started to follow.

****

7

Oliver's large hands shook, as he tried to calm down. His forehead, leaning on the trunk of a white birch tree, perspired with rage. It was a dark, horrible, primeval rage drilled into him by the army. In an era where you had to face your enemy, kill him with your bare hands you had to drop to a subhuman frame of mind to perform your duty. His shaking physically represented this type of rage Oliver was wrestling with now.

Instinctively he had dropped down to that sub-consciousness when Jon Coe had charged at him. Survival was well rooted in the ex- soldier's reactions, even if it meant dropping out of humanity for the duration of combat.

Again he looked at his shaking hands trying to focus his attention back to Litchfield and the picnic. "Why did you do this?"

"Why did you allow yourself to spin into this terrible black world of blood and death?"

"Why had you allowed yourself to reenter the world you've placed aside?"

On top of his loss of humanity, Oliver also gained back the memories he struggled to forget each day. The swordplay had triggered them to life again. There in his mind were his uniformed friends and comrades sparring lightly at the campfires not only with swords but also with verbal barbs. Jokes and brags filled his mind as if they were said seconds before. And Oliver traveled back in time.

The smell of horses rubbed down after a day's ride once more congealed in his nose with the smoke of a wood fire brewing a pot of camp coffee. "She is an excellent mount," Sergeant Major Zachary Ryan spoke from the distant past. Oliver was once more standing in front of his government issued chestnut stallion, rubbing its warm flank down for the night. It had been a typical day's march over several miles of the northwest, heading toward the Canadian border. "But not as fine as that girl in Harrisburg." Ryan's masculine, lustful laugh echoed across the camp field. "What do you say Squirt." He clapped Oliver on the shoulders, nearly sending him sprawling to the ground. "Are you looking for another mount like that?" He added in front of a husky, lustful laughter. The sound again filled Oliver's head. And though it was not physically possible, Oliver in his memory could see his own face. It was a toothy grin, with the patchy stubble of a 16-year-old's beard and tired, dark eyes.

"Yeah, a mount like in Harrisburg," Oliver answered back in a voice that squeaked and broke with adolescence.

"Well lad, stay with me, and you'll have plenty of fillies to mount. That's for damn sure." The older man smiled a soldier's knowing smile and clapped Oliver on the back again. As if fog cleared, Oliver could clearly see the Sergeant Major again. His face soured to life all covered with creases and crevices from his long hard life in the service, and the millions of small skirmishes he had found against the country's enemies and his own.

Thick nose and lips dominated the Sergeant's face. Between the scares of battle and small pox, the smile of his lust for life dominated the landscape of his face. Any extra folds of skin on his face or body shook with his laughter causing mere acquaintances to think he was a simple minded jolly old soldier.

But the Sergeant's blue eyes were bright and full of energy no matter what time of day or night Oliver ever looked into them. Behind these spheres of blue was a brain any commander would sell his soul to obtain. Ryan had been in too many battles and scrimmages to count, but enough to know when to duck, when to charge and when to run. He could smell an ambush, and taste the enemy's retreat in the air.

His whole life was the army, had been and would be "until he couldn't stand inspection," Ryan had once said to Oliver. Even the man's constant stubble of a beard held a military attitude.

Oliver idolized the sergeant major of the Fourth Infantry's Dragoons. The older man had served on the frontier for years against the western Indians. He had taken Oliver under his wing when the boy had arrived at camp one day. Oliver's horsemanship and horse sense had won over the respect of the older soldier. Now that the British had invaded America, he and Ryan were making ready to fight and die for their country.

Die, the word sank like a rock in Oliver's stomach.

"Die," the word echoed around his memory.

Sergeant Major Zachary Ryan would be one of many that would die at the Raisin River Massacre in January of 1813. The battle took place near Detroit. It was a major disaster for the Americans who were taken by surprise. After surrendering to the British, the prisoners were left in the care of the Indians who butchered the nearly 900 Americans. Oliver, already slightly wounded in the chest, had been sent away the day before the battle on a courier mission for his commander. That fact saved his life, but it also haunted him. He should have died with his friends, a nameless soldier buried in the western woods. Instead, he had been plagued by their faces ever since.

In a sense of regret and honor, he had tried to live out their lives for them.

"Why did you allow yourself to venture back there?" He asked himself again as he remained leaning on the birch tree in Litchfield. "It was Janet." His mind spoke. "Her eyes had enticed you. They had beguiled you into showing off." He looked again at his hands. They continued to shake with rage. "Those eyes had caused this." But no hatred came with the knowledge. Instead, her remembered smile brought a calming effect. It helped with his efforts to push the memories back into the dark recesses of his brain, back to where he wanted to store them. But they were strong so strong.

* * * * *

"Oliver?" Janet's light touch on the back of his shoulder startled Oliver from his nightmare memory. He hastily turned as if he was in battle again his hand in fists, ready to strike. His cold blue eyes met hers, and his hand shook. The unchecked sweat on his forehead dripped down his face. Janet stepped back, apprehension on her face. She had seen those eyes before. That morning when they had walked around the Green, Oliver's eyes had turned that color when he told her of his friends in the army.

It was her turn to shake. Her body reacted out of fear. It was a fear not of being attacked by the soldier in front of her, but of what was inside of Oliver. The pain and the memories that could cause such a reaction in this law student had to be so vile, so atrocious she could not bring her mind to imagine it.

"But he needed her," her heart spoke from within. "Now more than ever, he needed her." So she looked him straight in the eyes. She looked the evil that she had seen at the Green straight in the eyes and did not back down. "He needs to come back to this time, this place." She told herself, and tried with her eyes to reach into his soul.

Janet could feel his pain, not just empathy for the law student, but real physical grief. Her body shivered with despair, and her heart broke under the weight of sadness. "Lost friends," her mind spoke of her emptiness. Oliver's face blurred behind her tears, as she reached up her right hand and tenderly touched his face.

It was like the touch of an angel; his soul told him, the tender touch of an angel trying to reach out and save you. "To save me?" he questioned. Her touch reached a trigger inside opening the door back to reality and his heart and soul began to come back slowly from that sub-conscious state of the warrior.

He wrapped her smallish hand in his larger left hand. A blanket of warmth surrounded her fingers. He brought the hand to his mouth and kissed her fingers, intensely, passionately, not at all like James had that morning. She could feel Oliver's masculinity boiling behind that kiss. Their eyes stared at each other as he kissed her hand again. Nothing else registered in her mind, but the intensity of those blue dark eyes. They stared at her like the wide opened eyes of a tiger, ready to pounce. Animalistic in desire, murderous in intent Oliver's eyes bore into her as if he could read her soul.

But she was ready. She was ready to wrestle the evil out of Oliver, to bring him back to the man she had first met a week before at the Common. She was ready to do whatever was necessary to bring that happy-go-lucky smirk back to his face.

Her heart beat loud in her ears. An excited paralyzing fear like emotion filled her at seeing herself in the center of these warrior's eyes. Feeling like a mouse in the view of an owl, Janet did not know what to expect from Oliver. Hot blood flowed to her breast causing her to struggle for breath. And then he swept her close as his arm reached around her waist bringing her next to him. His strength almost lifted her right off the ground. It happened so fast, so unexpectedly that she did not fight it. Nor did she really want to fight it.

His warm breath tickled her face and her eyes instinctively closed. His lips, firm and moist touched hers, just briefly at first like a swimmer testing the water before diving into its arms. Then their lips met again in a long, heartfelt kiss.

Her heart jumped. "Had that really happened?" Her mind tried to bring sense to the abrupt kiss.

"God yes," her heart beat and rejoiced.

A taste of wine hinted on his lips, and she relaxed in his arms allowing him her full mouth. Their lips met again. This time, they touched for an even longer caress. Coaxing, flirting their lips pressed and danced together totally at ease. There was no awkwardness as she had experienced with James. No there was only desire, a desire to kiss again and again. His masculinity enclosed her in a world of passion.

Oliver knew how to kiss a woman, and he did.

Emotions flooded her. Drowning her with feelings she had only known in a dream. But this was not a dream, she told herself over and over. "This was reality!"

A burning, intense burning came to her cheeks. The heat of Oliver's lips traveled across her. Her heart stopped, she was sure. The whole world stopped, she imagined. And they kissed again. Warm wet lips pressed firmly against her mouth. Her lips reached back devouring his, begging his to come and taste again.

Like the floodwaters, once the sluice gate opens, her desire roared out of her heart. It rushed through her body causing her breast to ache and beg for caressing. Warmness settled between her legs. An intense tickling feeling sent goose bumps down her spine. Kiss after kiss, was all she wanted. His taste, bitter from the wine and sweet from his lust, lingered in her mouth. Dizziness spun her thoughts and she hoped, no prayed that she was not still drunk and only fantasying an alcoholically induced dream. But the spinning did not distract her. It did not turn her world to black. No, it made the kisses more passionate, more pleasurable.

Her legs buckled, drained of the blood that was rushing to her heart and head. Oliver's strong arm supported her, and she longed to be held like this forever. She longed to be held forever in his arms, feeling his heart pound, smelling his rich odor of cologne and horse musk, and tasting his sweet lips.

Fogginess, as powerful as the alcohol had been minutes before, cloaked her. It transported her away from Litchfield to that private world of midnight visits to her cavalier's arms. Sir Walter Scott's new book Ivanhoe had inspired her, now Oliver's kisses enthralled her. And she spun and spun in a downward falling that endlessly brought her into his solid muscular embrace.

Her breath faltered as Oliver's tongue ran along her lips, teasing them, beseeching them to open. A sigh erupted from Janet and her mouth opened ever so slightly. It was all the invitation Oliver needed, and he slid his tongue in her mouth. Softly, timidity it caressed Janet's tongue.

Passion soared from her heart filling her breast again with desire. It was her dreams come true! But it was better than any dream before. More intense, more vivid, she experienced every sensation every desire. Their tongues coaxed, danced, snuggled against each other, longing to join as one. Unaware, fogged by her emotions, Janet tilted her neck back allowing Oliver's free hand to caress and rub the nape of her neck.

His fingers so filled with rage seconds before became gentle ambassadors of love. Stroking behind her ears and at the base of her scalp, they sent a shiver of pleasure through her body. Effortlessly they crawled under her bonnet and touched her auburn hair.

Oliver's tongue left her mouth and traveled down her neck. Kissing, sucking his lips made their way to the bonnet's tie. With a simple, quick tug with his teeth and the headdress fell to the ground as her inhibitions fluttered to the winds. Once more his hand combed through her hair, releasing the tight bun holding it in place. Her long auburn locks floated down on her shoulders, a symbol of her freedom in Oliver's arms. He took a hand full of her hair and twisted it with his fingers as he pulled her tighter into his embrace.

His lips then savored the soft spot on her neck just below her right ear. New passions rocketed through her. "Oh God." she could not help but breathe and tears, tears of intensity came to her eyes.

Oliver sucked and nibbled once, and then abruptly stopped.

Stepping back, panic on his face he breathed barely able to speak himself. "I'm sorry." His eyes glared. "I made you cry."

"No," Janet refused to release her hold on his waist. When her arms had wrapped around him, she could not recall. "No." She could not say anything more her emotions were too acute.

But Oliver reached up and brushed a tear from her cheek with his right forefinger. "I made you cry." Sounding like a heartbroken boy, he licked the tear from his finger and then kissed her wet eyes.

* * * * *

No one, no one ever cried for him, Oliver's heart nearly burst when he saw Janet's eyes fill with tears. His lower lip quivered under the strain of his emotional outburst erupting from his heart. She then touched his cheek, and a passionate cloud shrouded him. He just wanted to hold her, to erase her tears. He just needed to hold her tight providing a safe haven for her. He felt guilty and ashamed at causing her tears. He only wanted to soothe them away. His heart pounded over and over in his chest. "Hug her," it called. "Hug her! Enclose her in your arms. Shelter her away from the evils you have seen."

Stepping close, he wrapped his arms around the woman and kissed her ever so softly on the lips.

She did not pull away, so he ventured again, this time with more meaning, more desire.

Lip to lip Oliver smelled lavender and port wine. Intense, passionate lips met his firm wet lips; lips that begged for more and more kisses. Kisses he was all too willing to provide. Drawn in like metal to a magnet, he kissed again and again. Her moist wet lips swelled with desire making the kisses even sweeter.

A lustful fever covered him. Heat flowed through his lips into Janet. She gasped, and his tongue found hers. It felt so soft and tender against his. A desire centered itself between his legs as he reached further into Janet with his tongue. She reacted unhesitant, devouring his passion, caressing his tongue in return, encircling his desire with a twisting hugging tongue.

Janet' passion sucked Oliver into her fervent embrace. Her arms wrapped around him, squeezing out her emotional cry. She was proclaiming a need, a longing need to be held close, safe and secure. Oliver closed his eyes allowing his self-defensive wall to fade. In so doing his rage disappeared and he found only thoughts of Janet. Campfires disappeared; faces long since buried vanished, leaving only this moment in time, this moment with Janet in his arms.

Her head tilted to his kisses, and he ran his tongue over the exposed slender neck. "Oh God!" she moaned, and he nibbled at her neck. Her skin soft and inviting more nibbles, more kisses. She shuddered in passion. The sensation caused him to forget proper form and etiquette. All that mattered was Janet, as their bodies snuggled in this fiery embrace. His mind only pictured this needy being pleading to be held encompassed in a desire new to both of them. A desire he never knew he could feel. But it was there full in his heart, undeniable.

Suddenly a tear crept onto his cheek. He paused unsure what it was. Then again a tear came.

Opening his eyes he saw them, crawling on Janet's cheeks. And panic seized him.

"God, you've hurt her!" His heart called. "You hurt her just when everything was right!" Words choked him. A distant pain twisted his heart, and he breathed. "I'm sorry." A thousand things flashed through his mind screaming to be said but only,

"I'm sorry. I've hurt you," came out. Unable to express anything else, he wiped a few tears with his fingers and then tried to erase them with kisses.

A salty taste filled his lips as he kissed one eye and then the other. The gesture brought the whiff of lavender again and focused him back to the wood path in Litchfield. Oliver stepped back and looked Janet in the eyes.

"I'm," he started, but she placed a finger over his lips.

"You did nothing wrong." Their eyes focused. Intensity filled the air, thick enough to be touched. "You did nothing wrong." Janet stressed each word for assurance, not only for Oliver but also for herself, as the fog lifted from her mind. "Nothing wrong," she told herself, "Nothing wrong!"

Janet took his right hand in both of hers and brought it to her breast. The action spoke more than her words ever could. "Feel my heart," she whispered, tongue-tied by the emotions within. "How could that be wrong?" Her heart pounded in her chest. Oliver's hand jumped, and he smiled like a little boy receiving a present.

He brushed back a few strands of her hair that had fallen over her face. She blushed, realizing what they had just done. Oliver smiled and could not say a word. They just looked into each other eyes for a few minutes, remembering, tasting the heated kisses again.

"Is it bad memories?" Janet finally asked trying to calm down her own heart, aware that the moment together had come and gone. It was more important now to show Oliver she cared about his feelings, about his memories.

The ex-soldier nodded.

"I saw them too, in your eyes and on your face." She paused in thought trying to find the correct words. Then she touched his face again with her hand. "I saw them when you turned around the first time after sparring with Jon. They were more dominant in your eyes the second time he came at you. I knew. No, I felt that you needed me."

Oliver bent down and kissed her lips silent. Her eyes closed to swim once more inside their pool of passion.

"Thank you." He whispered with a delight she had never heard in a voice before. She opened her eyes and smiled; internally pleased with herself and glowing with a satisfaction she had never known. So sweet, so soft, so special his kiss had been. It was not as extreme as the others, but it had been more personal.

"There are times when the past does not wish to remain the past." Oliver explained. "And it roars out of my mind like a stallion at full gallop, unstoppable, uncontrollable." Oliver looked at his hands afraid they would shake again. Janet squeezed them tight.

"I'll hold them." She said as if she had read his thoughts. "I'll stop them from shaking, forever if you wish." The statement hung there in the air, a hopeful wish. A bare naked wish directly opened to Janet's heart. Why she had said it, she did not know, but Janet could not take it back, nor would she. His kiss had awakened teenage dreams of love, dreams she had placed away with her hope of marriage. Seeing him so shaken by past nightmares, stirred her heart. She knew she could comfort him, make him whole again if Oliver would let her close.

Oliver hesitated for the first time in his life. Battles had hardened him to death, but this was life.

Janet was offering him life.

The ex-soldier looked over her shoulder at the trees and Bantam Lake just barely visible through the foliage. A bird sang out, and he wrapped his arms around her in a hug. "This was perfect," his heart said. The warmth of her tender body filled him with contentment, more than an early morning horse ride ever did. But his mind knew the truth. His situation trapped him between this comfort and the reality of his world.

There had been no place of rest for Oliver Block since he ran off from his father's horse farm in Sharon.

Across the western frontier, he had traveled with the Fourth Infantry during the war bringing death and destruction. His commander, a surrogate father figure, had died in his arms while calling out the name of a woman he had loved. In New York City where he had been part of an adopted family, he had been pushed out because of death. Even here in Litchfield, he had not been accepted inside the social norms and served as a symbol of destruction. He could not bring that curse onto the only person who ever cried for him.

"There is too much you don't know." He spoke hesitantly from his heart. "Too much that I can't tell you." Oliver looked away from Janet afraid that her brown eyes would make him stop. "I'm chasing a dream." He heard the words that had been encaged inside of him for years, suddenly escape. "There is a restlessness inside of me that pushes me on. Or causes things to happen that which demand I leave. In the army it was understood, battles and the enemy moved you from place to place. I never outgrew that. And then there was this vision." He looked at Janet. The long shadow of the shaded wood path made it appear almost like evening and for the briefest second Oliver recognized the face. "My God," His words stopped, and his heart stood still. A distant whiff of smoke and the crackle of burning wood filled his head.

"What?" Janet's concern came back; as she saw Oliver's eyes lose focus. He was falling back into the past again. She hugged him tight, hoping to hold him here in the present. His riding coat was coarse and itchy against her face, but she held on, held on tight as if that alone would keep him there in Litchfield. Then she asked. "What vision? Share it with me."

"There was this girl." His words came measured, unsure of his footing. Janet stepped back inside the hug creating distance between the two. Oliver could sense the statement disturbed her, but he had to express it. "There was this girl." He looked at her. Their eyes met, and he could see an anxious curiosity in her brown eyes.

"I know from New York City." Her voice quivered, unsteady as if it did not want to know what he was about to say. But Oliver knew she had to know. Oliver understood that nothing could move forward unless she comprehended his vision, his haunting vision.

"No, before her, before everything I've done to please the ghosts in my head." Images of his army comrades flashed through him. "She was," he paused, and Janet could feel the turmoil inside of Oliver. "She was my anchor. An old sergeant major once told me, that when you prepare to die, you need a reason. His was a little boy who had played on his knee once when he had camped outside of Harrisburg, Pennsylvania. He dreamed that one day that boy would grow up in a country free from the British and their Indian allies. Free to study the arts, not war. Mine was of this girl." He paused and licked his suddenly dry lips.

"She was a teenage girl who I saw only once in the light of a campfire. An aurora fanned out from around her face, like a hallo, if you want to be religious. I'm not. But I saw it, as plain as I see you now. And I knew she was the spirit of the whole country. She was the spirit of all those settlers out West who gave up everything and took a chance in a new land. I know it sounds ridicules and melodramatic, but when you are sixteen, and about to fight, you see things differently then when you are older or younger. I knew I could not let this young girl down, and I vowed myself to her like my sergeant major had pledged to the little boy." He paused again and released his hold on Janet.

Looking away from her he added softly, as if he was praying, praying to this vision. "There are times when I know I love her. I see her in my mind at least once a day. I wake in the middle of the night from nightmares where I've watched her walk away while I stand silently unable to speak to her."

Their eyes met again, and all the tension slipped away. Janet reached out and tenderly touched his face again, as she had done when he was struggling with his rage. He enveloped her hand in his, like before and gently kissed her fingertips.

"Did you ever tell her?" Janet asked, no longer put off.

Oliver looked at her in the eyes and released her hand, well aware of who stood in front of him now. "No. My troop marched away from that campsite and fought at the Raisin River Massacre." He looked down at the ground and Janet could tell tears were in his eyes. Slowly Oliver shook his head back and forth. "We never went back that way. We couldn't go back. There weren't enough of us left alive to be called an army."

Janet touched him softly on the shoulder; the emotions he was feeling caused her to hurt inside as well. "I spent nearly a year in an out of medical care, first in the army and then at the home of my commander's family in New York City. He had died but not before writing to his father of how I had become like a brother. His sister came to love me, but diphtheria stole her away. Since then I have been wandering searching for something. What I'm not sure."

"Could it be that girl?" Janet asked her voice quivering from a tear. Oliver looked up and they could see each had been crying.

"Yes, you," his heart wanted to cry out. It wanted to scream from the top of the nearest tree that the little girl was Janet. But the words strangled his throat. He wanted to cry, "I love you, and have loved you since we met so many years ago," but the words did not form. They remained unborn inside his heart.

Instead his lips quivered out. "No one has ever cried for me." His tongue tied lips trembled with the words. "No one has ever cared that much." Janet threw herself into his arms.

"I do."

"You can't." He summoned up all his strength to explain. "You can't. I'm cursed and you're too good."

"No." She stepped back again realizing what Oliver was doing. He was purposely breaking off their friendship. He was trying to push her away. "No." She declared unwilling to be brushed aside especially now that she had tasted the reality of her dream.

"You're too good for me. Hell you're too good for your damn little town in Ohio. You need to be loved by someone who can care for you, give you everything a woman needs and wants. That's not me. I'm too self-centered and to lost. I would tell you that I love you, but I can't put that burden on you. I do want to hold you and kiss you forever, but that could not be your type of love, just a soldier's love."

"No." Janet's fears came to the surface. "You don't mean what you're saying."

"Maybe," He looked away from her. "But I do know I should walk away now, if for no other reason than to save your reputation." He released her and walked away.

Janet stood there silently watching. It was as if her dream had become reality. Her cavalier was leaving just as he did every night she dreamt of him. Oliver's back faded away as he walked down the pathway toward the picnic and his chestnut mare.

"Damn you." She swore for the first time in her life. "Damn you, for breaking my heart and teasing me with these impossible feelings." She looked up at the sky to face the tormentor of her life. "Why?" Tears came. "What entertainment do you get from torturing the heart of a one-room school teacher?"

She breathed in deep, closed her eyes and regained control of her emotions. Christian chastity, proper ethics and social responsibility were concepts she had suffered with all her life. Now they were more of a millstone hung around her neck. She wanted to run after Oliver, tackle him and hold him until all the evilness had fled from his soul. She wanted to prove to him that she understood his needs and his pain. But those three concepts held her glued to that spot by Bantam Lake in Litchfield. It was not the right thing to do for a young lady to chase after a man. Luella had, and what happened to her? Janet asked herself. The pregnant 16 year-old was driven out of Harmony, Ohio.

Janet reached down and picked up her bonnet. She was not as free as she had thought a few minutes before. Twisting her hair into a bun, she replaced her bonnet and walked down the path herself. Oliver was already mounted on his horse when she came to the end of the path. He looked at her, sadness on his face that reached out and crushed her heart.

"Damn you," she whispered again this time cursing Oliver Block. He spun on his horse and rode off. His silhouetted figure in the sun, hung in her mind's eye so incredibly familiar she shook with confusion. And then she laughed the déjà vu feeling off as just a reaction to her broken heart.

8

Oliver spurred the seasoned horse on, giving it its heart to race the wind. He had been one with this horse since he left the service. They had become partners in a small stable just outside New York City, where Oliver watched the horse's birth. Oliver was allowed to train it any way he felt was correct. And this mare, along with several others, became the results. Each was a well sought after animals among the housemen of the New York, New Jersey and Connecticut area. The sable's owner, his semi-adopted father, was never prouder of his own flesh and blood.

The animal was getting old now, Oliver knew, but could not bring himself to think about what that truly meant. Few things had been as consistent as this horse in his life. Pegasus, named for the winged mount of Greek Mythology, was one of the few living beings in his life that did not question, or look down on him. The only other being that had not done that was the fifteen-year-old vision of Janet Fellows that daily played in his mind. Like Pegasus, Oliver now knew she too was coming to an end.

Age had crept up on both.

The horse's trot turned to a full gallop. Thump - thump - thump the hoofs of the horse pounded the hard dirt road that led to town. Their hollow sound echoed off the trees that lined the road and reverberated in the rider's ears. Only the hard breathing of the horse invaded that thumping - thumping - thumping.

Oliver's body leaned forward in the worn leather saddle. It felt the vibration of the charging horse and relaxed. Each thump brought the jolting earth all the way through Oliver's spine, clearing his head of all thoughts other than this freedom.

A laugh left Oliver's throat, a tension-easing laugh. It was almost a hysterical laugh of ecstasy and liberty. This laugh shook his body all over, cleansing him, freeing him from the world around him. It was as if he was in an independent universe, just him, the horse and the gallop. That is what riding full gallop felt like to the ex-soldier. He relaxed in the saddle and leaned further forward nearly touching the horse's neck. His body became one with the gait of the horse, balanced with the drumming hoofs, floating when the animal remained suspended in the air in mid-stride.

He was flying. Like the darting, singing birds above him, he was flying, free from the pull of the earth. Soaring like a hawk or an eagle, he drifted at the will of the horse as the raptures above drifted on the will of the wind currents. On board that horse, or any horse, at full gallop Oliver became the charging cavalier again, striking fear into a body of troops facing the onslaught of a company of mounted Dragoons with lances ready or drawn sabers.

A clear open grassy ground suddenly appeared in his head. The regiment formed to the left and right of him. Each man bedecked in his perfect uniform, his dress uniform, as if on parade instead in a battle's fray. Blue resplendent wool coats silky sleek from hours of rubbing and pressing, and white pristine riding breeches carefully bleached and cared for, shined in the sun. Flashes of sunbeams bounced in sharp pointed imitations of lightening here and there off the polished weapons of war.

A charge! The command was coming down the line. A charge! The regiment was going to perform a mounted charge, the most beautiful sight anyone could ever witness. The regiment was going to carry out a mounted charge the most awe-inspiring sight in which anyone could ever participate. White-plumed black leather helmets stood rigidly at attention, ready, waiting, eagerly waiting for the command.

All the muscles of the horses and humans, straining to be allowed to step forward, to be allowed to jump forward, to be allowed to race forward. A charge! The command was coming; the command was all that was needed to set this juggernaut forward, to release the tension felt in every nerve along the line. That was what streamed through Oliver's mind as the horse floated momentarily in the air. A charge!

"Aah!" Oliver cried into the animal's ear urging it faster as the visions in his mind kept changing every second that he was momentarily free from the world. From the charge, the rider sailed into the world of campfires and fields of white tents. Here the faces of tired warriors' ghosts sang and drank once again. Comradeship, lustful comradeship filled the rider's emotional void, and the once more smiling women of questionable social status appeared in the arms of comrades.

"Aah!" Oliver cried again urging the horse even faster. Janet's sweet fifteen-year-old face danced across the rider's field of visions. "Aah!" Oliver yelled trying to outrun the ghosts in his head. But he knew he would fail. Janet unknowingly had seen to that.

Campfires and the sound of duty drums played in his memory. Blue and white flashes of torn bloody Dragoon uniforms appeared in his mind. White plumes fluttering in the breeze all came back all interrupted his flight from Bantam Lake to Litchfield. But dominating all these visions, he tried to run from, was that of fifteen-year-old Janet Fellows.

It had been her, Oliver told himself. It had been her vision that had led him through the blood and gore of battle. It had been her, who had sat at the campfire so many years before. There had been times during the years that Oliver had sworn he had only imagined the haunting young girl in Ohio. The troop had been marching non-stop for weeks, endless weeks of little sleep. He could easily have had delusions, other soldiers did. This radiant vision of young womanhood could have been a delusion; Oliver had tried to convince himself throughout the eight years since he had first seen Janet.

But this apparition was more than a delusion to Oliver. It was an emotionally charged vision. Pure and white against the evening gray sky, the girl's face had been forever etched in his memory as deeply engraved as the Regiment's Silver cup with its battle's honors. Because of this powerful sensation caused by the girl's angelic face, a part of him could never let itself believe that the fifteen-year-old was not real. He had found her again. Today that part of him triumphed! She was real! She was here at his fingertips waiting for him to embrace her.

He pulled the horse up sharp. The deceased Dragoons instantly disappeared from his mind's eye. He was alone again, alone on the tree-lined, dirt pathway between Litchfield and the lake. He was alone to wrestle with his thoughts and emotions. Alone as he had been for most of his life, alone except for that haunting vision of Janet Fellows.

"What now?" He asked himself out loud. His baritone voice filled the void left by the abruptly silenced hoofs. "What to do?" His mind raced in a thousand different directions.

"You can tell her." He shook his head no. "You can run away." Again his head shook no. "You can just watch and say nothing." The three options battled for attention in his skull. They banged about and shouted for attention. They raised such turmoil inside him that he shook his head to remove them from his thoughts, but it did not work. He had to make a decision. He had to address them, now.

He eased the horse into a gentle walk as he talked to himself. "You could tell her the truth. She obviously does not remember you." The concept that his ideal woman would not recognize him had never occurred to him over the eight years since Oliver had first seen Janet. Nor had the fact that she might have grown-up ever crossed Oliver's imagination. In his mind, the campfire girl had remained fifteen and would always remain fifteen until he returned to her in Ohio.

"Funny how the mind hangs on to a vision of things and does not allow time to change it," he reflected, somewhat philosophical. But then he quickly returned to the issue at hand, already hearing the three options stirring up a commotion in his brain.

"The question is," Oliver paused in his argument. "Do you want to confront her? Do you want to bring an end to all those years of magical allusion that have played in your mind? Bring an end to all those secret desires and made-up scenarios you have lived out with her over the past eight years?" Oliver sadly shook his head "It's not the right time for that." He could not bring himself to kill those secrets dreams. "No, she would not see the significance of the vision I have carried all these years."

"You could ride away then." His time at the law school was coming to an end. He could easily move back to New York or elsewhere, leaving Janet behind and remember only the fifteen-year-old at the campfire. "But could you forget her?" His voice grew solemn. "She cried for you." His heart skipped a sudden beat. "She's that fantasy you've lived for these past eight years. How can you walk away from all your hopes, dreams, and aspirations?"

He paused as he remembered visions that had haunted him such as dreams of his returning to Ohio to sweep her off her feet. Dreams of weddings and family gatherings filled with fictitious children and in-laws. Christmases and Thanksgivings spent in each other's arms, aware of the mutual love that had been born at the campfire, nurtured over time and matured in each other's arms.

In these dreams, there were kisses, kisses, and hugs like what he experienced that afternoon. Oliver tasted Janet's kiss on his lips again. A lustful smirk came to him. It was a fulfillment of many of his haunting visions. "Those kisses of hers?" he smirked. Gently tapping the horse's flanks, he brought the animal to a lazy trot. "Yes, your vision has grown-up, gone is that sweet fifteen-year-old. But the kisses she gave today have made it worth the loss." The smirk stretched into a smile that hurt the corners of his mouth.

"Oh her kisses," his voice trailed off, and he understood that he could not just ride away from Janet, but how could he ever win her heart, as deeply as he had won the heart of his imaginary lover?

* * * * *

Abigail watched Oliver Block ride away before approaching Janet. "Well he looks a little calmer, but you're all red." She spoke in her slow southern drawl. "Did he get your blood up?" A mischievous smile came with the question. Janet's eyes flared at her, and the Southerner stepped away.

The smile disappeared, as the younger girl realized she had gone too far. "Well anyway, you-all seemed to have caused him to calm down." Janet nodded the anger slowly leaving her eyes. "Men, what good are they anyhow." Abigail joked trying to make Janet feel better and reached over to take her hand. Oliver had just held that hand, was all Janet could think about when Abigail's fingers touched hers. Oliver had just kissed that hand. The memory replayed in her heart.

Abigail tugged her toward the picnickers. "Now honey, you-all better get you bonnet back on, besides Arthur wants to go wading." She was chatting as if there was no one else in the world but herself. That was how it was; Janet had come to see from her teaching. Teenagers, whether boys or girls, were so self-centered that they would hold whole conversations with other people, and not realize no one was listening. It worked the other way as well. People could converse with a teenager, and the child would be so involved with something in their mind he or she would not hear a single word. Abigail was still rambling on about how the water would be colder than she wanted, but that the day seemed hot enough to venture the swim.

"Well, what do you think?" She looked at Janet. The older woman stood there staring at Abigail, not sure what to say, her mind was still recalling the savage kisses Oliver had implanted on her lips.

"He could not have kissed me that intently, that earnestly if he did not have feelings for me." Janet argued within herself. "He's hiding behind his past. I can help him overcome that I know I can." She looked down the dirt road the chestnut mare had trotted off on, and hope returned. Oliver Block would be hers; she smiled inside. All she needed to do was be patient. That was what all the writers she had read proclaimed love would come to those who did not push.

"Well, what do you think?" Abigail interrupted Janet's thoughts. "I need you to go." There was urgency in her voice. Janet blankly stared at her. "Weren't you-all listening to anything I was just saying?"

Frustration filled Abigail's voice. And then a giggle erupted from her mouth, and Janet could clearly smell alcohol on her breath. For a split second, she wondered how much of the wine Abigail had drunk and Luella's face flashed in Janet's mind. The vow Janet had pledged the night before to not let Abigail follow Luella's path, entered her thoughts. Her heart turned cold in panic, had she left Abigail alone too long?

The Southerner broke into her fears again with a near giggle. "You-all were thinking about Oliver. I can tell. It's written right on the red of your cheeks." She giggled some more. "I bet you helped him calm down." She leaned in close. "It's just our little secret if you-all come wading, but if you-all don't? I don't know if I can control that tongue of mine." She giggled even louder.

"Blackmail is an ugly habit." Janet warned.

"Yes, but it gets a lot of results." Abigail smiled back. "Are you coming?"

Janet nodded, "Only to save your reputation."

"And yours?" Abigail teased. Janet could not tell if the girl knew what indeed had just happened down the path from the picnickers, or if she would make up something to fit her imagination. The two girls walked back, arm in arm to the other students.

****

The water was cold, freezing cold. Why she had allowed Abigail Stuart to talk her into wading was beyond Janet's comprehension. But here she was, nearly knee deep in Bantam Lake. "It's too cold." She shivered and Abigail giggled. The curly red head was standing next to Janet, her dress likewise drawn up to their thighs revealing her thin, pale lower legs to Arthur.

The Willimantic native's eyes remained glued on the younger of the two girls wading in the water. Pure lust filled his charming hazel eyes, just as Janet had expected. A twinge of excitement shuttered around her body as she realized her figure was just as responsible for Arthur's stare as Abigail's figure. "That lucky man," Janet thought. "He has two beautiful women showing off their enchanting legs for his pleasure. Oh, I wish Oliver were here. His eyes would warm me, and I would be able to stay in the freezing water forever."

She pictured the blue of Oliver's captivating eyes and shook again, this time not for the cold of the water, but from the heat, his lips had caused earlier. She tasted again the bitter wine and the salty tears that were his lips. The vision froze her in her progress through the water. All her attention was zeroed in on the memory. "Could he be my cavalier?"

Once more her mind replayed Oliver's exit down the wooden path. His back, his whole personal on board that horse struck the remembrance bell inside of Janet. She had last seen her cavalier in the same disposition, riding away from her on board a horse into the morning sun.

Tears blurred Janet's eyes a moment. She wiped them away. Her body shivered either from the cold water, or the realization that Oliver and her vision were actually one and the same. "How will I know?" she spoke to herself. Oliver's exiting replayed over and over in her mind's eye. "How will I be able to confront him?"

"If he is the same boy than I'll look bad not having remembered him."

If he's not the same person I'll look despite as if I was making up a story to convince him to stay with me." Tears again came to her eyes. "He'll think I'm crazy."

"You're turning blue." Abigail giggled again and leaned closer, physically invading Janet's dream world. "Do you think Arthur has seen enough?" Her meaning came out in her tone. She wanted Janet to judge how much dress should be raised, to regulate how much leg was being shared.

"I think this is deep enough," Janet smiled back at the younger girl. "I mean I think your modesty is in danger."

Abigail laughed out loud at Janet's witty remark. The hint of alcohol on her breath once more warned Janet that the younger woman had been drinking a little too much.

"I do want him to remember this." Abigail whispered loud enough for only Janet to hear. "Do you-all think he will?"

Janet quickly nodded. "Almost any male I know of would remember such an immodest sight." Abigail nodded also and the two headed back toward shore.

"Why didn't you join us?" Abigail confronted the gawking law student as they stepped out of the water.

"It's too early for swimming." Arthur said. "In eastern Connecticut, you can catch your death of cold swimming too soon. Besides, you two wouldn't want to see me in my long johns." He laughed. "You might never erase that vision from your heads." They all laughed, and Janet knew Abigail was trying desperately to put that image in her head.

Stockings and shoes were discreetly placed back on, while Arthur sought to snatch a second look at the girl's slender legs. Janet again found pleasure in the idea of her own attractiveness. Ohio was so different than here, she told herself. There she was a respected, but isolated member of the community. She lived under the constant supervision of the elders. Wading in a brook like this would never be permitted. Attending a picnic with alcohol and fiddling or dancing might even lead to her dismissal. Social decorum was paramount in Harmony, especially for a teacher.

As Janet finished buttoning her shoes, she looked over at Arthur and Abigail. They had opened another bottle of port wine. They were holding hands, behind their backs, so others would not notice. Janet smiled remembering Oliver's hand in hers. Looking down, she could almost feel its warmth and the gentle squeeze of his fingers between hers. Moistening her lips, she closed her eyes and again tasted Oliver's kiss.

Unexpectedly, for the first time, Janet actually considered not returning to Harmony. "How could that be arranged?"

Janet pictured herself refusing to leave Litchfield at the end of her school. "I could simply refuse to board the coach." She thought, watching the imaginary Janet standing there at the Green, suitcase in hand, as the red coach headed down West Street. "All the other students would watch me. The teachers would scorn me." She paused in thought. "Everyone would be so shocked they would have nothing to do with me. Maybe even Oliver would frown on me for not following through with my contact."The thought played around her head a moment.

Suddenly Janet pictured herself boarding the coach, and heading west toward Ohio, when suddenly a tall lone dark clothed rider appears on the edge of town. "Halt that coach," Calls a rider, his face masked from recognition. The driver, fearful for his life stops the vehicle, and slowly the equine mounted figure pulls a hand gun.

"I'm not interested in any gold of jewelry today," the man's voice rings across the hollow where the coach rests still. "I have plenty of those. I'm looking for something even more valuable. I seek the other half of my heart. It is in the procession of a passenger on this stage. If she would simply disembark, I'll let the rest of you go unmolested."

Janet Fellows steps down from the coach, her heart beating loud enough from the passengers to hear. There is subtle hush among the women, keeping their children and husbands from spoiling the scene.

"I believe I am the possessor of that treasure," Janet nervously state as she approaches the rider.

"Indeed you are," Oliver responds, holstering his drops his weapon simultaneously. Then as quickly as the humming bird flies, he reaches down and sweeps the young lady into his arms. Placing her on the back of his horse they ride into the night.

Abigail's laugh abruptly transported Janet back to reality. The vision in Janet's eyes transform into the afternoon picnic area around Bantam Lake. She looked quickly around her, but saw no horse nor rider or stage coach. "It was all a fantasy made up in your mind."

Focusing again on Arthur and Abigail, she noticed the two had separated themselves from the rest of the picnickers. They had found a shaded are with several fallen trees to sit on. A small patch of young saplings provide a privacy hedge from the remainder of the picnickers.

The younger Academy student laughed again, as she sat next to Arthur on a fallen tree. The law student had his head tilted toward Abigail, as if he was whispering in the girl's ear. Abigail's hands were covering her mouth hiding her teeth from view.

Vanity, Janet thought. "The girl is too full of vanity."

"Janet," Abigail called over. "You should hear Arthur's stories about the law school. You-all won't believe what happens there."

"Tell me." Janet said as she sat down on the fallen tree alongside the others. She suddenly felt like a teenager again, with nothing but gossip about which to worry. It was strange how only a week in Litchfield had erased the role of matron teacher from Janet's heart.

"Well," Abigail turned to her, a flush full in her face. "It seems that Mr. Reeve can't talk above a whisper. The whole class has to remain silent, writing down notes as he speaks about his cases, and law."

The younger woman's speech came out slightly slurred which explained for her silliness. "It seems that your Mr. Mathers had a problem with keeping up on his note takings." She eyed the older woman. "It's a rumor he paid for someone's notes, a big no, no among the students." Rocking back on her heels in disgust, Abigail tapped her nose. "Well, James thinks it's Oliver, who spread the rumor when it really wasn't. Arthur here says it's none other than Jon Coe. You know the idiot with the fencing swords." She leaned in close to Janet as if to tell her a secret, the now strong stench of alcohol on her breath was staggering to Janet.

"You better go tell your sweetie to take that Jon out and really show him what a sword is for." The words left Abigail's mouth, but her eyes glazed over, as if she was fighting with a concept that words could not express. She looked at Janet, then at the ground, and finally at Arthur before rubbing her face with her right hand. The fingers played with her lips, feeling them, to make sure they were still on her face.

She wanted to say something, but the words would not leave her lips. Abigail pictured Oliver Block, and then James Mathers. Their names spun around her head, as did their faces. First there was Oliver kissing Janet and then James kissing Janet. Then there was trees and the ground spinning around with Janet and the others.

Staggering to a full upright sitting position, Abigail tried to focus on Janet's eyes but did not succeed. "But then you don't know who your sweetie is. Do you?"

Abigail looked back at Arthur and then at Janet. Her face paled as her lips sagged a second, a little drool came to its corners. "I don't feel too good," she slurred as she slumped to the ground and closed her eyes.

Arthur was there is a second, holding Abigail's head up off the grass. He looked up at Janet, a panic in his eyes.

"How much has she been drinking?" The older student sternly asked.

The law student shrugged his shoulder. "I think this is our third or fourth bottle. I lost track." His own voice showed signs of drunkenness.

"Well we better sit her up then." She stooped down next to the couple and struggled with the weight of unconscious Abigail. She never heard the sound of approaching feet until; James Baldwin Mathers was kneeling next to her. The Maryland student effortlessly took Abigail's full weight on his shoulders. Then with little strain he lifted her up in his arms.

"I'll put her over here by this tree." He spoke to the other two. "Then I'll get the wagon I brought from town." He looked over at the other two. "Are you both alright?" Janet hastened her step so that she was alongside of James.

"I'm fine, but Arthur and Abigail here have tasted too much of the vine." She tried to sound mature and in control. But something had happened to her reasonableness. She wanted to be the teenager again in James arms, not the old unmarried teacher of Harmony, Ohio. And she laughed an infective laugh that caused James to chuckle as well.

"I guess holding one's wine is not something they teach you at Mrs. Pierce's Female Academy is it." He looked over at her, a sparkle in his hazel eyes. He was happy at that moment, happier than he had been in a long while. Janet noticed that he had changed out of the formal outfit he had been wearing at church into one of dark trousers, muslin shirt and navy blue riding coat with red velvet cuffs and collar.

Squatting down when he reached the tree, James gently placed Abigail on the ground. Janet eased her against the tree making sure she would not fall back over. Arthur thumped to the ground next to the unconscious girl.

"Is she still breathing?" Arthur asked. His eyes were unable to focus.

"Yes, no thanks to you." James turned his eyes dark. Janet was amazed at the effect. James' presence was overwhelming. The way he took command of the situation caused her to feel safe and secure. The same secure feeling she had when she was in her father's home. Admiration filled her as she stepped away, mentally from the situation and watched the law student in action. He used just the right method to gain Arthur's attention and then compliance. There was no wasted effort, no overbearing, just simple command of the situation.

"Don't you know you are the host of this gathering? It is your responsibility to maintain the reputations of these two fine young ladies. A trip down Bacchus' lane is uncalled for and irresponsible. If it was not for me, you would have caused great disgrace to fall upon yourself and these two ladies." His angry words came like slaps to Arthur's face. The other law student visibly shook the effects of alcohol on his body. "Good God, man what were you thinking?"

"I guess I wasn't. It was such a pretty day, and the girls were just as pretty." He looked over at Janet and then at the snoring Abigail. "I'm sorry." He looked at Janet again. "I'm so sorry. I think I was just so excited at being in Miss Stuart's company. She is the prettiest girl I have ever been able to speak to." He bit lower lip as the confession poured from his mouth. "I have spent too much time working in the mills, to ever believe that such a wonder as she could ever spend time in my company." He looked at the ground and Janet could feel his sorrow surge inside him.

"It is fine," Janet reached over and kindly touched him on his arm. "She will be alright." Arthur smiled somewhat relieved.

"A little foggy in the head and possibly nauseous," James spoke. "We will need to get her home, before anyone else comes in this area. This could ruin her chances to study at Mrs. Pierce's." He sternly looked at Arthur for affect and then he looked over his shoulder as if he expected other picnickers to come through the clearing between the lake and the picnic site. There was no movement their way by the others.

"Fortunately I have a wagon." He looked at Janet. "I had to finish up some preparation work for the mock trial this week, before I came to the picnic. I borrowed one of those new small Buck wagons that we use a lot of in Maryland. The Governor's just bought it." He explained, not really sure why he was explaining. She nodded. "The mock trial will be held later this week, it would be an honor if you would come and listen." His eyes scanned her whole face looking for some glimmer of her acceptance.

"I heard about it from Oliver Block." James' hazel eyes shadowed at the mention of Block's name.

"He also invited me."

"Well I guess the sweetest rose draws all the bees." The wit impressed Janet and she smiled embarrassed. The red flashed across her face, and James felt his heart beat faster. He reached out and touched her hand, as he had done on the Green earlier that day. "It would be a great honor if you would come and support me." His smile was entirely different than she had seen before. It pleaded with her to name him her champion, like the knight of Camelot.

Once more the vision of her cavalier rode through her mind. Ivanhoe and the knights of King Arthur were constant readings of the schoolteacher. The poor lonely, isolated teacher of Harmony, Ohio who knew there would never be such a hero in her life. But that lonely person was not standing there in the Litchfield woods, instead there was a new person, well the rebirth of the older Janet Fellows, was standing there in the woods. This individual wanted one of these knights to come and take her away from the dark castle called Harmony. That new person wanted to be rescued by a shiny armored knight. Was James that knight?

"You do not have to answer me," he cautioned. "I'll simply look for your presence on Friday. Now let's get these two back to town before Abigail wakes." He stood up. "I'll go for the wagon." He hesitated a second looking from Abigail to Janet. "Do you know what might happen if she wakes?"

"Yes, I have seen drunken people before." Janet answered making full eye contact with James. She had seen her brothers and father throwing up, after a day of celebrating. Her father in particular was not a happy drunk. He often woke from short slumbers to want a fight or with thrashing of his fists. "Yes," she repeated again, sadness in her voice. "I have seen drunken people before, waking out of a stupor like this.

He nodded, a smirk barely noticeable, but noticeable enough for Janet.

"Don't be so condescending!" Janet's anger flared. "It has nothing to do with my western manners. You know just as well how drink is common among all the people of this nation. I have dealt with drunken people as I am sure you have, by the knowledge you so adeptly applied here." James held up his hands in an artificial surrender gesture and then walked off.

She had made a point with the future attorney, he thought as he walked to the wagon. Westerners were not savages just Americans like the Americans in his own state of Maryland. Ohio was made up of all types of people.

He smirked to himself. "What a fireball Janet is. She is the kind of woman that would help any politician making his way up the ranks to the highest posts." He reached into his suit coat pocket and pulled out the two poems he had written her. It was time to share them.

The ride back to town was bumpy and quiet, as both Arthur and Abigail, riding in the back of the buckboard, slumped into a sleep. Evening set in, during the trip, and in the fading light James ventured to touch Janet's hands a number of times as she sat next to him. James realized that the condition of the rural dirt road, prevented reading, so he did not present Janet with his poetry until they pulled into the rear yard of the Academy.

"Please read these, at your leisure. They are the ones I teased you with this morning." His shyness came out in his voice and he looked away when he handed over the folded sheaves of paper. "Now let's wake up these two and try to get everyone inside without making too much of a disturbance."

That was easier than either Janet or James had thought. Abigail woke from her sound sleep, drowsy, but not nauseous. She appeared more like a sleepy child than a drunken teenager, as the two women made their way to the school's back door. James helped steady Abigail about half of the way to the house. At that point discretion caused him to back into the shadows. As he did so, he requested Janet meet him in an hour at the same spot.

Janet nodded and James kissed her hand once in the dark.

* * * * *

A shiver of excitement rushed through her body. Janet could not control it. It had a mind of its own, sweeping though her, shaking her tickling her heart and landing square inside of her breast. Heat followed the excited shiver, and she swallowed heard remembering all the passion that encased her body that day.

It had been quite a day, she thought. First James had kissed her hand on the Common that morning, in front of all her instructors. That sensation was made even more intense by the knowledge others, the matron teacher likes herself, had been watching. "Public exhibition," Janet smirked to herself as she stood in the shadows of the Academy.

Then Oliver had kissed her lips, that afternoon in the woods. That memory shook her as feverously now as the actual moment. The taste and the presence of the ex-soldier loomed over her, watching her, as if a god looking down from heaven. She smiled, uncontrollably smiled, so that the corners of her mouth hurt.

Now James, was again present with a tenderness that surrounded her. His affection hugged her emotionally, not physically. It was a feeling of contentment and safety enveloping her within his personal aura connected through the lips that softly touched her hand in his kiss.

Fokker

How had the world turned topsy-turvy for her? Janet could not think of anything else as she made her way with Abigail to their bedroom. Fortunately not one was present in their shared room when the girls arrived. Janet quickly untied the other's dress, unlaced her soft cotton corset and removed them. Placing a chemise on Abigail, Janet laid her down in the middle of the bed.

Sitting down in the only chair in the room, Janet opened the two poems. James' strong, bold writing jumped from the pages. Fancy curlicues and crisp black letters spoke their magic to Janet's ears as she heard James' voice read to her.

From Across the Room

Faint allusions
Filter through
Filling hopeful
Fanciful dreams
For eternity.
From across the room
I watch you.

Janet pictured the dance. It had only been a day before, but it seemed like an eternity had passed between then and now. Just as the poem said, an eternity in which James had stood there watching her, studying her, finding the courage, she now knew he struggled with, to approach her.

"From Across the Room," She read the words as a sentence, out loud. Her voice quivered with the emotions she allowed to flood over her. "Faint allusions filter through filling hopeful, fanciful dreams for eternity." Tears blurred the words for a moment. "God, do I know about dreams," she whispered, "Dreams that haunt you with a hope that can never come true."

Abigail moved in her sleep, and Janet looked over at the younger woman. "What dreams do you have," she questioned the slumbering figure. "When everything you desire will come true."

Janet leaned back in the chair she was sitting in, and thought. "What do you desire?" She did not dare answer the question; her heart and soul were in too much turmoil to allow a reply to be formed. Instead, Janet picked up the other poem from James and read it out loud.

"From across the room,
I have seen you for days - weeks - months
From across the room.
I have watched you for days - weeks - months
From across the universe.

But it was when I started talking, talking, talking to you
That I started falling, falling, falling in love with you.

I had considered you for days - weeks - months
From across the room.
I had noticed you for days - weeks - months
From across the universe.

But it was when I started talking, talking, talking to you
That I started falling, falling, falling in love with you.

Conversing with you
Sharing wit with you
Debating with you
Opened mind to mind - soul to soul,
Creating perceptions

Bridging thoughts

Marrying hearts.

I had kissed you for days - weeks - months

From across the room.

I had embraced you for days - weeks - months

From across the universe.

But it was when I started talking, talking, talking to you.
That I started falling, falling, falling in love with you."

Janet put her head down on the small table that stood next to the chair. Too many things whirled around inside her head. Faces, smells, tastes, feelings merged into a collage of desires, reality and hopes that Janet Fellows had felt since she was fourteen years old. Everything hammered at her heart, causing her to drift back and forth from the cavalier to Oliver, to James. All three spoke to a different part of that overall fantasy she had been holding secretly within for all these years.

What to do now?

9

There was a slight fuzzy motion in the corner of her eye, and Janet smelled the musk of a horse. Oliver! Her mind told her without having to look up, who had caused the fluttering motion, and goose bumps covered her aroused skin. Oliver was standing in the doorway! She could feel his blue eyes upon her, watching her, craving her. Blissfully her heart jumped as a fever crossed over her face. He had come back. He had come where he should not have come. She knew she was turning scarlet with excitement.

She turned, and that ruggedly handsome face smiled back at her.

"What are you doing here?" She questioned. The delighted smile on her reddening face covered the fact that having him in her room was the one cardinal sin that never overlooked by the academy's governing board. Quickly looking over at Abigail to make sure she was still asleep, she playfully added. "You need to get out of here." Her eyes then grew wide with anxiety as she tussled with the knowledge that if anyone knew a man had come to the academy's back door; there would be immediate expulsion.

But Oliver had placed his whole reputation on the line to see her, now at the Academy, in her room! Her heart's voice spoke to her. That was as gallant and chivalrous as her knight should be! The heart could not stop telling her, how amazing, how tremendous it was that someone would risk everything for her company. She looked at Oliver, trying to convey his need to leave with her eyes, but they must have only reflected her excitement at seeing him again, for Oliver remained standing there smiling, a silly happy smile of youth. Finally, in desperation Janet added in a stage whisper so as not to roust Abigail. "I mean that. You can't be here. Mrs. Pierce will kick me out of here faster than the crack of a whip."

Oliver shrugged his shoulders "I seemed to have forgotten which way is the exit." He teased and simulated confusion by looking around his eyes rolling in his head. Turning back to her, he leaned on the doorframe and remained standing half in the hallway, half in her room, just to see what she would do. He knew full well the risk he was taking and the consequences it would have on Janet and him. But it did not matter at that moment in time, all he wanted was to see her, talk to her, kiss her.

Janet stood and came to him as he leaned in the doorway. Excitement filled her, at the thought that she was breaking the rules. She had always been the one upholding the standards. As a teacher, she was the maker of the rules, but now she was deliberately breaking them. There was a new enticing appeal almost a delightful tension brought on by the fact that she had a man in her room. It thrilled her, more than she wanted to admit.

His arms instantly wrapped themselves around her welcoming waist. "I just needed another." He leaned in for a kiss, and she parried him away.

"No, not here," She looked over his shoulders, afraid that someone might come down the hallway. She pulled him into the room and slipped the door closed. As she turned back to face him, he kissed her. Full on the mouth his lips caressed hers. She did not resist. She could not resist. His warm wet lips came again, and she responded with a passion she had not known she held inside of her. Her arms wrapped around him, as his did the same around her. They squeezed each other making the kisses even dearer and more intense. A delicious anxiety rushed over Janet; excited by the fact Oliver was kissing her again, and the fact that he was there illicitly in her room. She fell into a daze allowing his lips to press harder against hers. She matched his desire and actually pressed back. The warmth of his body blanketed her, and she drifted away from the present.

Falling, falling she allowed her heart to guide her into a world of colors and allusions. She was in her dream world, but Oliver was there, not the cavalier. He had entirely taken the place of her long sought for nightly visitor. His face, younger and less troubled, but clearly his face occupied the uniform of a Dragoon, and she was kissing him. Her heart skipped a number of beats, forcing her to breathe erratically.

Their mouths parted a little, and their tongues joined in union. Once more they caressed each other, stirring rainbows of colors that filled Janet's mind. Gone was the vision of the cavalier only to be replaced with bright hues of reds, yellows, and oranges. She tipped her head back, allowing Oliver a long lingering passionate kiss. Their tongues coupled together in a sensual dance. And her body tingled with hot and cold shivers. The colors in her mind cooled to greens and blues. Suddenly she was transported to a wide-open rolling hilled field of tall grass, where she stood looking up into the blue sky, Oliver at her side. Then just as quickly, just as unexpectedly, she was wrapped in his embrace as the sun descended in a fiery evening sky. Oh to be held forever in those strong muscular arms as the world around her moved endlessly through time. That was all that mattered now. James' poems, Mrs. Piece's rules, the contract she had with the Harmony Board of Selectmen all vanished behind the visions of being with Oliver.

The bed creaked as Abigail rolled over in her sleep. Janet snapped opened her eyes and pushed away from Oliver.

"Stop," she said, coming up for air. "You can't be here. You can't be doing that."

Oliver looked at her, a passion in his clear blue eyes, that she and never seen. His whole focus was on her, she could tell. His entire mind was centered in on only her, and her kisses. There were no longer any memories playing in his head. They had vanished from his eyes, and she smiled at her success. She kissed him softly again on the lips, to keep that clear focus alive. "You must leave. I'm so sorry. You can't be here. You must leave." She struggled to calm her heart and get her breathing back to normal.

Oliver smiled a silly sloppy smile. What was he thinking, Janet asked? But she would not know, for once again the bed creaked, and Oliver slipped quickly out the door. Janet looked at the bed, but Abigail seemed to be still asleep. Without another thought about her roommate, Janet followed Oliver out into the hall.

* * * * *

Earlier Oliver Block had noticed that the buckboard was missing when he first had returned to the Wolcott's barn from the picnic. He had been allowed to board his chestnut mare at the stables in exchange for caring for the horses of the Governor's household. It was a duty the ex-soldier and horseman did not find troublesome. It allowed him a chance to ride anytime he needed to escape the Litchfield environment. It also allowed him free use of the family's various wagons and carriages. These had come in handy during his year's stay at the school. He had swept many a young lady off of their feet by his appearance in one of the Governor's prestigious carriages.

He had also made the acquaintance of one Benjamin Arts, the groom for the Governor's stables.

The older man had become an instant friend. His natural philosophy had been one akin to that of Oliver. His rustic ideas and love of horses had been a refreshing change from the law school students solely concerned with reputation. Whenever Oliver found himself needing an escape from the law students,

Benjamin was there to talk with or silently work together.

After caring for his horse ridden so hard after the picnic, Oliver returned to his room, to discover that James Baldwin Mathers was out. On his small study desk, the other law student had left his papers open. Oliver availed himself the opportunity to scan them. The majority of the writing concerned the case the two were going to argue later that week. Tapping Reeve, feeling that his students needed to be properly prepared to face any judge had selected a Supreme Court case for the two to argue. The real case of Hall vs. Mullin would open soon before the nation's highest court. This case wanted the justices to rule whether or not a slave could be declared free if that slave inherited property from its owner. James was arguing against the declaration of freedom, while Oliver was to present the case for freedom.

Looking over James' papers, Oliver noted that he had addressed all the same facts in his approach to the case. There was nothing new in his discoveries. Flipping through the papers, he then discovered scratched out copies of poems. "Rough drafts," Oliver spoke softly to himself as if he was in church. "I didn't know James fancied himself a writer."

He paused in his scanning and actually read the words. James' meaning became very clear to Oliver. "The boy has a heart, and it's captured." He would have laughed out loud if his own heart was not ringing concerning the same the fact. He continued to read, and fear crept into his heart. "There is no way you can compete against this." He read the words again and found himself picturing James at the church this morning studying the young ladies from the academy. His eyes had apparently been taking in all that was beautiful about Janet.

"From Across the room," Oliver's voice filled the attic. "God he's good." His thoughts raced to memories of the fifteen-year-old Janet sitting across from him at the campfire.

Oliver had seen the same beauty James was capturing in his writing. He had felt the same longing for Janet then, a desire to hold Janet eternally. "Why didn't you write it down?" Oliver had to ask himself but knew very well that his words did not come in poetic form, but presented facts and opinions, unflattering with style and grace.

Placing the poem copies down, he found another paper with the beginning of a letter addressed to Janet. Once more his eyes scanned the content.

"Thank you, Miss Fellows, for the opportunity to converse and promenade with you today. Your sparkling conversation was only enhanced by the singing bird's sweet voices. Together your voice and theirs dispersed all thoughts of the recent winter. Spring has arrived as clearly as the touch of your hand has stirred emotions within me.

God's magical skill so awes me. What incalculable odds it is that our kindred souls should have found each other. It sparks of a divine power concerned with fate. Our destiny cannot go counter to this fate."

Here the letter stopped, and Oliver placed the paper back as close to its original position as he could recall. Anxiety at the possibility of losing Janet to James tugged at Oliver's heart.

"If James was in court the judge would have thrown out his argument." He reflected on the words in the letter. "The poor boy does not know his audience." A knowing smile came to Oliver's face. "Janet is too practical to fall for such sappy words. Actions are what will gain her heart." He remembered the long passionate kiss they had shared. A chuckle erupted from Oliver. "He'll never have the fortitude to sweep her in his arms." Oliver relived the moment. His excitement triggered the longing to escape as a groan of passion. A warm shiver crawled over his body and his thoughts zeroed in on another kiss. Pivoting on his heels, he immediately headed out the door. If he hurried, he could get to the picnic for one more kiss.

* * * * *

As he was heading back to the Wolcott stables located to the left and behind the main house, he caught sight of the buckboard coming back through town. Its progress was clearly visible across the plowed fields off of South Street that leads from the old Governor's home to the common area. Janet's kiss played on his lips as he watched the buckboard. Its taste lingered, and his heart dictated his next action, a step toward the school. Once in that forward motion, he just naturally followed the small wooden vehicle to the backyard of the academy. All thought only on seeing Janet again.

Arriving shortly after the buckboard, he quietly hid from view among some lilac bushes. From there he watched as James and Janet tried to deal with Abigail, whom Oliver instantly recognized as being drunk. He had seen the same sloppy walking and floppy head to many times in the service not to know Abigail's condition. The scene brought a slight smirk to his face. There was nothing funnier than watching people struggle with a drunken person, while also trying to remain silent.

Silence was something that his years in the army had taught him. He was able to sneak up on a company of British soldiers with little trouble. But James was not a soldier; otherwise, the Southerner would have simply placed Abigail on his shoulder and strolled up to the building. Oliver knew that trying to have the young lady walk, would only increase the amount of noise they made, as well as increase the chances of being caught.

But Janet and James insisted on walking the other young lady. Placing themselves on either side of Abigail, and wrapping their arms around her waist, the two struggled with Abigail's unco-operative feet, trying to get them to work instinctively. But the alcoholic haze in Abigail's head made that nearly impossible. Twice Oliver watched as the two nearly dropped her to the ground, but somehow they managed to get Abigail to the academy's back porch. From a distance, the whole affair looked like two friends helping a sleepy friend. It would appear that way to Mrs. Pierce if the matron teacher happened to look out of her window. This appearance was fortunate for the two women because Oliver knew that the headmistress of the school did not put up with anything that would cause a spot on the school's reputation. He had seen young ladies removed from the student body because of an errant kiss in public, or a little too much intoxication.

Oliver held his breath hoping that the later did not happen, for that would have put an end to his chances of kissing Janet. Her face, seen from across the yard, even in the evening light was just as radiant as it had been at the lake. Her lips full and delicious in his memory called to him. They aroused him, and he sought only to devour them again with his warm mouth. A bulging against the buttons of his trousers warned him he was fantasying too much, but she had sparked to life all the passions he had felt over the years since first seeing her in the glow of an army campfire.

Looking at James now, struggling with Abigail, his arm touching Janet's arm, Oliver could not help but notice that the other law student was thinking along these same lines. Just as the three reached the porch, James stepped back and whispered something to Janet, who nodded. Oliver could not make out what was said, but could clearly see that the Ohio teacher's eyes were intrigued.

Oliver's heart thumped, concerned. A smile, a simple smile crossed Janet's face, and he was suddenly jealous. Jealous not of James per say, but of the fact that he, not Oliver, had not gotten the sweet smile given so quickly. Oliver feared it was a sign that she had been wooed carefully with words, words that he just could not use so skillfully.

Forgetting the scene in front of him for a second, Oliver closed his eyes and remembered. Time slipped away. Years vanished in the fog of memories and emotions. She was there again in front of him; his hand slipped through her arm, as he escorted her around the camp, on orders of his lieutenant. Her smile beamed on his face, and he acted tongue-tied and shy as only an adolescent male could. Every word stuck in his throat, ever action came awkwardly, and every look from her caused him to look away, embarrassed. How he had ever survived the camp tour was beyond belief. But he had touched her then.

He had held her then, and now in Litchfield, he had done the same.

He looked down at his hands, the same hands that had touched her nearly eight years before. How they had changed, yet remained the same. He knew them, but she had not recognized them. No wonder, Oliver thought. She saw little of his face most of the time they had spent together. His voice had not deepened yet and but broke far too often in her presence. His figure, well it was just lanky. And his hands were not as calloused, not as exposed to the evils of the world. Tears blurred his vision for a second, but then departed with the memory, the most precious memory Oliver had. A memory he had almost forgotten. The kiss at the lake, however, had rediscovered it in the very back of his heart. The kiss, he thought and licked his lips.

Oliver looked up from his hiding spot to see that the two academy students had disappeared into the school building, but James still stood in the backyard silently staring at the door, as if he was still watching them. Finally, he turned and walked back to the buckboard. Still, he did not leave right away, and Oliver festered with doubts about if the other law student would ever leave. Then he saw Arthur Griswold slowly rise from the back of the buckboard parked near the far edge of the academy's yard. He must have been asleep in the back, Oliver thought, and James was waking him, before leaving.

Arthur shook the sleep from his head and crawled onto the front seat of the wagon. James joined him and snapped the reins to get the horses going. When the sound of the cart had faded away, Oliver finally emerged from his observation post alongside the building. Silently, as if he was in the woods of the Indiana Territory again, he crept to the back porch and tried the door. It swung easily in his hands. Peering in, he confirmed that no one was there. Looking down the hallway, he saw one door of the five that lined the hallway open. It had to be Janet's.

Heal to toe; he eased his way down the hall. Riding boots could be the loudest pair of shoes anyone wore if they did not stealthily approach. Oliver did. Heal to toe, heal to toe, slowly shifting his weight has he progressed was his method, and it worked. Soon he was standing in the open doorway looking in at Janet with her head down on the small table next to the only chair in the room.

Oliver's heart stopped. He had infiltrated the holy sanctum of the Female Academy. Never before, with any other student at the school had he dared to enter the building unescorted. Even he understood that if caught at that moment everyone in that room would be suspended from the schools. But Janet was there; she was the only thing that mattered to him. He had to prove to himself that the kisses they had shared earlier were not simply to calm his troubled soul after the sword fight. He had to see if the word, no emotions were meant for him. He had to earn an easy smile like James just earned. He wanted a smile meant only for him.

Janet looked up at that moment, and his heart melted at her smile. It was a smile so full of life and joy that it jumped out from her. It kissed his doubts away, and he didn't even hear her words, as he was too mesmerized by her brown sparkling eyes.

He knew she was talking to him, but the words did not register in his mind. All that was comprehended was her smile and her sweet ruby lips ready to be kissed. All that mattered was the delight in her luminous brown eyes that warmed his heart. No one, his mind reminded him. No one had ever felt for him like she did.

It scared him. Deep inside of him the concept of dreams coming true filled him with fear. What would happen next now that the world was perfect? What could happen next? The thought burned in his heart. He would be happy for the rest of his life. No, Oliver did not believe in fairy tale endings. He had seen too much in his short life ever to believe in fairy tale endings. But here she was, the vision that had taken him through battles, walking toward him. He reached out and tried to kiss the image. She parried him away, and for a second he knew that he was right all along, there were no fairy tale endings.

Then her hand pulled him inside the room, as the white wooden door closed behind him. The rich brown circles inside her eyes grew wide with anticipation. He was as deeply drawn to her, as she was to him.

There was no fighting it now. They kissed. Her lips were just as sweet as they had been in the woods earlier. They kissed again. Their lips pressed hard against each other in an exclamation of longing to marry. She squeezed him in a mutual embrace that spoke of togetherness, comfort, and commitment. He held her tighter, and her body relaxed into his arms.

Gone were the visions of the battlefield. Gone were the doubts he had about her interest in James. Gone were his fears of actually finding the end of the rainbow. Only the sweet pleasure of tasting her kiss remained in his mind. And his whole body concentrated on just that one desire.

Coaxing with his tongue, she parted her lips. Once again he tasted her tongue. His heart pounded in his chest sending hot blood throughout his body.

Janet's body felt warm, and alive in his arms as if it was meant to be there. Her head tilted just at the right angle for his lips to caress. She was made for this, he told himself. She was made to be in his arms and no one else's. Destiny, James had written. Oliver recalled in between kisses. James did not know how true he was, Oliver almost laughed out loud. But Janet was Oliver's destiny not James'.

His hands reached up to her back and embraced her close to his chest. The calico material of her dress was soft to his touch, but the cotton corset underneath teased him into wanting her bare back in her hands. A twinge of lust filled him with dreams of virginity yet to be won. It was a prize that he would give his life to obtain.

His mouth slipped down to the soft spot on her neck he had discovered earlier. Janet softly moaned to his kisses and the excitement grew inside of him. Warmth centered itself between his legs and he felt his manhood respond. Embarrassed and fearful that its firm presence might dismay Janet from further kissing, he tried to hide his arousal by changing positions. But Janet refused to release him. She pulled him tighter against her as she seemed to fade into a trance. Her hips leaned up against his manhood and her firm breast pressed hard against his chest causing him to desire a taste of them. His lips and tongue guided over the soft spot on her neck and she moaned deeper in pleasure. Flames roared to his groin.

Just then the bed creaked.

Oliver jumped back startled. He had forgotten about Abigail. His whole focus had been on Janet, just Janet and how she was now the dark haired woman standing in front of him. For the first time in nearly a decade no other voices or visions played in his mind. All that was there were Janet's longing brown eyes, her moist red lips, and her sweet, tender tongue. And the firmness between his legs, she had caused to bring to life.

He drew her close for another long passionate kiss. His firm hot groin pressed hard against her.

She matched his request, sending her tongue deep into his mouth. Embracing her hot body against him, Oliver could feel the moisture between her legs. The lust within her was demanding, coaxing, begging to be held tighter, closer, almost to become a part of him.

The bed creaked again. And Oliver quickly slipped out of the room before his passion exploded.

Breathing came hard to the law student as he tried to stealthily make his way down the hall and out the back door. His heart was pounding so hard he could hear it. He was sure that anyone near him could also hear it. His manhood remained firm, longing to erupt, longing to know the pleasures of a woman. No, he confirmed with his heart, only the pleasure of Janet.

Suddenly Janet's hand tenderly touched his shoulder. A moan of pleasure escaped from his mouth as he spun to face her. Her deep brown eyes reflected the moon and stars of the evening sky. But they screamed out to be kissed. Urgency filled them to the point of overflowing. Oliver could feel her desire. It hung in the air waiting to be grabbed, hugged and conquered.

Totally out of control, completely under the spell of those eyes, Oliver seized Janet and kissed her with all his heart!

The crunch of a footfall came seconds later. "No," Janet called as she flinched out of Oliver's arm appearing as if she was being forced into the kiss. A rough hand slammed down on Oliver's right shoulder and spun him around. A full open hand swept into view. Warrior instincts took command.

Blocking the incoming slap with both hands, Oliver locked his hands around the wrist of James

Baldwin Mathers. Pivoting on the balls of his feet, Oliver turned to the right bringing James' arm with him, and over his own shoulder. The Southerner lost his balance. Snapping the arm downward, as he knelt, Oliver brought James' body over his shoulder and dropped it to the ground.

The stunned Southerner looked up at Oliver, now standing over him. "You bastard," James said, anger erupting from his eyes. "You bastard, she is an innocent child, and you're not going to ruin her." He rolled and bounded to his feet. His body stood upright, and he again tried to slap Oliver.

Once more the ex-soldier dumped him to the ground by using the enraged man's own momentum. James again bounded to his feet. This time, however, he did not repeat his efforts at challenging Oliver to a duel. "Why the hell don't you fight like a gentleman?" He demanded.

"Because I'm not," Oliver looked over James' shoulder at Janet. The statement was directed more for her attention than James' "I wish to live to see the next day. Gentlemen have a nasty habit of dying too young."

"Well it will be you this time that dies too young." James said his voice cold and calculating. "I'll expect to see you tomorrow at..."

"Don't expect to see me any time," Oliver cut James off. "I don't fight duels."

"Coward," James called as he stood upright, his dignity once more in place. "You don't even think enough of Miss Fellows to face me for respect." He glanced over his shoulder at the Academy student, as if to say - see what I have saved you from. Janet just looked away, not sure what to think.

"I'll hunt you down then," James, continued his threats. "Like a dog."

"You do, and you'll never see your precious Maryland again." Oliver looked again at Janet, hoping to catch her eye. Hoping that she would give him a sign that his actions were what were in her heart. But the lady only looked to the ground, totally confused as to what she should do. The doubts returned. The knowledge that fairy tales did not exist for Oliver Block filled his heart and he sighed heavily, his heart breaking. "I warn you leave me be, or it will a sad day for all." He turned and walked away into the shadows of the night.

* * * * *

Janet's heart was pounding so hard that she could feel it nearly exploding in her chest. Her breasts filled with a fever she had not felt before. They ached for Oliver to touch them, maybe even kiss them. She gazed into his blue energized animal eyes as they stood in the backyard of the academy. Her only thoughts were on the little voices screaming within her. Touch him! Kiss him! Hold him! The voices called over and over.

A warm moist feeling crossed her body and centered between her legs. Nothing in her life had been this intense. Nothing had ever prepared her for the look of pure desire in Oliver's blue eyes. She melted, under their passionate stare. Gone were all thoughts of proper Puritan demure or even the restrictions of a small community teacher.

"God" her heart called out to the divine spirit. "Let him take me. Now and forever, let him have me." Lust mixed with her wishes. As in her dream, her cavalier swept her in his arms and kissed her full and thick on her awaiting mouth.

It was then that she saw James Baldwin Mathers approach from the shadows. Rage was evident on his bearded face. Despite the dark, Janet could clearly see a fire in his hazel eyes. His hand shot up, and Janet jumped back out of Oliver's embrace. "No!!" She screamed.

Why?

She was not sure if it was to stop James, or to prevent others from seeing her kissed by Oliver. She had fallen completely out of control under the spell of Oliver's stare, now the reality of the moment was roaring in her mind. It was not permitted. It was not right for a woman to give herself that quickly to a man. Her tuition would be returned, her purse packed and the miracle of this Litchfield would come to an abrupt end. She could not let that happen. She could not face the return to Harmony in disgrace.

Too much was happening at once. It was all too fast for the young lady from an isolated community of Ohio. It was not to happen at all like this, she told herself trying to ease the confusion in her heart and mind. She was there in Litchfield to learn how to teach, not be the object of two men's fight.

But you are the object, her mind told her. You are the cause. She looked at the two facing each other like lions facing off over a kill. She was the cause. A pleasure filled her. A sick, exciting pleasure filled her. What had Guinevere wished? She asked herself, to have knights fighting duels over her, came the answer. Well here was Janet with two men ready to fight - fight over her.

She watched as the two men grappled in front of her. It was like watching the young boys in her school fight at recess. Oliver clearly understood how to hurt James, and was trying hard not to do so. But James did not have a clue. He assumed that the other man was only scared or a coward. Things that Janet knew full well were not the case. But James kept after Oliver, like the bullies at recess, needling, believing they had the upper hand.

Hard words were called out. Words that made Janet hide her face. She had seen these words lead to death. But Oliver parried them like he had the sword thrust of Jon Coe earlier. He allowed insults to fly in the air that Janet knew hurt his pride. But she could not make eye contact with him.

She simply could not bring herself to his rescue. All those years of being drilled by her mother in proper etiquette, came back to her, filled her with embarrassment, a desire to run, and shame at being caught outside in the arms of a man.

Why? Her heart demanded. Why are you so confused? Don't you love Oliver?

There was only silence in her head. No answer. What was love?

Before she could answer, Oliver walked away.

10

James suddenly grabbed Janet hard by the shoulders, turned her and intensely looked into her eyes. Despite the darkness of the night, Janet could still clearly see the alarm in his hazel eyes. "Are you alright?" He asked concerned evident in his voice. His strength not controlled, but enraged by the recent action. Its power moved Janet, physically moved by this outpouring of concern and virility.

"Yes." She answered still confused by what had just happened in front of her eyes. Ensnared by this new sensation that had taken over her body, Janet could not form more words.

James' strength now prepared to surround her for protection thrilled her a little. It opened a part of her soul that needed the knowledge that she would be safe. And she looked into his eyes, hunting for an answering glint in his eyes.

"Did he hurt you?" He asked as concerned as before.

"No," She answered flatly, unsure of her voice and the feelings that were racing through her body. "What would make you think that he was hurting me?"

"It appeared..." James stated and released his hold on her and stepped back afraid of the thoughts that jumped into his head. These same thoughts then abruptly dribbled from his lips as words. "You mean that you wanted to kiss him. After I've told you," his words trailed off as his mind fought with the reality becoming clear in his mind. "You mean even though you know how I feel."

"How you feel?" Janet came to her senses finally. Pausing to line her words up, she adjusted the calico dress, even though it did not need to be adjusted. "How do I know how you feel? All I have is two hand scribbled poems, and a kiss on my hand." She held up her right hand as if to show James the kiss. It naturally was not there.

The law student stepped back another pace totally at wit's end. No woman had ever addressed him in this manner. He had never had to explain himself to any woman other than his mother. He breathed deep and let out the air slowly in thought. He gained, even more, time, through picking up his brown hat and placing it firmly, squarely on his head.

"What do you expect?" James confusedly asked. "What do you want as a token?" He shook his head in disbelief. "I have given you my heart. Wrote it out for you on paper, and even ventured a sign of affection in public." He threw his hands up in dismay. "You damn Puritan, Federalist Yankees." He turned away for a second to compose himself. When he turned back, Janet met his puzzled eyes. "In Maryland, we would have been holding hands in public by now, and sneaking behind the barn for a kiss or two."

Janet could not help but smile. James was becoming more like Oliver when the specter of another man hung over his head. She ventured a tease just to see what would happen. She knew now that Oliver would sweep her into his arms and kiss her deep till her toes felt the pleasure. That thought lingered in her breast as she looked to James and said. "Well as Shakespeare wrote, here is a Pilgrim's kiss for you."

Janet folded her hand in a mock praying gesture.

James reached over and took her two hands, and then drew her into his arms. Their eyes remained glued to each other. His body was warm and inviting. Janet could not deny that. It was almost as comfortable as being in Oliver's embrace, but there was something missing. There was no tension of Oliver's strength sweeping over her, ensnared her in the tightest trap she could ever imagine. It was a trap that she found harder and harder to desire to escape. James' embrace, however, was gentle, controlled and caring. It was safe there, pulled up against his vest and musk smelling cravat covered white shirt. She listened and even through the layers of clothing, heard a thin thumping of his heart. She closed her eyes and wrapped her arms around his waist, returning his embrace.

"How can you not know how I feel?" He whispered his voice resounding in his well-defined chest. "All these days I have been thinking of you walking in the sun with me, hand in hand, arm in arm. What would make you think I could not feel anything but a desire for you?" His warm breath tickled her face, as his passion became more intense in his voice. Tension filled his embracing arms, as he pulled her tighter to his chest. "From the first day that you arrived here, I have watched you. I have envisioned nothing but being able to hold you in my arms." He breathed deep as if he was struggling with his emotions. "Have I dreamed of a prize unredeemable?"

It was a question Janet knew she had to answer. She had to answer it while looking into his eyes, she told herself. She had to see his face. It was impossible that two men could feel the same thing for her! Her mind shook her with doubts about her sexuality. Her mind warned her again about slipping into a dream world that was ruled by the heart. No, her mind spoke loudly to her. Two different men could not be experiencing the same feelings, the same intense feelings that she was experiencing.

She leaned back in his embrace and looked up. His square jaw, covered with the brown beard framed against the night sky was powerful. It seized her with an unwilling urge to kiss him.

Janet shook her head, in surprise at the craving. Their eyes met, and James' eyes burned into hers. She felt his muscles tighten his embrace and tense throughout his body. "Miss Fellows I beg of you, please give me the sweet taste of your lips."

His passionate voice came quiet and steady. Heat again crawled into Janet's cheeks, the hairs on the back of her head stood up. She had excited this Southerner to the point of no return. Her mind teased her heart, and she felt excited. This time, it was the words, and gestures, not a physical touch that triggered the response. James slowly, awkwardly tipped his head and touched his lips to hers. Her eyes closed in anticipation of falling into a daze as with Oliver.

Tender, afraid, cautious were the first three words that came to Janet's mind. Sweet was the last word that came, and it was that description which remained. His lips tasted of nothing definite but hinted at many different flavors simultaneously. Her head spun but only a little and she remained in perfect control of the situation. His lips came again, this time, wetter, firmer and more determined to provide pleasure. They tickled her lips with a slight touch and then a full kiss. She responded in kind, allowing James her full mouth to caress.

As his lips departed, she leaned back and waited for the spinning in her head to stop. She smiled, delighted as a schoolgirl. The burning in her cheeks told her that James had connected to some emotional cord within her heart.

What? Her heart screamed. What are you doing? It thumped, in reaction to the kiss. A sigh came unchecked, and James moved his lips away to look again into her eyes. A silly smile crossed his face, and

Janet knew there was one equally as silly on her face. "Thank you." He whispered almost embarrassed.

Turning away, he walked a few steps back toward the shadows he had emerged from minutes before. Janet stood silently actually afraid that James was going to leave her in the dark, in the back of the academy wanting another kiss, longing for another kiss from James. Not that his kiss was as sexual as Oliver's, but they were just as potent. Their shyness had an attraction that had made her head spin. She shook with a shiver of delight at the idea that James was as inexperienced as she was concerning sex or even kissing. They were two virgins exploring the world where every turn brought a new wonderful discovery. She rubbed her arms to erase the goose bumps on them.

Suddenly James turned back after bending to pick up something from the ground. "I brought you these." He held a hand full of spring wildflowers, among them violets and clover. "I will bring you wildflowers every day if you would let me." His smile reminded Janet of the look she sometimes got from new young male students. The look of infatuation, or puppy love, her father had called it. But for the young boys, it was as powerful as the love her parents had felt for over thirty years. That thought planted a seed in her mind.

"Thank you," Her voice almost giggled. Reaching out, Janet took the flowers from the law student.

Was this just an infatuation? Janet had to ask herself. Was she simply the object of a schoolboy's crush? Yes, James was a graduate of Yale. He was in his twenties, but he was mental so young.

He stepped closer and kissed her again. She could have resisted, but a little voice inside stopped her from fighting. "Let's see where this leads," her curiosity said. A mischievous feeling inside the academy student agreed, and she kissed James back. The flush in her cheeks tickled and she nearly laughed with excitement.

James' lips pressed hard against hers. They were dry, nervously dry. Janet giggled to herself. He smelled of sweat from the fight with Oliver. It was not an unpleasant odor, just a notable one. His hands at first awkwardly held her, as if he did not know where to place them. But then they found her back, where they had rested before, and drew her in for a full embrace and tender kiss. She closed her eyes and kissed him back; wrapping her arms again around his waist pulling him into her has much as she felt his strong arms pulled her.

Their lips played together, coaxed each other to relax, as if unsure of what had happened a few seconds before. Janet almost believed that this was their first kiss yet again. She realized that James was completely ill at ease with her in his arms. But she enjoyed it all the same.

It was not threatening to be in James' arms, Janet's heart thumped. With Oliver, there was a tension, a fear of falling out of control, of becoming an animal desiring complete carnal knowledge. There was also a strong yearning to gain that full carnal knowledge. The two-edged sword, so to speak, Janet's mind had reflected after their first kiss by the lake. But with James, there was no pressure. There was no hidden desire to go beyond what was happening at that moment. It was exciting without the fear.

It was cozy.

Janet looked at him as he tipped his head back from the kiss. Concentration filled his eyes, and Janet felt his arousal through the calico material of her dress. "Twice," the wicked side of her mind spoke. "Twice in one night you've teased a man to firmness." Heat shot up through her at the thought, and she knew her face was scarlet. If only this were Oliver instead of James, Janet told herself, she would easily have surrendered her body. But James' arousal did not affect her as much. She hugged him tight to reassure herself that his manhood was excited. It was.

Moments before, she had been floating in a rainbow of colors, triggered by the touch of Oliver's lips. Moments before, she had been moist with passion, wanting to be held forever within the walls of Oliver's heart. But now, the mood was different. She was pleased, almost comfortable in James' embrace, but the thrill was far less, far from the pinnacle she had felt minutes ago.

She stepped back from James and looked at the ground. If I close my eyes, she thought. Then Oliver will come back. He will be here in James' place I wish. I wish, I wish. Looking up James stood there puzzled by her actions.

"Did I do something wrong?" He asked an alarm in his voice.

"No, I just was taken aback." Janet said. "It has been quite a day." She smiled trying to ease the awkwardness. "I'm..."

"Embarrassed," James tried to help. "I should not have been so bold." He stepped back himself creating a safety of space between them. Deep inside of him a voice of panic called out to beware. He was going too close, it told him. Janet was not ready for what he wanted to say. She was not willing to hear the words that wanted to form on his lips. But he had to confess. Unwillingly his heart pounded searching, reaching for hers. He was swept away by what he wanted to be love. He was out of control of the fantasy that he had developed to write his poetry. But he also did not want to consider his feelings simply made up. He wanted them to be real, to have a life in Janet's heart. He looked into her eyes but did not see a returning sparkle. You've moved too fast, his heart told him. You need to step away. He took a deep breath and sighed. "I was too forward," he apologized. "But I thought it was right at the time."

"It was." She looked into his eyes trying to read his thoughts. Nothing came. With Oliver, she had been able to see right into his soul. But James was too much of a closed book. His confusion was evident, but that was all she could see. She added awkwardly. "I needed to be comforted."

"Is that what it was?" James snapped suddenly changed in mood. "I'm glad to have provided the service." His tone became distant, and Janet knew she had hurt him. His voice filled with a superiority tone, the same tone she had heard him use after the dance. "I must tell you Miss Fellows that others would consider what we just did more than comfort."

"You are right. It was more than just comfort, but I am not sure of my footing." Janet defended herself, feeling that odd sensation of fear she had felt the night before while having tea with James. He was reprimanding her as if she was a servant or a child, not his equal. That was why she had felt at the tea the same way she did when the elders of the town observed her teaching. It was a feeling of inferiority, such an employee to her boss.

"Your footing is sound." James countered her statement like a lawyer pressing home his argument. "I can't help but state the obvious again. I have feelings for you; strong feelings that affect my thoughts each and every minute of the day." He paused in mid-thought, hoping that his words could trigger a reflection of Janet's heart. He eyes studied her every breath, searching, hoping for that sign.

"What can I do to make you understand that I am enthralled with you?" He spread his arms out like a defeated warrior. "I can't spend an hour away from you without your vision filling my mind's eye. And when we are near, I can't help but watch you do the little things that make you, you. I have them memorized already. The way you brush your hair from you face. The little biting of your lips you do when thinking and the nervous smile that comes to your face when I talk to you." He looked away for inspiration. "The stars can't last as long as what I am feeling right now for you." Looking back, Janet thought she could see his hazel eyes moisten. "I am not a little boy chasing after a pretty face. I am a man who has seen a good part of this country."

The second James claimed to be a man; Janet knew the truth. He was lost, drowning in his whirlpool of emotions. They were emotions that he, himself had caused to lap over him. Love, the word came to Janet, and she shivered with delight. He was in love with her, truly in love with her. No one had ever said that to the matron teacher of Harmony, Ohio.

She looked at James in a new light. Could she return the feelings?

What are you doing? She suddenly asked herself. What are you thinking about? You don't even know this person, and he does not know you. This realization about James acted as a candle being lit in a dark room. Her eyes opened wide, figuratively and she looked at the man in front of her. Neither one of them had known each other's name merely a week before this moment. How could he be standing there professing an emotion that brought with it a lifetime commitment? The question shook the matron teacher to the depth of her marrow. Could she bring herself to believe in love at first sight?

Only with the cavalier, her heart called. Only with the cavalier! Janet knew that her heart would never forget her first and only love.

Oliver's face came to her mind's eye. That was different her heart argued. There was something utterly distinctive yet so very familiar about Oliver. Somewhere deep, deep inside of Janet a chord of recognition had been struck. She looked again at James, scanning him from head to foot. The same chord did not resound in her heart. James was not her cavalier.

"James," She stopped him in the middle of his discourse on his feelings. The law student looked at her, his facing slowly turning gray as the evening turned to a warm spring night. "How can you feel this way? We have only known each other for a week." She paused trying to read his face, but could not because of the shadows. "You don't know me. You don't know anything about my family or my past." She sighed. "And I don't know you at all."

"Do you believe in love at first sight?" His voice came slow and precise.

"I don't know." She lied. She had been in love with a mythological soldier all these years, without even knowing the man's name. She had fallen for him, by just watching him ride away on his horse. But that was not love as James was trying to argue. That was adolescent fantasy.

"This place is something special." James continued not actually hearing Janet's words. His mind set on making his point as if it was a last ditch effort to win her heart. "There is a magic in the air that affects everyone who comes here to study. Haven't you noticed?" Janet nodded. "Think about how many weddings you have seen in the past week."

It was true that the Congregational Church was busy as the site of ex-students weddings. In the past week, Janet had been aware of three large weddings and a number of smaller affairs. She had been involved in two of them as a member of the school choir. Abigail had said it the night of the dance. She was there to get married, not to study to advance herself, but to marry to advance herself. Janet even had to admit she felt the same electricity in the air concerning love and marriage. But she did not tell that to James.

"Most of those weddings were the results of students meeting here. Law and Academy students are brought together for one purpose to provide the leading families of the nation with proper spouses." He stopped afraid that he was getting to clinical. "I mean to say that this town of Litchfield has been set aside for the creation of perfect unions. It is in the stars that we have meant here. I honestly believe that it is our destiny to be friends. I tried to write that down once, but could not finish the thought logically. But it has dawned on me, that what is happening here in Litchfield is not logical. It is an emotionally charged environment. Love is not rational."

"What do you know about love?" Janet had to ask.

"I know that you have taken control of my thoughts. I find myself thinking of ways I can spend time with you. Take this morning and the Sunday before. I'm Episcopalian not Congregational, but I was there because you were. I made excuses throughout the week to be near you. I can't help but picture you enjoying the summer breezes on the porch of my family home in Fredrick, Maryland. Isn't that love?"

"I don't know."

"Well if you don't know, then how can you say it's not love?"

"Okay," she held up her hands in surrender. "I yield to your argument. But explain how you can feel this way when you don't know who I am. You have no clue to my past or goals. My likes or dislikes."

"I know you like wildflowers." He smiled, and she giggled. Leave it to an attorney to have wit.

"And from there I can discover more about you if you will let me." Janet nodded her head.

Oliver hung back in the shadows after throwing James to the ground twice. His breath came fast and cumbersome from the excursion. But he breathed through his mouth to maintain his silence. He had to see what James and Janet would do. As he watched the little drama unfold, he could not help but admire the southern law student. He had learned to take the initiative. Oliver almost cheered when James reached over and took Janet in his arms for the first kiss. For some unknown reason, there was no pain of jealousy. Maybe it was because the kiss was so juvenile, or the look on Janet's face was not one of attraction. It didn't matter, what mattered was that now Oliver knew there was a genuine rivalry between the two men. He waited just long enough to see the second kiss before he silently walked away.

* * * * *

Janet's head spun as she reentered the academy. Two men, two entirely different men, were spinning her heart. What was she to do? Abigail was sitting up in bed when she entered their shared room.

"Well, look who's back, the blushing trophy." A lustful smile covered her face. "It must be nice to have two men fighting over you." Her eyes zeroed in on Janet's blushing face. "Now don't deny it. You-all just love all the attention." Janet could not help but nod her head. "Well doesn't it beat all to see such honesty from the educators of this country's youth?" Abigail moved off the bed and came alongside Janet. "Honey, you-all better watch behind you, if you-all expect to return to that wonderful position of yours in Harmony. I tell you, Janet, Mrs. Piece will not be too kind if she catches you-all kissing in the backyard of the school." Her eyes grew wide. "And you-all never can tell what it might take to keep these lips closed about a particular young gentleman paying a visit to this here room."

"You won't," Janet gasped.

"No, but you better be careful in the future."

"I didn't ask him to come here. He just showed up."

"I could tell that you-all were distressed that he did. That wrestling hold you-all put on him seemed to have nailed him right to the door. What was that move called a lip pin?" She giggled, and Janet could not help but laugh herself. The two hugged in excitement. "Isn't it wonderful here?" Abigail added after they had stopped laughing. "All the men you could possibly want to know in one place, for you to sit back and choose. My cousin told me it would be this way. I didn't believe her. I thought that modesty and social norms would prevent the sexes from merging together. But that is just not the case is it." She looked into Janet's eyes. "You are falling for one of them aren't you?"

"I don't know."

"Be honest. No one kisses a man the way you-all did Oliver unless there is something inside."

Janet looked to the ground, feeling her face flush with color. "I can't say. It's all happening too fast." She looked at Abigail. "Don't you think things are happening too fast?"

The younger girl suddenly appeared older. Her eyes hinted at a piece of knowledge that Janet did not know she had held. "My sister spoke to me before I left to come here. She described Litchfield as a mini world unto itself. The streets were filled with ambassadors in fashion from Paris, statesmen in training from around the country and women impressed with the idea their role is to create and educate the next generation of demi-gods to the United States Senate." She snickered. "She went on to explain Litchfield this way. The people who come here to study are the royalty of this country. We will be the kings and queens of government and industry." Abigail paused and looked at Janet. "I see it this way. Unlike Europe with its great families and connections, we have Litchfield, where the next generation meets. But Litchfield is better than royal connections because we, the students here, have the free will to pick a spouse."

"Don't fool yourself into believing you are here for an educa-tion," Abigail continued, after regaining her breath. "We are here to pick a spouse. It is our duty to create the next generation of demigods." She pushed back a few strands of red hair that had fallen on her face from her animation. "Think about it. Our founding fathers are dying yearly. All of them have retired from public life. A new generation is in power in Washington, Daniel Webster, John Quincy Adams, and my cousin John

Calhoun. We have to parent their replacements."

She smiled suddenly aware that she had been rambling. "Well, that's what I see." She smiled embarrassed. "All I know is that there are a lot of men here that you-all wouldn't mind melting into their arms if they would let you. And most of them will let you-all." She grinned.

"Like Arthur?" Janet finally spoke. Abigail's cheeks turned ruby red. "You know he's not from a top Connecticut family. None of his relatives have been senators or governors."

"I know," she brightened. "That's what makes Litchfield so spe-cial. Our father's wishes don't always have to be followed, but in the end, I'll be happy and so will he. I'll be the wife of a distin-guished man, which my father wants. And I'll be able to live a life of luxury and leisure, which is what I want."

"Don't you feel it's all too fast? All to set-up?"

"So is courting down in South Carolina. There I'd be allowed only to see certain members of the community based upon my father's wishes. I would be expected to marry one of them and only one of them, or become an old maid." She looked at Janet and grimaced. "I guess that was your decision."

"No," Janet responded not at all hurt. "I never had a choice persay. There were only married farmers or children in Harmony when I was 16 to 18. After that, I was already well entrenched as the teacher. What widowers or bachelors that happened a long found brides among my students. I guess I never was even considered." Her voice trailed off depressed.

"See there; that's why Litchfield is magical. You're the focus of not one but two eligible bachelors." Janet smiled, delighted at the thought. "Be honest, do you really care now if it is too fast or contrived?"

"But what if you didn't want a life of leisure? What if you wanted to change the world?" Janet spoke from her heart.

"You heard Mrs. Pierce. We will change the world by raising our children to be the leaders; to have high moral and social ethics; to believe in their abilities, God, and country."

"I want to touch more people than just my own children." Janet argued. "I want to bring about a world where we are as important as the men." She looked the southerner in the eyes. "I want to see the dreams of Abigail Adams brought to life. You know as well as I do that a woman's work is just as important as that of a man's. In a house or on a farm, we have to be equal partners. So why can't we be equal in the eyes of the courts and government?" She paused for a breath and then continued. "Mrs. Pierce, herself, said it in this room that she was looking for the same thing, equality among the sexes. But you and she both want it to take a lifetime. I want it to happen sooner. I want all the children raised with the ideas we are being taught here. A daughter, anyone's daughter, not only needs to be able to say to her father whom she wants to marry. She needs to be able to say no to her father or any man."

Abigail shook her head. "I guess you-all in Ohio have a different culture than we do in South Carolina. It is not the place of a daughter to ever question her father's decisions. I guess you are much more independent in Ohio. But think about it, what leaders have you-all produced? Whom do you see coming out of that wilderness to lead us to paradise, to quote the good book?"

"We have William Henry Harrison." The name of the military hero left Janet's lips without any thought. It had been his troops that had camped in Harmony on their way to fight the British. It had been his troops that had caused her best friend to fall in love. It had been his troops that had dramatically changed her life, making her an adult long before she wanted to be one. It was his troops that had brought her here to Litchfield, to be fought over by two men.

She looked away from Abigail and sat down in the single chair at the table. It was his troops that had brought the cavalier into her life. The fog lifted from her mind erasing time's hold. She pictured Oliver, the boy from her dreams. His face, so familiar, his kiss so real appeared within her heart and mind. And she tasted the coffee again and smelled the wood fire.

"No," she gasped. "No." Her mind watched him ride away with the rest of the army. His tall, lanky body silhouetted against the rising sun. Clearly, he was the master of the horse he rode. Its gait hinted at his control as well as at the pleasure of an early morning ride. And a silhouette of that afternoon flashed in her mind. It covered and then merged with the silhouette of her dreams, becoming a perfect match.

"It can't be." She murmured barely audible. "It can't be."

"What?" Abigail came and stood next to her. "What?" She asked again unable to hear the confused thoughts in Janet's mind. But they were there screaming in Janet's head all at once. The memories and visions combined with experiences and present time thoughts. Every sense, every emotion Janet had ever thought or felt rushed about again in her head.

It was. It had to be. Oh God!

She jumped to her feet, a frenzy in her eyes that nearly scared Abigail. "She took the younger woman by the shoulders "It is. By God it is him!"

"What?" Abigail responded totally confused.

"I've been blind this whole week. But I know now." Janet shouted between a hysterical laughter. "It's him. It's him. All these years I have thought it was just a fantasy, but it's him. My God it is him." She shook Abigail in excitement and laughed so hard she cried. "I don't know why I didn't see it before." The tears blurred Abigail's face from her vision, but Janet didn't care.

It was true! It was real!

The dream, the haunting dream was real!

Tears came unchecked, and Janet slumped into the chair again, exhausted from the emotions roaring within her body. Abigail simply hugged her, not knowing whether Janet was mad or having a religious experience. And the two sat, arm in arm as the night crept into the room.

11

Abigail was completely baffled at the sudden outburst from her roommate. Fear for Janet's sanity enveloped her. Her mother had raised Abigail on the southern belief that if you kissed a boy before you were married, you would go insane. And here was her roommate babbling and crying unprovoked. At that moment Abigail was ready to swear what her mother had told her was the absolute truth. In her mind, she was already swearing off men, even Arthur.

The hysterical outburst at discovering the truth caused Janet's logic to be thrown completely out the window. Words and other babble came from her mouth, as the emotions were too severe within to form coherent sentences or even thoughts. Then slowly, ever so slowly it seemed Janet began to settle down. Abigail released her embrace and looked at her friend in the eyes. "Are you alright?" She questioned unsure of what else to do. "Janet?"

The older student rubbed the happy tears from her puffy face and smiled. The world came back into focus again. Abigail's face cleared from the blur and Janet could see the concern in the younger lady's eyes.

"Yes," Janet exhorted. "I'm fine. In fact, I'm better than I have ever been in my whole life!" The tears slackened, and Janet came to her senses again. What are you doing here, she questioned herself.

What are you doing here in this room when he's right outside, just down the road!! The dream is real!

"What can I do for you?" Abigail questioned concern very evident in her voice. Janet looked at her and only smiled. It was a silly sort of smile that nearly brought tears of joy again. It was a silly sort of smile that caused Abigail to question her roommate's sanity.

"Nothing, nothing at all," Janet said, her eyes darting toward the door. "You see all my dreams have been answered! All my hopes have come true!" She laughed again, and it hurt her stomach. The pain caused her to double over, but when she looked up, she smiled at Abigail. "Don't worry I'm quite fine." She looked out the small window in the room, noticing it had become very dark. "I think I'll go for a little walk before it gets too late." She said, aware of a desire to be with Oliver at this time of discovery.

"Not unless you take me along," Abigail firmly demanded. "You've just had a frantic laughing and crying attack. I can't let you go out."

"But I need to." Janet looked the other in the eyes. "I need to." Janet said with all the conviction of a converted sinner. She had made up her mind to see Oliver again that night, no matter what it took. She had to see him. She had to tell him she knew who he was. She had to find out if he knew who she was.

"Then tell me why you suddenly burst into tears and laughter."

"Because I'm so happy, so incredibly happy," Janet gushed.

"Did one of them propose?" Excitement filled Abigail's eyes.

"No something even better has happened."

"Good God you're pregnant." Fear filled Abigail's voice, and she physically moved away from the Ohio student in an effort to avoid becoming pregnant herself.

"How could that happen?" Janet lashed back. "Don't be a silly child. You know as well as I do that could not have happened."

She paused and realized the young lady in front of her did not have any idea from where babies came. Raised on a farm, Janet knew firsthand about mating and the need for sex. But Abigail had been raised in a segregated southern household, where the conversation was always prim and proper. Janet leaned over the table and took Abigail's hand. If she did not tell the younger woman, who would? She might end up making love to Arthur and unknowingly become pregnant.

Visions of Luella came to Janet.

"God, why do men keep women ignorant?" She asked herself. "What benefit does it give them? What pleasure does it give them?" Anger filled her, and she began to outline how to conceive babies.

Abigail became visibly shaken and disgusted. But the truth had to be said to the teenager; otherwise, Janet kept telling herself. Otherwise, Abigail would be another disgraced woman. Tears fought to come to her eyes. This time, they were tears of sadness and regret long stored in her heart for Luella.

"You were the cause." Her heart spoke over and over throughout the explanation about babies. Janet never got over the fact that she had brought her best friend to the camp where she met the lieutenant. She was the cause of Luella's disgrace. She was the reason that community sent the young girl away from Harmony. She was the cause of her imprisonment in the one-room schoolhouse in Harmony. All this repeated year after year in her head, and now hammered like the largest church bell Janet had ever heard.

But today, she told herself. Today she was starting a new chant ringing in her head. This new chant will repeat how happy she was. It would repeat how Janet had saved Abigail. It will repeat over and over that the only love that a heart remembers is its first true love, and Oliver was that first true love.

"Oh, how wonderful Litchfield was!" Janet screamed within

herself. "Oh, how wonderful fate was! Yes, the Greek goddess sisters had led her back to the cavalier, her midnight cavalier!" She almost wanted to throw out her Congregationalist beliefs and return to paganism just because Oliver was right down the road from her.

She looked over at Abigail, as she finished explaining about birth. The southerner was slightly paler than she had been when the conversation had begun. Surprise filled her eyes, and a perplexed look covered her face. "My mother never told me anything like that." She said in genuine awe. "That's the truth you told me."

"Yes, dear," Janet maintained her teacher's voice. "For your own good, that was the truth." She tenderly touched the Southerner on the cheek. "Do you believe me?"

"I guess I have too." Her eyes still held its wide, astonished look. "But I never..." She did not finish her sentence; instead, she only shook her head.

"Now remember all this when you and Arthur."

"You don't worry about Arthur and me." She looked Janet in the eye. "That man isn't going a touch me until the preacher says 'you may kiss the bride." And even then I might have to think a second about it." She looked down at her ample breast and for the first time since they developed wished they had never grown. "So that's why all those men keep staring at me."

* * * * *

Just then the door to their room opened. Both ladies jumped as if they were trying to hide something from the new arrival. They were embarrassed by their topic of conversation, Abigail in particular. Janet, on the other hand, had a small hope and fear that the new arrival would be Oliver or some other male. To their dismay and relief, it was only the three other students who shared the room. All three were under thirteen and easily distracted. They had been sent to the school from the local surrounding comminutes to obtain some education beyond what the local one-room school could provide. They were the daughters of prominent businessmen in Western Connecticut and as such needed that additional education in order to navigate the social society they would be a member of with ease.

Because of their ages, and their sizes, they had been assigned to share the room with Janet. She acted like their mother hen. The teacher inside of her naturally took over concerning their grooming and hygiene. She also served as their surrogate mother when they did not feel well, as the youngest one, MaryEllen Clark already discovered the night she felt homesick.

Seeing the younger girls, Janet came to her feet and wiped the last of her tears away. All three were dressed similarly to Janet in flax linen off-white work dresses, with light chemises and cotton corsets underneath. It was the custom to get the younger girls ready, for the heavier rigid bone corsets by having them wear cotton ones even though they were undeveloped. When the fashion changed from hard bone corsets to the cotton ones, the practice with the younger children did not change.

"Have you been crying?" The ten-year-old MaryEllen asked her eyes wide with curiosity.

"Mommy use to cry all the time when she was with child. Are you with child?"

"No," Janet smiled. That was the second time MaryEllen had asked the same question in less than a half an hour. Was there something in her eyes that hinted at the desire within her? She shook off the thought and looked at the new arrivals. "You can't be with child unless you're married." She lied to the child and looked at Abigail who nodded her approval. Visions of Luella crossed her mind, followed by the taste of Oliver's kiss. That desire rose inside again, and Janet could feel his hands warm on her face. "And I'm not married." She concluded, trying to brush off the hot throbbing passion crawling through her.

Mary-Ellen sneezed. "Bless you," all four said almost simultaneously. The youngest looked at them and smiled. Janet noticed a reddening of her cheeks. She had not been looking well for the past day, but then she was only ten and youngsters were always sick.

"Are you feeling sick?" She asked.

"Miss Peck sent us down here because MaryEllen couldn't stop sneezing." June, one of the two twelve-year-old twins who shared the room said. "She said that she could not conduct another minute of class with all that disruption." June looked at her sister April for confirmation. The other twelve-year-old nodded. They were from New Milford, Connecticut, the daughters of a local merchant. "Who had learned the trade from Roger Sherman," the two bragged over and over. Miss Peck was the school's sewing teacher. In the evenings she had small class for the younger students who did not have any skills in sewing.

Janet walked over to MaryEllen, brushed back a strand of her long black hair that had fallen on her face from the pinned bun to the back of her head. Heat rose from the girl's uncovered head. Janet then felt MaryEllen's forehead. It was warm to her touch, as was the girl's whole body. The child's blue eyes were watery and sad. Janet knew the youngest girl needed some bed rest. She also knew that MaryEllen would fight lying down if no one else was making ready for bed. "Well it's late; let's get you ready for bed." She hugged the little girl as if she was her own child.

"Would you read to us?" MaryEllen asked in her sweetest voice. The angel inside of her was always apparent when it came time for bed and a story. "Your voice is so pretty, and it makes me fall asleep faster." She smiled at Janet and the older woman's heart melted. She wanted to have a child like this, just like this.

Janet nodded and pulled her Bible from the top of the shared dresser. The worn volume had been in her family for a number of generations. Her mother's mother gave it to her. An heirloom that a middle child received since everything else of value went to the older male children.

Opening to the book of Rebecca she read out loud as the younger girls undressed, washed their hands, feet, and necks and brushed out their hair. Abigail took over the reading when it came MaryEllen's turn for brushing. She had become fussy and only wanted Janet to touch her. The teacher did, noting that the young girl had become hotter.

When the younger students crawled under the covers, the twins snuggled in the center of the shared bed. Mary-Ellen, however, leaned on Janet listening to the Ohio student read. The words spoke of Rebecca's love for her husband, and her defiant attitude toward the village elders. Janet mouthed the words, but her thoughts were on Oliver. Mary-Ellen snuggled tight, reminding Janet of the ex-soldier, and his long passionate embraces. Slowly as the words stretched across pages, the youngest student began leaning heavier and heavier on Janet, signaling that she was dozing. But it was not a sound sleep as the fever made her toss and turned. Each time that Janet was sure the child was asleep; MaryEllen would move, cry out a faint "don't go" and snuggled tighter.

Eventually as the book on Rebecca came to a close, the little child was snoring sound asleep in Janet's lap. Her black hair plastered with sweat to her forehead and her breathing came shallow. Perspiration covered Janet's lap and most of the front of her dress. It had soaked all the way through her cotton corset to her skin. Janet carefully moved her body from under the sleeping child. The twins, though not asleep, continued to lie in bed undisturbed by Janet's leaving.

Walking over to where Abigail was working on needlework,

she stooped down. "I think I'll go out for a walk now." Abigail looked at her the concern still present in her eyes.

"Do you want company?" Janet smiled, and shook her head no, her thoughts only on Oliver.

"Well, then you-all better change that dress." Janet looked down and saw the huge wet spot left by the sweating child. It was then that she felt the unpleasant dampness all the way through to her skin. Nodding, she turned to allow Abigail to untie the simple bow fastening that held the light dress tight. It slipped off quickly as did her wet corset. Taking the discarded dress, she dipped it into the bowl of water the girls had used to wash up. She quickly ran the refreshing cold water over her warm stomach and breast, heated from the body of Mary-Ellen. She then slipped on clean chemise and threw a white linen dress over that without a corset.

* * * * *

Oliver Block brooded as he walked through the night. His mind was not on his destination, but instead on what had happened at the academy. Lust filled him, but it did not rule him as firmly as it had inside of Janet's arms.

"God was she beautiful." His voice whispered, "So soft, so warm, and so perfect to hold." He wrapped his arms around himself in a vain effort to relive the feel of Janet's embrace. Slowly his heart, racing from her kisses, settled back to normal. Slowly his excitement eased to normal, allowing his manhood to relax. She had done all that to him.

Tears came to his eyes, as he sat down on a tree trunk alongside the main road from the academy toward the green area. Across from him was the Tallmadge mansion and behind him stood the large home of another wealthy family of Litchfield.

Oliver looked at the Tallmadge's' home a while. Its white washed walls reached up toward the heavens proclaiming the wealth of not only the family that lived in the building but of the whole community here in western Connecticut. It was similar to homes he had envisioned he would live in when he was a teenager. The dust of endless marches filled his lungs again, as did the visions of the fifteen-year-old girl from Ohio. Dreams, endless dreams that had pushed him along his whole life always centered on her and a house like the one in front of him. The fear he had felt in Janet's arms returned. It could not possibly happen that his dreams would come true. What would happen then? He would be happy.

"How," He asked himself in the dark of Litchfield. "How are you going to make those visions come true?" He looked down at his hands. Soldier's hands, covered with scars from sword fights, covered with calluses from fighting the reins of too many untamed horses. "These are not the hands of a gentleman." He said. "These are not the hands of an attorney, senator or governor. No these are the hands of a worker. These are not the hands to hold that fifteen-year-old angel."

Oliver could not overcome the mystical aspect of his vision of young Janet. She had been too precious to his heart. She had been too important to his sanity to believe that the young lady he had just held was one and the same as his vision. But it was a reality, his mind told him, and he felt her lips on his again. His lust stirred to life, but also mixed with a deeper sense of the moment. Oliver smiled, as a feeling centered in his heart that brought contentment and simple joy.

Dark slowly surrounded Oliver, as candles in the various windows of the houses around him were blown out. As that darkness came, so did the voices of his comrades. Haunting voices, jokes shared, brags made, all resounded in his head. It was always worse after he had to fight someone. It was always worse when a situation threw his emotions any jolt from normality.

Both things had happened that evening. He had fought James and had nearly confessed his love for Janet

He listened for a second. There was his sergeant major's voice and that of his lieutenant. But their jokes were different. They were not repeating remembered moments alongside the camp-fire. No, they were giving him advice, advice for the here and now. Oliver's head snapped up as if called to attention. This haunting was different so different than it had been for nearly ten years. There was no sadness at the men's deaths. There was no longing to be with them again. Instead, there was brightness to the visions, a brightness that Oliver did not understand. But he knew what he had to do. He knew deep in his heart like he had known that Janet was the fifteen-year-old from his dreams. He stood and turned back toward the academy.

There was a longing inside of him that just wanted to be near Janet at that moment. This longing drove his feet toward the academy. He did not care if it meant just sitting outside of the building in which she was living. He just needed to be near her. And his feet began to quicken, to almost a full run. He just needed to be near her. Soon the building appeared in his sight. Its windows a blazed with evening candles, as the students worked or studied.

He slipped around the side of the academy and spied the basement window of Janet's room. The candle within allowed him a full view of the occupants. Janet was sitting at the table with Abigail hugging her. Softly he approached the window and leaned his head on the wooden wall of the school. He was close to her, which was all that mattered.

Sitting down, silently, he rested the back of his head against the frame of the building, so that he could no longer see into the window. The cold field stone foundation cooled some of the late spring heat from his body. If he remained quiet, Janet's voice could be heard through the sealed glass and wooden frame window. Her voice filled him with pleasure. He did not need to follow her words; just hearing the sound of her delightful voice caused this pleasant reaction in him.

He closed his eyes and quieted his heart. Her words came through; hung in his head, and then vanished as if they were a dream.

With her words arrived her spirit as well. It was the spirit of a strong-willed woman who could compliment and check Oliver. His heart reached out to his mind, set in its decision. Tears wet his cheeks, and he ignored them. He did not care what he looked like; he just wanted to hear her voice again.

"You are right," his mind kept repeating. "You are right."

He heard Janet's conversation about changing the world and how to conceive babies. His face turned a slight shade of red, even in the dark. Not that he was embarrassed by the topic, but because he had heard his angelic vision speak of the Christian sin. And when the conversation was abruptly interrupted, Oliver turned to watch as the mother side of Janet handled a sick child.

All this, he witnessed, knowing that his heart longed to bring about the completion of Janet's desires. But his mind told him over and over, that it was not to be. "Accept the facts," his mind spoke.

"Happiness was something Oliver Block would not know."

He sat again with his head against the building, taking his eyes off his vision, seeing only his dead friends. "The sergeant major, Lieutenant Premont, Grace Premont even the lieutenant's father had all suffered because of you," his mind spoke its vicious facts. "They had all died because you are cursed."

Tears came again. His father had seen that evil in his eyes so many years before and always told him. "You are a Jonah." He then cursed him as the young Oliver left the farm. "You think you're always right, well may you find out the truth about human nature. May you always know pain like the kind you are giving me today. May you wander always looking but never knowing the joys of love. And may you bring death and sorrow where ever you alight!" And so it was throughout his life, Oliver had followed the curse, discovering on the battlefield the truth about humans. They will do anything to their kind.

Happiness and been always just outside his reach, from his vision of Janet to his engagement with Grace.

He was indeed cursed.

"If you remain here Janet would suffer." The voices of the dead told him to leave. Tears came unchecked as he heard her wonderful voice again. He could not hurt her. He thought thoroughly depressed. He could not hurt Janet.

As he stood to leave, he heard the back door of the Academy creak open. Glancing into the room, he noticed that Janet was no longer inside. When he looked back up, she stood there right in front of him.

"You," She whispered, not scared or even surprised by his presence. "I..." She did not finish the thought but instead stepped into his outstretched arms.

Wet tears met her face as they embraced. They were Oliver's large wet tears of frustration and emotional turmoil. Her heart shattered, knowing that he was suffering inside. With the same mothering instinct she had just used on MaryEllen, she tenderly stroked his forehead and ran her fingers through his hair.

Their eyes locked on to each other. She longed to dive into them, to be able to read his thoughts. But most importantly she desired to ease away the pain Oliver was feeling. Her own eyes clouded, and she knew she was on the brink of an emotional outburst.

His hands reached up and framed her face in between. Their warmth reached inside of her, spinning her mind, thumping her heart. Not a word came. They just stared into each other's eyes. All the years of fantasy ended with that stare.

He brushed aside a tear that started to fall on her cheek, but his eyes never left hers. They reached inside her, touching her heart, singing out the secret they both now comprehended. Tension filled the air like electricity just before a summer thunderstorm. Janet shivered and felt a trembling race through Oliver's body.

Still silence cut the night as neither one spoke a word. They just stared at each other.

Her heart beat louder and louder. Her breathing came slowly and heavy, matching Oliver's breathing. She felt his eyes grow more and more intense in their stare. Her stomach twisted under their spell, like the mainspring of a clock. Twisting, twisting until it was taut, ready to erupt.

Words formed in Janet's mind: love, pure virginal love, first love, deep forever love. And the tears came. Love filled tears of happiness.

And then ever so slowly he brought her face to his. Their lips touched. Salty tears moisten their kiss. For a second they parted, and their eyes met again. The happiness rang out from them. Clear of all memories, Oliver's blue eyes shined even in the dark of the night. And they kissed again. This time with all the emotions that had been stored up over the past decade. Oliver's kiss exploded on her lips with passion.

She closed her eyes completely willing to be led anywhere by the warm, caring hands hugging her face. She was fifteen again, spinning around at the touch of the young soldier's hand in hers. He had been her escort around the camp. His touch was just as warm then as the rough hands on her face now. She pressed her lips hard against Oliver's. The salty taste lingered still from their first kiss. His lips pressed back, yearning to devour her. To draw her into him, in an everlasting embrace. She felt his pain, his delight, and his confusion. And she knew the same feelings.

"God," She whispered and it erupted in a moan. He caressed her lips with his and then tenderly ran his tongue over them, licking away all her tears. Once more their lips touched, caressed and embraced in a kiss that brought colors into Janet's mind. A rainbow flashed within her head. Bright, warm colors shined within. She felt dizzy and trembled.

Oliver's hands glided down her neck to her shoulders and then wrapped around her waist. He pulled her tight, squeezing the breath from her lungs. The embrace enveloped her in a passion stored for too many years in a dream. She surrendered and allowed him her full mouth.

This he took with pleasure. Lips to lips he kissed her and kissed her, the warm blood sailing from his heart to his mouth, bringing fire to her lips. Heat filled her, cuddled her, and wrapped itself around her like a blanket on the coldest winter night.

She struggled for her breath. And his tongue found hers waiting inside her mouth to dance with him. Tenderly like a feather on her cheek, Oliver's tongue slid alongside of hers in a coaxing dance of love. Their lips joined together, bringing his tongue further into her mouth. It explored, touching her in places it had never been before, tickling an aching in her breast to life.

He stepped back and brought his lips up to her tearing eyes. As in the woods, he kissed away her tears. "I love you," he whispered, almost afraid she would not return in kind.

But she did. "I love you." Her voice spoke the words she had so long to say to her caviler. He kissed her hard on the lips and then slid his lips to the soft part of her neck.

"Oh God," Janet moaned again, as the lips found her special place. More colors flashed across her vision, and she felt a falling sensation. Oliver sucked on that soft spot and dizziness roared through Janet. She tilted her neck to feel his lips again, and Oliver obeyed. This time, he licked the sweet spot with his tongue and then sucked on her neck. Janet just spun out of control.

Falling, falling she allowed her mind to go blank and focused only on the sensation of his biting her neck.

The sweet pleasure of pain mixed with passion rocketed desire through her. It centered in her stomach, releasing the taunt clock spring Oliver had just wound up. Her own emotions and passions roared to life. She reached up to the back of his neck and pressed his lips tighter against her neck.

A warm glow covered her sending a moist feeling to her thighs. Her breast filled with eagerness that urged her to press them against him. The sensation of her corset-less breast rubbing against the soft cotton of the simple working dress she had just slipped on excited her even more. Her nipples pushed against his chest, causing a new shiver to spread over her. They ached to be touched and to be kissed.

Oliver moved his lips down to her throat, as if he was reading her thoughts. Here her dress loosely drooped down, revealing a small portion of her breast. This he kissed, first her left then her right breast. Tenderly, softly he ran his lips over them, as if they were the most precious treasure he had ever beheld. He kissed them again, and her nipples harden against the thin cloth that separated them from his lips and their taste.

She drew his head to the center of the two orbs and rested it there. His hot breath tickled down her cleavage. "Oh God," She sighed so heavy, so loud she was afraid everyone in the academy would hear her. But there was nothing she could do. She was completely devoured by her passion. He kissed her breast again, and ran his moist tongue between them.

His right hand reached up and lovingly cupped her left breast. Caressing it, fondling it, he kissed it at the same time. She moaned again, and Oliver ran his tongue along the edge of her dress. He caressed her breast again, and then kissed her nipple through the cloth. Another moan escaped her lips and the moistness between her thighs grew warm. And then he nibbled her through the cotton.

Her head exploded in colors, warm intense sensations jumped throughout her body. And she pulled him closer yet.

Rolling her head back she felt his breath again tickling her cleavage. His tongue played some more with her burning aching breast, before moving it back up to her throat and her favorite soft spot.

Once again her head spun with desire as he sucked her neck.

And then he was kissing her again. Long passionate kisses with his tongue and without that took her to an edge. An edge she had never approached before.

Oliver's breath came hard and heavy as he worked his lips around Janet's mouth. Over and over he tasted her sweet lips. Their firmness called to him, teased him into caressing them and embracing them. "I love you." He choked almost in tears. "I've love you for years and years."

He stopped and looked Janet in the eyes. The clearness that had been there before fogged over for a second. Janet knew he was remembering her from Ohio. And she kissed him to bring him back to Litchfield.

Oliver stepped back, suddenly aware of his voices again. "No, you can't be here." He tried to push away her embrace. "I'll only hurt you. Look at me, there is too many deaths around me." He looked at the ground expecting to see the corpses. "My comrades, Lieutenant Premont, his sister, even your friend in Ohio. All of them I've hurt." He looked into her eyes. "You deserve so much more than I can give you.

I have to go. I couldn't stand it if I hurt you. I couldn't..." his words failed him.

"You live too much in the past," she cautioned in a whisper.

"But you are my past."

She placed a finger on his lips to silence them. "No, I'm your future."

He caringly kissed the finger. "I wish." He sighed and walked off without another word.

12

Janet stood there behind the academy in complete shock. Speechless she watched Oliver's figure evaporate into the dark of the evening. It was her dream! Her heart cried out. It was the reenactment of that haunting nightmare all over again. The taste of his kiss still lingered on her lips. The feel of his hand still rested on her breast. The heat of his aroused body still left her warm and eager between her thighs.

And he still walked away!

What the hell happened? She questioned her whole body. No part had an answer. What the hell happened? She asked as she watched the silhouette of her cavalier walk away just like it had for the past eight years. Embarrassment, bewilderment, utter confusion all whirled around inside of her.

The shame came to her at having been kissed, caressed and willing to surrender. Bewilderment filled her because of his inability to understand she was surrendering to him. The confusion came from the void caused by his walking away. The emotions whirled and stabbed at her heart creating the turmoil of feelings that brought tears, anger, and even a little hysteria.

"You bastard," Janet finally said the only words her voice could form. Looking skyward, she added, "Why?" A slight breeze came up, and she wrapped her arms around herself suddenly cold. An angry shiver shook her. "Why?" She asked the stars again.

"He's testing you." Abigail's unexpected voice scared Janet.

She jumped and looked behind her to see her roommate standing in the doorway of the school. "That's what the Baptist minister would say in South Carolina. He's testing you." Abigail came closer to Janet. Speaking in a voice of maturity that still shocked Janet, Abigail added. "That was too much of a kiss to let him go." She smiled. "Yes, I saw it. Lord, I hope someday to have a kiss as wonderful as that one. Someday I hope to be as immersed in love as you two are." She added with an understanding that came from her experience. "He loves you, and you love him. It's as evident as the stars in the sky. What are you doing standing here? If I were you-all,

I'd be a walking after him." She gestured with her head toward the direction Oliver had disappeared.

"What are you going to do?"

Janet looked at her all the emotions still hammering about in her head. She then glanced over her shoulder to where Oliver had disappeared. For nearly a decade Janet had been watching him ride off. For nearly a decade she had been helpless to prevent the repetition of her nightmare. "So what are you going to do?" Janet asked herself.

Her hesitation caused Abigail to reach out and touch her arm. The comfort offered eased Janet's frustration. She looked at her friend.

"I heard something about loving you from the moment he saw you at the campfire?"

"When I was younger, his troop camped outside Harmony. We knew each other than, as children. We just remembered today, just now." She looked at Abigail. "He was a fantasy I did not believe real, just an adolescent dream."

"Well what are you waiting for? Few people ever get to live their dreams. You do. Go. Get out of here." Abigail actually pushed her in the direction of the departed soldier.

"Thank you," Janet said, not sure why, but just knowing it needed to be said.

"Go," Abigail whispered again. "I'll cover for you here." Janet looked once more over her shoulder hoping Oliver would be there. He was not. The same hope that caused her to glance for Oliver had been the one she had lived with over the years. This belief had proven fruitless until today.

"Until today," Janet said to herself. A conviction seized her heart. All her life she had done what others wanted. She would argue, but in the end, she had done what others had wanted. "Until today," Her heart said. "Until Oliver had kissed you," the heart continued speaking, "Until you let Oliver kiss you!"

"Yes," She confirmed to herself. "You had taken the initiative. You had pulled him close for the kiss. You had come out here seeking to confront him. You need to go. Only you can end the dream the way you want it to end, snuggled tightly in Oliver's arms." His warm embrace sheltered Janet again and she sensed his presence surrounding her. His lips brushed against hers, tickling passions lurking just below her calm demure. She looked back at Abigail excitement sparkling in her eyes.

"You need to go." Her friend stated. "You need to go now." Janet nodded and skipped away.

* * * * *

Oliver weaved through the darkened village of Litchfield unnoticed by the residents. His mind was on Janet and what he had just done. His heart grasped the god awful truth of his exchange with Janet. His conversation had destroyed all the optimistic visions he had lived with for the past eight years. They would be compelled to slip forever away from his heart and mind, never to become reality. His desires sparked to life that afternoon were fruitless now. He would have to leave the village as soon as possible. The dye had been cast to paraphrase the holy book.

He reached the Wolcott home minutes after leaving behind his dreams in the academy backyard. His regular quick walking pace increased even more by the inner chaos brewing inside his heart. He had raced through the village unaware of what was around him, only knowing he was stabbing himself in the heart. Quickly he gathered together a change of clothing, a lantern and his legal debate notes. He then headed for the one place he would feel safe and at home. The one place where he could be alone, and fight off the depression he knew would be coming.

He could not face James Mathers in their shared room that night. Everything that James represented was what hurt Oliver at that moment. James was the symbol of the perfect people in the world. He had the money. He had the charm. He had the luck, while Oliver possessed none of that.

As he exited the back of the old governor's house, he heard James talking to himself. The Southerner was strolling down the dirt road from the Common, lost in thought and talking out loud. He paused and listened to Mathers act out what was in his mind. Vignettes of James' envisioned life with Janet came forth into the darkness, riding the words of the Southerner unaware Oliver was eavesdropping.

Oliver silently placed the items in his hands to the ground and edged closer to the approaching James.

As he did, Oliver remembered the words he had heard Janet say as he rested by the Academy window. He recalled the defiance in her eyes, as she demanded to change the world. She could do that if she were married to James. He had the money to buy out her contract. He could provide her with a respected family home from which she could change the world.

A sad smile came to Oliver's face, and he knew what he must do. Oliver slipped around the front of the house to see the other law student.

James slowly pranced through the night. He was acting like a male peacock with his plume in full bloom for the first time in his life. His thoughts were on only Janet and the kisses they had shared. They were his first kisses and they tingled through his body like fine alcohol when drunk. In fact, that was how he felt, a little drunk, a little unsure of his footing, a little off-balanced because of Janet Fellow's kiss. He hardly noticed the village green area and the lights from the candles in various windows as he passed by. All that mattered was that he had kissed the girl of his dreams. He had held Miss Fellows tight in his arms and tasted her lips.

"Oh, what a beautiful night it is! Oh, what a wondrous life it is!" His voice said out loud, expressing the twisting, tickling joy that raced through his body. His thoughts played with the idea of marriage and the important things yet to come with Janet by his side. His reading for the bar; his taking his father's place in the state senate; his bringing Janet to the family home all these thoughts filled his mind.

"Mrs. James Baldwin Mathers," His voice broke the darkness, while his mind pictured his father's home in the Maryland state capital. It had an eloquent reception hallway and a large front porch on which famous personalities were often discussing state politics. Here, in his mind, James pictured Janet and him arm in arm meeting visitors "I have the honor of introducing you to the Governor." He unconsciously bowed as he walked in Litchfield, playing out his Maryland vision, unaware of anyone who might be watching his progress toward the Wolcott home. "Yes my dear, you can join us for conversation on the porch." He continued to live this fantasy as he walked.

There in his mind, he was entertaining the upper crust of society in Annapolis. It was the Mathers' first social dinner, and Janet was at her radiant best. She would be dressed in a long flowing sky blue satin gown, brought in from Paris. His solid midnight blue frock coat would be designed to be a matching male counter to his wife's dress. Silver buttons clasping the neatly trimmed frock closed at the waist to enhance the multi-colored silk waistcoat that he would wear underneath it.

Champagne and wine also from France would flow for the guests. And Janet, beautiful Janet would be the center of attention of all the wives. Meanwhile, James, his father discreetly in the shadows, would be the focus of the leading men of the capital city, and the state government. "It will be a smashing success." His voice came again, his mind still picturing Maryland not the dirt road in front of his Connecticut lodging. "She will be the perfect hostess, saying just the right thing, demure and obedient."

"Come back from your fantasy world." Oliver Block's voice broke into the daydream. "She could never play that role." His shadow suddenly loomed in front of James. The Southerner stepped back in fright but then quickly gathered his wits.

"Out of my way, you scum." The southerner spoke, rage in his voice. Anger seized his soul as his fists instinctively formed. His pride hurt still from the confrontation the two had had earlier that evening.

"Didn't I show you once I was not afraid to fight," he stated boldly.

"No, you showed me that you did not know what fighting was." Block stepped within arm's length of the other law student and grabbed James' coat just below his collar. His breath burned on James' cheek as he spoke soft but crisp into the other man's ear. "Listen here boy, I would and could kill you before you take your next breath. I simply did not fight in front of the lady because I care for her. But you know the truth now. Feel this hand." He brought a hand quick and hard against the younger man's throat. "This hand has known death. It is not afraid to taste it again." He squeezed and James' breath cut off for a second. Blackness fogged the Southerners' mind. Then just as abruptly as the oxygen had been cut off, it was returned.

James's legs were weak, and Oliver's strong arms held him to his feet. "Do you understand James? I do not want to duel or play your fancy games with life. I only want Janet to be happy." He paused, his voice choked by something. "You can provide her with a queen's palace in Maryland. I know that. I can only give her an apartment in New York. But you can't give her want she wants." He leaned even closer to the young man's ear. "She needs to be independent. She is not a porcelain doll that you can bring out for entertainments and dinner parties. She is a woman with opinions and beliefs. Like a spirited mustang, she can't be fenced in. She needs her head. She needs to be able to gallop, not just prance as you hope."

He released James and stepped back. "I'm giving you her." He choked again, "If you can handle her? If you can give up the reins and allow her to run free, she will be the best wife any man could ever want. But if you don't." He suddenly grabbed the man's neck again. But this time he did not squeeze; he just held it in his vice like grip. "If you don't you will be the most miserable creature that God has ever placed on this earth."

Oliver moved in close again. His hot breath fell on James' right ear. "One more thing, if you hurt her in any way, I will hear. And I will make you pay." With that, the vice was released from James' throat, and Oliver's shadow disappeared almost silently into the night.

James stood there a moment, his eyes following the shadow that was Oliver, his right hand rubbing his throat. Was he giving her to me? He repeated Oliver's words. Their meanings slowly dawn on him, and the anxiety that was on his face from his encounter turned to a smile, a deep, deep smile of relief. He almost shouted at the top of his lungs but thought second of it once again feeling Oliver's hand on his throat. "There will be time to celebrate later," he said out loud, "Plenty of time to celebrate." He rubbed his hands together to release the energy now racing through his body. His night could not have been better. "God, what a beautiful evening," He said and walked into the Wolcott's house.

* * * * *

The warm evening gave way to a chilly night as Janet made her way through the dark town. She regretted having slipped on only a light cotton dress over her chemise, but once committed to chasing down Oliver; she was not turning back. She reached the Common with no problem. For the past week, she had walked the exact same route daily from the academy to the church, across the common to the law school as part of the student's required singing promenade.

Now, however, she began to worry when she reached the Common. She had no idea where the Wolcott house was, other than that it was across from the law school. How was she going to find the house? She asked herself. How was she going to find the law school? She had never been to the law school other than in the daylight.

She paused on the common and looked at the buildings that surrounded her. The steeple of the Congregational Church stood out against the rich dark of the Connecticut spring night. Stars flirted with the tip as if the structure indeed reached into the heavens. She remembered what she had read to the younger girls that night. Rebecca had been a strong woman; a woman who would not stand back and allow the world to walk over her. She had loved her husband and had stood beside him no matter the trouble. So would she, stand beside Oliver, no matter what had to be done to eliminate the past.

"I'll make me his future." She defiantly said looking at the stars. "I'll replace his dreams and nightmares with the present, just as he will replace my dream with a warm hand to hold each and every day from hence." The spirit of the biblical heroine reached out of the church and tapped the young woman in the heart. Janet brush aside the doubts she had about finding the Wolcott house, she just knew she would. Resolute and determined she turned and headed down South Street in search of the law school and the Wolcott family house.

The dirt road grew darker as she ventured away from the common, and its commercial outlets. With each step, she began to formulate what she was going to say. The frustration inside of her dissolved into a commitment to fulfill her fantasy. "I'll be damned," she muttered to herself. "If I'm going to let Oliver just walk away, like he has for the past eight years." A rage caused by her feeling of helplessness nestled in her stomach and worked its way into full anger as the cool wind of the night bit at her. Her nose became cold to the touch as did her fingertips.

"I'm tired," She muttered. "I'm tired of being trapped. Stuck between reality and what I want." She breathed deep. "Damn it, I'm smart, I'm pretty, and I'm a stupid teacher." She looked at the houses that lined the road. They were not as large as the Tallmadge's house, but they still spoke of wealth that she did not know in her life. "Why am I trapped?" She questioned no one but herself.

"Because you were dumb enough to bring your friend to the army camp," She answered herself in spite.

"That damn army, what good did it do anyone?" She answered remembering Luella Bates, "If I had not taken her to the camp?" The thought had also haunted her for years. How would her life be different?

"I would be married now. I'd be married to some broken back farmer in Ohio with at least five or more children." She paused and looked again around herself. "I would never have come here." The houses filled her eyes. "I would never have known Oliver and felt his kiss." She touched her lips and smiled, from deep within her heart.

A shiver shook her, and she wrapped her arms around her. The sensation reminded her of his hugs. The smile grew, as it mixed with a little lustful desire to kiss Oliver again.

Then in the corner of her eye, she recognized the small single room building that served as the law school. She had been reminded of her own Ohio school the first time that she saw it. It was here that the leading men in the nation had been coming since before the turn of the century to study law. It was strange that so much greatness could come from such a small place.

"Will they ever say that about my school?" She wondered out loud. Deep in her heart she knew that she loved teaching the children. She could not see herself doing anything else as rewarding as that, even if it was becoming Oliver Block's wife. There was just something about knowing you were molding the mind of a child. That power to change the life of a child was inspiring. In her hands was the future of her community in Ohio. It was a daunting challenge but one she had managed so well for the past eight years.

Walking to the law school, she turned and faced the road. These, almost directly across from the building stood a large whitewashed central chimney house. Silhouetted against the darker sky, it spoke clearly of its age and dignity.

"The Wolcott's home," She whispered almost afraid to speak out loud. If caught out of the academy at this late hour, she would be sent back to Ohio immediately. She knew that fact, but she had not thought of it until this very second, as she stood ready to cross the road. If sent back to Ohio, would she ever see Oliver again?

"Fate is not that kind." She said summing up her courage and boldly crossed the dirt road.

* * * * *

TONY KANE

Oliver Block was having what he called a soldier's mess. Standing in the stable of the Wolcott's homes, he had before him a plate of cold meats, bread and a cup of coffee. After taking his change of clothing to the stable, he returned to the kitchen of the old governor's home and smiled at the cook. He had learned in the army that it was the sergeants and the secretaries that ran the world, not the generals and mill owners. In a house, it was the cook.

The Fredrick Wolcott's servant fell to his natural charms and found some cold meat for him to eat. The house did have a habit of maintaining a boiling pot of water for tea or coffee. Soon he returned to his studying in the stables with his meal. He knew that keeping his mind busy was the best medicine he could use to forget Janet.

Now he stood dressed in his brown trousers, riding boots and long evening shirt. The linen shirt hung down to his knees and served as his sleeping garment. Shortly he would be removing his boots and trousers for sleep. Keeping the slight chill off the stables was a small fire Oliver had lit in the Franklin stove situated in the front of the building.

Sipping his coffee as he paced between the small, well-worn tack table and the nearest stall, Oliver looked over his notes for the mock trial. The words on the pages of his handmade notebook danced in his head making connections that Oliver was well prepared to argue. "A slave is a slave in name only," He began to rehearse out loud, his voice filling the stables with sound other than the neighing of the dozen horses living in the building. "From ancient time forward, slave owners have maintained the right to free their charges, when the person has been productive, loyal or because of a great many other emotional bonds. This liberation has often taken the form of a bequest in the property owner's will. The court recognizes these bequests with little dismay or questioning." He paused and sipped a little of his coffee.

"It is also a common practice to bequest a little property or financial gain to a newly freed man in the same will. Once more I say the court does not venture into the examination of these requests, but simply administers the requests, producing new citizens of the community."

"The question we face today is a logical sequence or continuation of this practice of emancipation!" He looked up from his notes and hammered home his point to the audience of horses in their stalls using his right forefinger to write in the air the dot at the bottom of his exclamation point. "Instead of issuing a separate declaration of freedom, a property owner should be able to free his slave simply through a bequest of tangible property to the slave's name. As is recognized in all states, a man can own property, but a slave cannot. So by the simple act of becoming a landowner, the slave becomes a free man. It is simplicity! It speaks to the American hatred of massive governmental bureaucracy! In all it is the most American thing to do, to rule in favor of such a simple system of creating freedmen!"

The door creaked, and he turned instantly aware of human eyes watching him.

* * * * *

Janet walked into the dooryard of the Wolcott house and then froze. How was she going to find Oliver? A knot tightened in her stomach. She was going to be discovered here, and it would have been all for nothing. She would not have talked to Oliver; she would only end up ridiculed by the community and sent back in disgrace to Harmony.

"Why did you come?" she questioned. "What a fool you are." She cursed herself for falling to her desires. "Good God Janet, you are a mature woman. You came running out here like some lovesick child."

The knot in her stomach tightened further, and tears blurred her vision. "You're not going to see him again." The words left her mouth and hung in the air like a tapping on the marital drums of an army camp. They were fatal words. Fear gripped Janet. "You are so pathetic. You are just a lovesick child."

The truth blurted out from her, and she could not help but picture the cavalier from her dreams. "Oliver." She whispered out loud. "Oliver of the past not the present," She whispered and looked at the house tracing the line of its architecture by the glow of candles in various windows.

Which one of these windows looked in on Oliver's room? The impossibility of the task at hand overwhelmed her desire to hold the law student. She allowed the tears to come to her eyes, and she shook her head in despair. "It's impossible." Her voice said out loud. "And then there's James." She suddenly remembered that the two were roommates. Even if she could find Oliver's room, who would be in it?

Defeated she turned away from the house to head back to the academy. Then she noticed it, a thin line of light coming from under the double door of the stable.

"It's a sign," She excitedly whispered. A shiver raced through her. "Where else would a horse trainer be? She almost laughed out loud at her discovery. Oliver just had to be in the stables, she thought.

Her body again shook with excitement. "I yelled at God enough to send me a sign and here it is."

She crept up to the detached stables. The double door was slightly ajar, and she could just see in. Oliver Block stood there in his white linen shirt and brown trousers. The shirt pulled out so that it hung down to mid-thigh. His hair was loose and in his hands he held a tin cup and several leaves of paper sewed together into a tablet. His back was turned toward her, as he directed his speech to the horses. Janet listened enthralled by his baritone voice and its intensity.

Unaware of his human audience, Oliver continued to argue his case before the equine judges. His words reached out into Janet's heart. She was not a social reformer, as many of the residents of Ohio were, but she did have an opinion about slavery. It was hard not to have a view about slavery growing up in Ohio. That area was noted for its abolitionist tendency, and Janet's family was among the first in the Harmony area to start an anti-slavery discussion.

Not only did Oliver's words affect Janet's heart, but also the conviction in his voice stirred her heart. She leaned against the door to listen closer. "No one could be that convincing if they weren't sincere," she thought, and a smile of compatibility crossed her lips. Oliver's presentation reached a fervor pitch as he addressed the concept of an American way. It was another cord that struck Janet's upbringing. Her generation had the knowledge that they were the first-born Americans. It was their generation that would create the model for other Americans to follow.

Janet stared at Oliver's well defined muscular back. Yes, this was the model she would have designed if she were a sculpture. Like Michelangelo's David, Oliver could be the bronze figure of his age.

A tickling smirk came across her face, and she rubbed away the heat that suddenly filled her cheeks. The quick motion caused her to lean too hard on the door, and it creaked open.

Their eyes met.

Oliver's clear blue eyes widened with shock and delight. She was there, suddenly appearing like the girl in his vision had done throughout the eight years. She was there, but this time, it was a reality. His heart stopped unwillingly to accept the fact that his yearning for her had been fulfilled. His face showed the confusion in his mind and then a slow mirth came to his lips. "Janet." His words came excited and full of love. "You came here."

She nodded, afraid that her own voice would not be as calm as Oliver's. The excitement inside of her shook her. Her stomach knotted and then released with a spasm of delight that caused her to dig her fingernails into her palms to prevent her from showing the adrenaline rushing through her. She stepped into the stable and closed the door behind her. Her actions caused Oliver's eyes to widen even further.

There was only one interpretation that could be made by the gesture.

Oliver stepped toward her, dropping his papers and cup along the way. The items bounced off the floor, but their crash did not interrupt the kiss the two lovers shared.

Coffee, hot coffee lips met Janet's, and she was transported back in time to Harmony. All the fog of the previous eight years disappeared with that kiss, revealing a hidden memory of the army campsite.

Darkness surrounded her, as the wind came up bringing the acidic smell of campfires. Corporal Oliver Block stood next to her, his dark blue uniform of the Dragoons smelled of horse musk and fresh air. He was escorting her around the campsite, on orders from Lieutenant Premont. Luella was receiving a personal tour as well, but hers was with the young lieutenant. Fifteen-year-old Janet was still naive enough to believe that the personal affections of the Lieutenant were honorable.

Oliver's young voice babbled in her ear, while his arm looped together with hers in a proper escorting manner. The words he said were not remembered over time, just the sweetness of his voice. Suddenly his ungloved hand slipped into hers. Its warmth surprised her, but she did not pull her hand away. After all, it was a miracle that a soldier would be paying any attention to this fifteen-year-old girl from a backwoods community. Janet was awestruck by the presence of all these soldiers. Oliver in particular, stirred her heart because he was so tall and so close.

He continued with his walk and his narrative, but Janet just looked at his face. His curved Dragoon helmet, with its white plume, was set down to his eyebrows, giving his face a more majestic look. So it would appear for the next eight years. His body held a ramrod posture, providing Janet with a vision of an older man, than the aid's actual sixteen years. But it was the warmth of his hand combined with the smell of horses and fire that caused the most lasting memory, a memory that was to haunt her.

Then suddenly, unexpectedly, the aid turned to her at the edge of the camp. "Well, Madam that is the tour." He nodded his head as if to note the end of an assignment. "With the exception," he held up a mischievous finger, "of the company's traditional kiss." He quickly added a nervous squeaking in his voice. Then shyly, awkwardly Oliver tilted his head and sloppily placed his lips on hers. And she tasted the coffee on his breath, a taste she now experienced in the stables behind the Oliver Wolcott House in Litchfield, Connecticut.

13

She was floating. Free falling off a cliff into an endless well. Flashes of hot, bright colors lit up her mind, spinning her emotions, even more, bedazzling her heart, and shading all that were beyond the touch of Oliver's lips into darkness. Wrapped in his strong arms, Janet did not have a care. All her emotions, all her senses were focused only on his touch, his taste, his smell.

His kisses came tenderly savage to her lips. A tingling electrical sensation raced through her body with each touch, each caress of his full talented lips. All his pent up emotions demanded release through each long, juicy, passionate kiss. His breathing was heavy and warm on her cheeks, and she could feel all his muscles tense in anticipation of sweeping her away into the world she had only dreamed. The intensity of Oliver's kisses excited her more than the warmth of his palm on the back of her neck.

And she knew, yes she knew why. Finally, the river overran its banks inside of her and Janet finally knew why Luella had done what she had done. The flood of emotions, of intense pleasure, stepping higher and higher with each touch of Oliver, fogged her mind but opened a door she had never opened before. It must have been the same door that Luella opened with the army lieutenant. Once opened, Janet knew she could not close it again, and so it must have been with Luella.

Janet's head spun under the onslaught of Oliver's kisses. His strong, intense kisses caused her heart to skip with each caress. This intensity twisting her stomach into a frenzy over and over, tighter and tighter with each kiss, each touch of his tongue, each pass of his fingers over bare skin.

She melted completely willing to surrender to Oliver's desires.

His body, silhouetted against the flames of the woodstove filled her eyes when she dared open them. His solid shoulders, shared from endless hours of manual labor, spoke of an unleashed strength that she begged to feel wrapped around her frame. His arms, like steel bars, supported her as she melted. Not a hint of struggling, not a hit of weakness came through. Oliver's presence dominated all around her. She forgot all else.

Their lips touched firm and wet against each other. They had become partners that knew each other well now. They caressed, twisted and coaxed each other to make the kisses come alive with fire and desire. Like dancing partners who had practice for years, their lips glided gracefully across the dance floor of yearning lust. An intense, almost tickling feeling raised the hairs on her arms as lips traced the line of her jaw to the base of her right ear.

Janet's breath deepened as her heart quickened. Oliver's presence overwhelmed her. Its intensity reached into her own body stirring her heart to pump hot blood quickly to her chest and a hunger between her thighs. She closed her eyes and drifted with her senses. It felt almost as if she had left her body, and was floating above the couple in the stables. She swore in her mind, that if she opened her eyes, Janet would be watching them, from above, but Janet did not dare open her eyes for fear it was only a dream, the same dream she had live so many times before.

The smell of horse musk, wet and dry hay and wood fire from a small Franklin stove in the corner mixed in her mind, and she flashed between Litchfield and Harmony.

"Was it real?" She had to question. "It has to be," her lips called back, swelling from the passionate blood racing to them. It had to be her breast called out urging her to press them against Oliver's chest. It had to be craved her arms longing to encircle Oliver's body in them.

Suddenly Oliver's own musk filled her senses, reassuring every inch of her that it was a reality. These kisses, this moment of absolute pure joy was actually happening to her. And she did not hesitate any longer. All inhibitions vanished behind the knowledge that what she was doing was fated. It had all been written down by the three fates the day that she was born, according to the ancient Greek myths, something the teacher inside of her had studied and taught. What she was doing was the culmination of her midnight dreams for the past eight years. What she was doing was right!

His arms pulled her tight to his lightly clad chest. The sensation spun her deeper into her fantasy world. His chest was warm on her cheeks, and she relaxed into it, hoping to crawl inside of his body. There she could be a part of him, a part of his essence. She would become the most valuable part of him, his love.

She pressed her ear against his chest and listened. His heart beat loud inside, a symbol of his spirit. His hands stroked her bonnet free hair, and it fell from its bun, down to her shoulders and beyond. His lips tenderly kissed the top of her head, as his fingers combed through her silken auburn hair. The sensation raced down her spine tickling her with pleasure.

Oliver's embrace shrouded her in love, and she dreamed again of a future with him. In the distance, she heard his heartbeats, the thumping of the horses in their stalls, and their whispered neighing. The animals' breathing was low and heavy like Oliver's. For a moment, Janet pictured the animals, their large brown eyes, looking on, watching the lovers' intimate moments. A new tingle of excitement prickled her.

It was as if the whole world was watching her, as she boldly gave into Oliver's embraces.

"They could be caught!" Her mind called out to her to run away: to leave at this moment, while no one would know that she was there. But her heart spoke calmingly that this was how it was to be. This place inside Oliver's arms was where she had to be, inside Oliver's warm, loving embrace for the rest of her life. Yet a third voice tantalized her at the thought of being caught. The vision of others watching her, holding Oliver, kissing Oliver brought an unknown guilty like pleasure, to her. She almost wished Mrs. Pierce was there to see her in the soldier's arms. That would have made the kisses even more wonderfully delicious. And she hung on to her lover tighter than before.

Oliver's hand slipped down her hair to shoulders bare but for the straps of the light dress and her chemise. His lips moved down her neck to her shoulders. The tingling roared again in her stomach, and she sighed deeply. His war, lips brushed ever so tenderly on her neck and shoulders, and she unwillingly dug her fingers into Oliver's back. The soldier responded with a hard sucking kissing on the soft spot of her neck. Her eyes suddenly filled with a flash of hot red and yellow.

Slowly her hand crawled down his back, searching for the hem of his shirt. What she wanted, more than anything else at that moment was to rest her head on his bare naked chest, just to be as close, to him as physically possible. Her hands found their way to the bottom of his long shirt and slipped up underneath the linen. She felt the warmth of his bare back. His skin was muscular and firm to her fingertips. It was a muscle development known to most men of the 1800's, brought on by the woodpile and other routine daily chores. She edged her fingertips up his back to his firm shoulder blades. His bare skin felt almost hot to her fingers as her hands crawled up his body, feeling all along the way what she knew was his true self.

His lips came with more intensity as she reached beneath his shirt and scratched her fingernails gently along his spin. Oliver turned her face to his. Their lips met together in a full mouth embrace that sent a shudder through both of them. Strong, passionately they caressed and tasted each other. His tongue edged along the seam of her mouth teasing and tantalizing her to part her lips just a little so their tongues could meet.

She refused, longing instead to be kissed and kissed lip to lip like before in the woods. Oliver's body tightened, as his desires were teased and then denied. Oliver stepped back and looked at her. She could feel the animal inside of him. She could see it in his bright blue eyes. That tiger-like look from earlier that afternoon in the woods had returned. She was his prey, and she loved the idea of being devoured by Oliver.

A tingling filled her from head to foot. Her breast ached to be touched. And still, his eyes bore into her. She closed her own and tipped her neck back. Oliver took the request and ran his tongue up and down on her soft spot. A falling sensation spun Janet's body. The intensity caused her mouth to open in a moan.

"Oh God," her voice came, and she did not know if it was a yell or just a whisper. She was too far inside the tiger's pounce to be aware of anything else.

Her heart beat loud in her ears. Hot blood flowed to her breast causing her to struggle for breath. His warm breath tickled her face and neck. His day old beard growth scratched her cheek, in a delightful pain.

A taste of coffee lingered on his breath, and she lay back in his arms allowing him her full neck.

His tongue and lips sucked and nibbled sending new flashes of tickling intensity through her body.

Deeper moans erupted from her voice and echoed in the stillness of the stable.

Their lips met again. Coaxing, flirting they pressed and danced together totally at ease. There was no awkwardness only oneness they each felt, as they were enveloped together, in a shroud of devotion.

The world was perfect. This surrender was contentment, Janet told herself and glowed.

* * * * *

Oliver looked up from his speech at the sound of the barn door creek, and the fulfillment of his dreams stood there. Not a word broke the silence of their surprise and passion, as Janet closed the door behind her. His body literally shook in anticipation. It was as if he was facing combat again, fear and anxiety filled him. Would he fail? Could he possibly return to her what she had given him? These questioned haunted him, as he swept her into his arms.

She was soft there, small inside his muscular embrace. Like a newborn foal, searching for the shelter of her mother, Janet's love sought the shelter of his embrace. An intensely excited shiver shook Oliver as he kissed her. Like electricity racing through the night sky, it prickled Oliver's skin, causing the hairs on the back of his neck to stand on end. It was right, so perfect to hold her like this. He pulled her into his chest longing for her to become a part of his soul.

Her vision, as a fifteen-year-old had been there, now Oliver wanted this Janet to replace that first image. She would become the all-encompassing reward that he searched for throughout his daily life. All that would matter from this point on would be her happiness, her gratification.

He squeezed her and ran his fingers through her long auburn hair. Its silkiness shocked him and delighted him. Like petting a horse or dog, the gesture brought a relaxing pleasure to Oliver. No one, he told himself over and over. No one had been this close, this important to him. No one had allowed him to be this comfortable.

He turned her lips to his and showed her how much she meant to him. Wet, firm kisses responded to his lips with a passion that he could not help but feel race into him. A fever soared through his chest, into his lips, and through his fingertips into Janet's heart.

She moaned, and his heart pounded harder in his chest. A new wave of obsession, more intense, more devoted to achieving its goal seized Oliver's' mind. His tongue and lips pressed hard against the soft spot of Janet's neck as her fingers touched the bare skin of his back.

Her fingernails tickled his skin, a sensation that the ex-soldier had not felt in years. Yes, he had known women, but none as powerful, as seductive as this one in his hands. All others faded from his mind, as she ran her hands over his back. Oliver sucked deeper on her neck and nibbled a little harder.

"Oh, God," Janet breathed in his ear. Her breath was warm with a desire Oliver longed to touch.

She cooed and relaxed into his arms. She was his, his mind told him. All his to do with what he wanted. Like a lake held back by a dam, Oliver's lust pressed hard against the earthen works to be released, to conquer Janet's body.

The desire swelled him with heat and passion. Janet felt his manhood awake. She grabbed the end of his shirt in her hands and pulled it slowly upward revealing his well-defined chest. A small tuft of hair brushed against her cheek and lips as she kissed on and on.

A small purple scar rested just below the tuft. It was here he had given his life to the country and her. Now she was going to reward him for his courage. She knew it then for certain, as she had known it before she had even walked into the stables. She was going to give Oliver her most precious gift.

A gift she had been holding in wait for the cavalier of her fantasy.

He finished removing his shirt, as she rested her head centered on his breast. The white linen garment dropped silently to the stable's wooden floor. His heart echoed in his chest, filling her with a new excitement. She was really here. She wanted to pinch herself to make sure everything was real. But she knew it was. The passion, the excitement, the desire were too strong to be a dream anymore. Running her hands over his bare chest, she touched the old wound tenderly afraid it still hurt. Oliver showed no sign of pain or even recognition.

She had to ask, and looked up, breaking the mood, breaking the moment.

"Does it hurt?" She tenderly asked. Her voice was a surprising sound in the quiet stable. She looked at his eyes bright blue, completely vacant of memories. All that was there were a lust and excitement she had brought forth, and that made her smile with a blush on her cheeks.

"Does it hurt?" She pointed to the wound, and Oliver finally understood.

"No." Oliver said. "It doesn't hurt anymore, now that you're here." He embraced her with a kiss. "Nothing hurts, in my body or my mind anymore now that you are here." He smiled, and she could clearly see into his soul for the first time. It was clean, completely cleansed of the misery he had known in battle. His heart was alive, filled with only her love. His body was also very much alive, filled with his love for her that she watched it give off a shine, a happy glow of warmth.

"Good." She leaned again on his chest, and he wrapped her tight once more with his strong arms. The heat of the embrace touched deep within her body comforting her. "I'm glad." She felt his manhood against her and a new wave of heat crashed over her.

Oliver started kissing her neck again. New emotions flooded her body, drowning out all inhibitions she had ever had. A burning, intense burning came to her cheeks and thighs. The heat of

Oliver's lips traveled across her. Her heart stopped, she was sure. The whole world stopped, she imagined.

Their lips found each other again, and this time she allowed his tongue to play inside her mouth. The taste of coffee vanished behind the other sensations that rocked her body. His fingers crawled up her back and eased the straps of her dress off her shoulders. The fabric fell mid-way down her breast revealing more than she had ever thought she would show a man.

Oliver's teasing mouth ventured down the front of her throat and onto her cleavage. The heat of his breath, the firmness of his wet tongue shook her with intensity. She closed her eyes and allowed his lips to taste the top of her breast. Then ever so slowly to his touch, she turned her back to him. He ran his wet, searching tongue up her shoulder blade to the nape of her neck. Lifting her auburn locks up, his lips ventured to pet, tease and tasted the back of her neck.

Then ever so slowly, as if time had come to a standstill, Oliver progressed inch by inch down her back. He reached one of the two ties holding the light cotton dress on her body. With his teeth, he secured an end of the bow and gently pulled it loose. The dress dropped even more on her breast, but Janet did not stop it. Her hand did not even attempt to hold it up. Instead, they reached back and pulled up her hair to give Oliver a full clear run to the other bow.

Yes, she thought. Yes! Yes! This moment was the climax of her fantasy. This moment was what she had been hoping for the past eight years. Her body, naked in Oliver's arms was all she desired at that moment. All thoughts of social responsibilities faded behind a tingling sensation caused by Oliver's lips timidly caressing the back of her neck.

Oliver's lips kissed the new bit of naked skin revealed by the untying of the first bow. Then he took the string of the second bow in his mouth. Another gentle tug and it was free. The dress fluttered to the floor of the stables.

* * * * *

She knew the wind that must be blowing through the stables was cold. She knew the night had turned chilly from her walk through Litchfield but all Janet felt at that moment was heat, a burning fire throughout her body. The chemise she wore was nearly see-through. Her brown nipples pressed hard against the linen cloth, demanding to be released. Her breath came hard, heavier than if she had been running. And Oliver continued to kiss the back of her neck, sending wave after wave of heat through her body.

His hands wrapped around her thinly clad waist and pulled her tight against him. His trousers bulged where his manhood was fully excited. It pressed up against her, warm against her nearly naked rear. She could feel it yearning to explode. And she leaned back, feeling its heat through the cloth, feeling it pulsate with desire. A tenseness came to Oliver's' breath, and his lips moved to the back of her left ear.

His tongue played with her ear lobe, tickling her with yet a new sensation.

She leaned back into him forcing his hard manhood to throb against her body. He suckled her neck from behind totally out of control. She took his hands in hers.

It was all up to her now, she thought. All up to what she did next. Was she going to surrender? The question spun in her mind, like a whirlpool, twisting and twisting adding to her already confused thoughts.

She opened her eyes and saw the stable. The horses in their

stalls still thumped their hoofs on the wooden floor. The smell of hay and horses lingered in the air. But they were distant compared to the smell of Oliver and the feel of his wet, luscious lips on her neck. The whole world appeared distant, remote from her as she snuggled deeper into Oliver's arms.

She could feel his wanting her. His manhood firm against her body throbbed in unison with his pounding heart. Its cry reached into her soul and heated it with a fire of desire she had only felt in her dreams. But this was not a dream; this was as fundamental as love itself. She was as animalistic as she could even remember allowing herself to fall.

She felt his callused hands. The scars of his battles evident on the thick fingers she fondled in her hands. Hers were so small, so needy compared to his, but at that moment, hers were in command.

Janet knew it. She was in complete control of Oliver's large hands. Those hands that she had dreamed would someday caress her breasts.

That thought sent another wave of heat through her. This time, it landed in her breast, causing them to tingle in anticipation. Hot blood filled them, swelling them, causing them to urge her hands upward. Her nipples reached out hoping to be kissed, to be pinched ever so gently in between his fingers.

"Do I?" She asked. Standing there in the middle of the stables, she knew, in reality, she was on the edge of a cliff, a cliff that did not allow one to climb back up, once you had fallen. She looked down that cliff. The sides were steep and dangerous. But there was a monstrous passion for falling. There was an unbelievable urge to step forward.

"Just take one tiny step." Her heart panted, "Just one tiny step forward." Its voice came in heavy urgent sighs as deep and as hard as her breathing was coming from her throat.

"Do I?" She panted again. "Do I?"

Closing her eyes again, Janet watched as her vision whirled with colors. Every nerve in her body stood on edge.

And the voice continued to pant in her head, "Just one tiny step."

The abyss flashed through her head. And she grew dizzier and dizzier thinking about right, wrong, feelings, love and reputation. Twirling and twirling her head spun and her stomach tightened to the warm kisses on her neck, and the pressure of Oliver's fully aroused manhood barely contained by the linen of her chemise. "What would it be like to fly?" She asked and stepped.

Her hands commandeered Oliver's up her stomach to her aching breasts.

"God, yes," she moaned as she cupped his hands over her breasts with her hands. Gently, tenderly, she showed him how she loved his touch. Softly she rubbed his fingertips over her excited nipples. "Oh God," She moaned again. Her voice sounded far away, as if on a distant island. "Oh God," she murmured too swept up even to care what came from her lips. His hands, his hands were on her, caressing her, fondling her. That was all that matter!

Warm colors filled her mind. Red, yellows, purples all danced within her sight. The intensity she had never felt busted within her, twisting her stomach tighter and tighter until she wanted to explode. Oliver's hands continued to caress her breast as his lips found the soft spot on her neck again and again. "God, more," her voice called. "More!" Her mind spun. "More!" her heart cried.

Intensity!! Intensity!!

Her mind was confused by all the sensations boiling inside of her faded from reality. It spun. It clouded over. It turned to night and came back even more confused. And all the while Oliver continued to fondle, pet and kiss.

Floodwaters of desire and passion overwhelmed her. She submerged in a hunger for more of Oliver's body. An animalistic demand roared from her heart. It rushed through her body causing her breast to ache and beg to be sucked and cuddled. Warmness settled between her legs. An intense tickling feeling sent goose bumps down her spine. Kiss after kiss was all she wanted.

She turned her body to his. His taste, sharp from the coffee and sweet from his lust met her mouth. Dizziness spun her thoughts, and her legs buckled, drained of the blood that was rushing to her heart and head. Oliver's strong arm supported her, and she longed to be held like this forever. Forever inside his arms, feeling his heart pound, smelling his rich natural odor and horse musk, and tasting his sweet lips.

Fogginess cloaked her, and his lips ventured down her exposed bosom. Once more that day, his lips tasted her cleavage. Once against his lips rounded her left breast and momentarily lingered on her excited nipple. His teeth, timid, shy almost, encircled the brown tip and nibbled.

The sensation was too much for Janet, and she cried out in ecstasy. Her breath faltered, and if his muscular arms had not been there, she would have fallen to the floor. Another nibble followed, and her voice again cried out its ardor. Oliver's lips then gently caressed as his tongue circled the nibbled nipple.

Janet's nerves prickled with an intensity she could not even remember. It was so intense that her thighs quivered, and she swore to herself, "God Damn."

Suddenly Oliver's lips had found her other breast. It too experienced the delight of its sister. Once more the colors flashed in her head, and the curse left her lips, "God Damn."

More intense, more vivid, she experienced every sensation every desire she had only felt in fantasies of her youth. Their tongues met in midair danced and snuggled against each other as Oliver returned his attention to her lips. These kisses were more viral more extreme than any she had felt earlier that day. It was as if Oliver was trying to release his complete obsession for her through his kisses. Fogged by her emotions, Janet tilted her neck back allowing Oliver's free hand to caress and rub whatever pleased his fancy.

However, Oliver stepped back, his breathing difficult. His stare bore right into her. His tiger-like eyes were wide with passion and lust, anxious and hungry to consume her. She was his prey and longed for him to attack.

His eyes took in all of her. It was as if he had grown another pair of hands. Janet could feel them scan her from head to toes. Modesty would have caused her to grab her dress quickly from the floor and cover herself. But she was well beyond modesty! In fact, she was delighted by his stare. She was elated by his leer. She welcomed all his attention focused on her firm naked breasts.

He had dropped into an animalistic state almost as deep as if he was in battle. His body sensed, instead of felt. His eyes zeroed in on Janet's body. The desire, pure desire to have it, filled his every thought, but one. That one was his conscience. It was the only part of him that could always bring him back to civilization after battle. It spoke to him now, well aware of his heartbeat, keeping time with his heavy breathing. It was well aware of the throbbing between his thighs that demanded release from his trousers.

He shook his head to clear it of the instincts powering his other thoughts. "No," He whispered more to himself than to Janet. "It's not right." He summoned up a courage he did not know he had. "You need to go." He spoke to Janet. "You need to go now." He stressed each word. As ferment as his kisses had been. "If you don't go now I can't. I wouldn't be…"

"I want you." Janet hoarsely whispered. "I want you. I love you."

"I love you," Oliver breathed deeply to gain some control of his body and thoughts. His eyes, however, refused to leave their focus on her breasts. "God do I love you. I've loved you from the first time I kissed you." He finally looked away breaking some of Janet's magnetism. "That's why you have to go."

He stressed the words again, and Janet could tell he did not actually believe them.

"Why?" She stepped into his arms and began to tease his chest with her lips. His taste triggered another round of heated excitement inside of her.

"Because if you don't. I'll want you to stay here with me all night." He pulled away. "And that you know can't happen. Let's face the truth."

"Truth," Janet looked at him in the eyes, her lust subsiding. "Truth?" she questioned. "The truth is this. In six months I will have to go back to Harmony, Ohio and be an old maiden teacher the rest of my life. You will go on to be an attorney in New York City, far away from me. And what will we have? Just this moment, just this night." Tears filled her eyes, and Oliver's heart broke.

He had done it again. He brought pain to someone that was close to him. He reached out to wipe the tears away from her eyes, but she brushed him off. "I love you." She said. "When I'm in your arms, I don't care anymore what people say or think. I don't care. I have followed your vision throughout the years, until it brought me to you, here in this stable." She waved her arms around her. "It's not the best bridal chamber, but it is what fate had brought me." She looked into Oliver's eyes. "I believe we are meant to be together. Here! Now!"

Oliver shook his head no. "You and I have been fooled." He tried to calm down both of them. "I too have been following a vision, one of you. I have been trying to find that fifteen-year-old who I kissed on a dare from my Sergeant Major. You have brought me safely home from battle and more. But this can't be our bridal chamber." He looked around the stable. "It's just not right. You deserve much more than that."

"But you said you can't give me more."

"I was wrong. I see it now. I can give you what you have been searching for. I can give you my heart, my whole heart." He leaned over and kissed her gently on the mouth. "This I do, tonight." He looked her in the eyes. "I give you my whole heart. The heart you captured that night in Harmony."

14

Oliver tenderly kissed her on her sweet longing lips. All the emotions buried inside of him for years pulsated through his kiss into her soul. Janet wrapped her arms around his neck and held his lips to hers tasting the coffee of the Harmony campsite again.

"I love you." She whispered and leaned into his naked chest. The tuff of hair felt soft on her cheek. "We only have this night." She added. Oliver stepped back again. His eyes once more took her full mature body in. A lustful smile creased the corners of his mouth as his eyes scanned every inch of her body.

Her light chemise hung across her shoulders, exposing both of her breasts all the way to her small brown nipples. The linen attire then hung loosely to about mid-calf on her. It was not a flattering piece of apparel, but it still provided some sense of mystery concerning how the rest of her body looked.

Oliver could just imagine. Midway down her scantily clad body was a dark shadow beneath the chemise. The sight caused his manhood to stir again, pressing hard against the four buttons that contained it within his trousers.

In Janet's mind, the idea of mystery or fantasy was more erotic than actual nudity. Looking at the shirtless Oliver, was more tantalizing than if he was nude. Her eyes took him in. His white breaches reached only his knees. The large bulge in the center of them told her all she needed to know about Oliver's desires. His chest, even with the purple scar enticed her. Well developed from the years of chopping wood and handling horses, its muscle tone physically excited her, especially now that she had rested her head against it.

"Only tonight," she repeated.

All the instincts that made males, males, bombarded Oliver's thoughts. Every hormone in his body was calling for release. His eyes, his heart, his soul all longed to reach out and rip the chemise from Janet's eager waiting body. The feel of her soft body, the taste of her tongue, the smell of her lavender perfume all twirled around in his head. This moment was what he had been waiting for all his life.

This night would be the ending of the haunting vision that had guided him all these years.

But that little voice, that voice from the farthest point of his heart still spoke. "You love her," it said. "You love her more than the horses, more than the soldiers, more than yourself." The words cut through the fogging lust that blanketed his mind. "It's not right."

Oliver felt the throbbing in between his legs. Its heat and desire pulsated through his limbs into this very soul. It demanded attention. It demanded to know Janet.

"How easy it would be." Another voice spoke. A voice Oliver had forgotten he had inside of him. "She is willing. Take her in your arms, and she will melt to your every desire." Oliver licked his lips in anticipation.

Janet's eyes grew wider as she envisioned his desire. She bit her lower lip. A teasing tickle filled her as she felt Oliver's eyes followed the curve of her neck down her throat to her exposed white breast.

Their taste had been sweet to his tongue. Their lavender smell had been stronger than any other part of her body. His manhood throbbed for attention.

"But it's not right." That voice echoed its power weakened behind the flash of manhood. Oliver closed his eyes for a second, trying to gain some control over the lusty thoughts within him.

Then tenderly, timidly even, he ran his fingers along and over her sweet, gorgeous breasts. Hooking the chemise with his fingers, he looped it back into place, covering her. His will power had prevailed. He then kissed her ever so softly on her lips. It was a kiss that spoke of true love; of true commitment and respect.

"I love you," he said, "Now and forever. I love you so deeply that I would rather love you than make love to you." Janet blushed. Modesty reared its head, and she crossed her hands over her bosom. Oliver understood instantly, he stooped and picked up her dress. Handing it to her, he immediately turned toward the horses.

"We need to get you back." He began to talk, not looking back out of respect, as she dressed. "But we need to do it without anyone noticing you." He walked to the horses' stalls, remembering she could ride. He grabbed a bridle from its hooks on the side of the stalls. "Can I look back yet?" He politely asked.

"Yes." Janet responded, still adjusting her dress. Oliver turned aware of her blush, and his burning cheeks. Shyness came over him. It was something he had never known. He placed the bridle down on the corner of the stall gate, as he saw Janet struggle with her dress. Awkwardly he crossed to her and offered to tie her dress. Janet smiled and turned around.

It was so natural to her to just turn around. Feeling like an old married couple, Janet did not exchange a single word but allowed the caring fingers to lace together the ties of her dress. Once finished, Oliver's arm encircled her waist for a brief hug and a kiss on her cheek. This embrace was contentment, she told herself. This feeling was the miracle of love.

She patted his hands and felt comfortably warm throughout her body. "People are used to seeing me ride at night." Oliver explained his plan, still hugging her from behind. She leaned back into his still naked chest and listened. "I'll saddle up Pegasus, my mare; give you my coat and hat. You then ride to near the academy. Dismount and sneak back into the back door. I'll follow on foot, and bring the horse home." He squeezed her to note he had finished.

"Why don't I just walk?"

"There's more chance someone will see and recognize you. Then there will be questions as to why a young lady was out alone at night." She agreed with a nod. "You'll have my hat and coat on. From a distance, you'll look like me. A man can get away with a lot more."

"I know," she flushed with a guilty anger. "Your Lieutenant proved that." Janet turned and faced Oliver. "You knew he fathered a child." The statement came as a shock to Oliver. His face grew pale as he shook his head no. "Well he did, and that's why I'm a teacher."

Their eyes bore into each other as memories flashed through their thoughts. Lieutenant Premont had spent several evenings with a young lady as well while encamped in Harmony, Oliver recalled. The same young lady that he had entertained the night that Oliver had managed his "traditional kiss." It all became clear to the ex-soldier. All these years he had been so centrally focused on his vision that he had forgotten the other girl. Another memory then roared into his consciousness. Its presence had also been blocked, not out of ignorance but out of necessity for its pain was too great to bear daily.

"Her named was Luella Bates." Oliver's voice came quietly almost in a sorrowful whisper.

"You remembered." Janet's tone was sarcastic. "That's wonderful. I wished he had." She turned away. "When the town found out she was pregnant, they dismissed her from teaching. She was forced out of town, in disgrace." Janet turned back tears in her eyes. "But your Lieutenant didn't remember her."

"Yes, he did." Oliver's face paled further. "I know he did. Her name was his last word." He locked onto Janet's eyes, with his. "I was with him as he died. I held his hand." He looked at his right hand envisioning the Lieutenant's dying hand clamping onto it again. "I held it as he squeezed to keep life. But the wound was too great. The blood loss was too much. And as he closed his eyes, her name came. Luella, Luella."

Janet's eyes blurred behind tears, and the two lovers embraced.

Minutes passed, maybe even hours passed as the two hugged in the center of the Litchfield stable. Time had no meaning; there was only the need for comfort. There was only need to hold each other as if in a fortification against the barrage of miserable, painful memories. And they cried, each over the loss of another life that they could not resurrect.

Janet allowed all her loss to pour forth as she buried her face in Oliver's chest. His warm body that had brought lustful excitement minutes before now comforted her like a parental midnight reassurance. The world spun turned and progressed, but Janet only snuggled contented to be ignorant of time's march.

Oliver too did not prevent his sorrow from speaking. Visions of comrades raced around his head, triggering long suppressed tears to escape. The feeling of Janet's trembling body in his arms brought forth a new desire in him. It was the desire to protect her, to ease her pain, and to make her whole again. He understood now that soldiers were not the only ones wounded in wars, and civilian wounds were just as deep, just as terrible to heal.

"What happened to her?" Oliver finally asked as the tears subsided.

"All I know is she returned to her brother's home in New London here." She nervously smiled. "When I first heard that I was coming here. I was hoping to go there and see if I could find her. I didn't know how far away New London was from Litchfield. I had always heard that Connecticut was such a small state. It really isn't." She grew sad again. "When she left I wasn't allowed to write to her. We didn't stay in touch." Tears came again, as Oliver's warm hands stroked her back.

Janet's helplessness shook Oliver to his core. A hollow feeling came to his heart as he realized there was nothing he could do to help her. The pit in his heart moved to his stomach, where it settled annoyingly reminding him of his situation, Janet's contract and the love he felt for the first time.

Helplessness was something Oliver did not allow in his world. But Janet's situation forced it upon him. That fact gnawed at him, deepening the pit in his stomach. It was a pit he now knew he had to fix.

How? He questioned himself. How! He puzzled over the problem as he hugged Janet to his chest. Her rain softened hair brushed against his cheek. It tickled his nose and brought a contented smile to his face. The mixing of these emotions inside of him was like oil and water in a jar. His lip quivered from the emotions suddenly boiling up inside. Frustration filled him, frustration at his helplessness to ease Janet's pain. It was a helplessness he could not change.

He smelled her lavender perfume and kissed her auburn hair. "Somehow," He proclaimed, "Somehow." James Baldwin Mathers face flashed in his mind.

Just minutes before he had been willing to give Janet up to James. The thought nearly caused him to laugh. "How could you ever leave this?" His arms, so tenderly engaged, asked. "How could you ever not want to smell Janet's hair, feel Janet's beating heart or taste her lips again?" The question hung inside of him unanswered.

Janet stepped back, wiping her tears. 'I'm sorry. I don't know what's come over me." She looked at the ground embarrassed. "You're right. I need to get back to the school." Oliver nodded and then tipped her face to his. Ever so sweetly, he kissed her lips and then each of her eyes.

"Please," his voice choked. "Please, I want to stop these tears. I just don't know how."

"Hold me." Janet also responded not sure. "I guess just hold me." They embraced again unable to separate, unable to walk away from this day of discovery, this day of rediscovery.

* * * * *

Minutes past again as the two just sealed themselves off from the rest of the world. The boundary of Oliver's arms became the edge of Janet's universe. There was absolutely nothing beyond the encircling embrace. There was only his warmth in her world. Only the quiet, reassuring thud, thud of his heart filled her conscience.

Calmness slowly came over Janet. Incredible contented peace enveloped her. She cooed, almost purred in Oliver's arms. He echoed with his own sigh.

"Do you really think we'll fool anyone with your coat and hat?" She asked once again in control of her thoughts and emotions. Though she did not want to leave, she knew she had to. My reputation is damned, she thought, but it was all she had left.

"I have found that people tend to see what they want to see." Oliver argued like an attorney. "They expect to see me on a horse riding. They'll see my coat, my hat, my horse and want to know it as me. Ride tall, that's all you'll have to do." He kissed her and then picked up his shirt. The notes for the mock trial scattered to the floor as the shirt brushed them off the small tack table on which he had placed them.

Janet watched the paper float to the ground. "I heard you rehearsing." She said and helped gather up the paper. "You sounded sincere."

"Thank you." Their eyes meet, as did their fingers. The passion was still there, floating just below the surface conversation. She could see it in his blue eyes, waiting to pounce. Just a thin layer of manners and respect prevented her virginity from being extinct. Lust filled goose bumps quivered over her body.

"I mean it." She forced herself to remain focused on Oliver's summation. "I liked the appeal to American's desire for efficiency."

A smile blossomed on Oliver's face. "You were listening!" Excitement, as great as that of his love for her, filled his eyes. Their blue irises sparkled as if she was naked again in front of him. This excitement exploded from his lips in a diatribe of the case's argument, his position, the law school's requirements, and the fact that he had glanced over James' notes. A mischievous smile crossed his face at the last point. Janet giggled.

"That's one way to have the advantage." Her laugh turned into words.

"Yes - but having you is the greatest advantage," Oliver blushed. Janet smirked not sure if he were serious or just fishing for something to say that would make her cooed some more. But one look into his clear blue eyes showed Janet that Oliver was serious. She was his advantage over James and the rest of his memories.

The thought pleased her. "If it is true, then you have given him a great gift" She smiled. "Now what idea can you share with him that will allow him to defeat James?" The questions revolved in her head as she stood there longingly staring into his loving eyes.

Oliver smiled and touched her face with his open palm. "Thank you." He spoke confidently. "This day has been..." He struggled for a word to finish his thoughts. As he paused, Janet turned her face into his open palm and kissed it.

"There are no words." She spoke from her heart knowing full well the turmoil within. "There are no words to express what had happened." They made eye contact and blushed again.

"Other than I love you." Oliver finished, and Janet looked to the floor.

"Can I help with your argument?" Oliver looked at her puzzled. "For the mock trial," she clarified. Oliver shrugged his eyebrows and handed over the paper to her.

It was a simple gesture, but it spoke louder than if Oliver had yelled he loved her in the center of Litchfield Common. By handing over the papers, Oliver was telling her she was his equal. Other men of the times would have brushed her off as being just a woman, just a pretty item to look at in their homes. Some would patronize such a request from her by quickly reviewing the papers out loud. But here Oliver was making her an equal. He was allowing her to edit his work.

Janet's heart warmed as if he was kissing her. She was his equal. No man had ever treated her that way. Even James had been unwilling to see her as an equal. But Oliver unhesitant placed her on that level.

She looked at the papers and noticed a slight shaking. Doubt caused it the moment he put the papers in her hands. "Are you ready to be his peer?" She asked herself. "Hell Yes!" Janet took a deep breath and consumed Oliver's writing.

The penmanship was not as neat or as fancy as James' the teacher Janet immediately said. And she scolded herself for the surface observation. "You must focus on the content not the visual." She warned her teacher's eye. "This is where you can truly help Oliver. Here is where that advantage can be made real. Bring your passion into the subject of his argument." She continued to read the firm determined script.

Oliver's oral argument in the case, were centered on the economic and judicial points of probate. There was no moral objection. There was no cry for liberation. Oliver had not even referred to the slaves as human beings. For the Ohio native, these last two points were ingrained in her consciousness and could not be separated from the overall issue of slavery.

Though not sure of probate laws, Janet followed the flow of Oliver's argument. It was crisp, to the point and efficient - similar to his overall basic principal of America's desire to save time.

Finishing, she placed the papers back on the tack table. Oliver's blue eyes eagerly awaited her comments. Like so many of her students, who had turned an essay or short story in for review, Oliver had that half pride filled, half scared look in his eyes. Janet had found writers were more possessive of their words than orators. It was always a tricky almost difficult task to edit these artists, even if they were only children. Was Oliver such an artist? She puzzled.

If she made a false step would he ever trust her with his writing again? Doubt seized the teacher.

"Well?" Oliver nudged with his one-word question.

"Socrates would be pleased by the logical and simple flow." She began apprehensively.

"So would Tapping Reeve." He retorted. "But what do you think about the content of the argument? Do I have a good heart?"

The anxiety inside of Janet bubbled up. Janet was sure it showed on her face. Oliver smiled. "You can't hurt my feelings." He reassured her.

She nodded and summed up her courage. "If he didn't want an opinion, he shouldn't ask for one."

She breathed in deep.

"Well, I think for law students it would be fine." Her voice became confident as the conviction escaped. "But for a jury don't you think you should appeal to the emotional?" She looked at Oliver's face. There was no sour expression. There was no stand-offishness. There was only genuine interest on his face. Relief came to her heart, and it warmed her throughout.

"The emotional," Oliver quizzed.

"I don't mean advocate mass abolition. But at least note you are addressing human beings." The trembling in her voice eased away as she gained confidence in his interest of her opinion. "In ancient Rome, the slaves were allowed to earn money, attend schools and purchase their freedom. Freedmen could gain citizenship and acquire property. These freedmen contributed to the rise and prosperity of Rome.

Why can't that same philosophy be applied here?" She looked into his eyes waiting for some indication she had made a point in Oliver's mind.

He just continued to stare at her; his interest in her not wavering, but there was no indication in his eyes of acceptance. "If you don't like that argument," She continued. "Why not appeal to the very reason we're a country." An excitement filled her voice. "We," She spoke with her hands as the excitement brewed within and needed some physical outcropping. "Americans were born with a new sense of right. I think Benjamin Franklin first explained it. We were rougher, coarser than Europeans and so our law system needed revision from that of England and Europe." A fire filled Janet's eyes as she began to articulate her passion.

The fire reached out and touched Oliver's mind. The enthusiasm tickled his skin and triggered goose bumps to race over him. The sensation stirred him, stroked his imagination and drew him to the edge of his seat.

"Our society also needed to be remodeled." Janet continued. "We Americans have thrown out the concept that what your parents were dictates who you will be." The whole frontier allows people to start anew in this country. And so it should be whether that settler is from Ireland, an ex-slave or a poor New England farmer." Her voice rose with emotions. "You know how hard it is to survive in the territories. We must depend on our neighbors. And we judge our friends not by who they were in the past but by who they are now! That's the argument you should make. These ex-slaves should be freed by the simple fact that this nation must allow every man to be judged on their own accomplishments not those of their fathers."

Oliver leaned back on his heels. An astonished smile crossed his lips.

"Yes," He whispered, his eyes indicating he was in deep thought, "Yes," he murmured. "That does ring true." He rubbed his hand down his chin pondering Janet's thoughts along with his ideas. Janet sat back against the tack table, silent. He needed time to organize his thoughts, the teacher within told her. A smile of delight came to her. She had done it. She had given Oliver something of value.

The smile grew into a daydream. The stables turned into a book-lined study. Oliver sat on the edge of his writing desk; papers from some case's closing argument in his hand, Janet meanwhile looked on, as she was doing now, aware of his thoughts, and his planning (scheme). Every now and again she would venture a word, or an idea as Oliver plotted out is defense. They would be a team.

The thought brought even more details to her daydream. Causes - abolition, education of women, property rights, citizenship, all echoed in her head and verbalized in her dream. They would be a team determined to change the status quo where it needed change for the better.

"Yes, I can see it now." Oliver's voice brought her back to the Litchfield stable. "I can combine your ideas with mine to create a two-prong defense of the law. James will be forced to argue that slaves are chattel not humans."

"Does he believe that?" Janet was horrified at the possibility someone so intelligent could hold that position.

"I'm not sure, but he is from a slave holding family." They made eye contact. Oliver could read her mind. "I don't. We had some freedmen in my company against the British. They bleed the same color as I did. They died the same as well." His eyes grew distant and Janet immediately reached her hand to him. Its touch instantly eliminated the darkness in Oliver's eyes.

"You've given me a cause to wrap around my logical argument. With that I shall win!" He seized her hand and kissed her fingers. "With you there I can't help but win."

"I'll be there." She beamed. "I'll be there Friday and every time you go to court if you want."

"I do." Oliver added so sincerely he sounded as if it was a marriage in front of the Litchfield Congregational Church.

15

The intensity of Oliver's "I do," hung heavy in her heart as Janet rode Pegasus across the Common. It teased at her lips; still tasting the last long passionate kiss she and Oliver shared. His tongue had played with hers in a longing last caress before sending her home.

Heat crawled up her thighs sparked by her memories of Oliver and the horse's warmth. She was forced to ride astride the animal, with her dress and chemise pulled up to her waist if she was to appear like Oliver. Her bare naked legs rubbed against the animal's warm, soft fur, tantalizing her. The sensation of their tongues dancing together just seconds before only made the warmth between her legs more seductive. It had been a minute or more since she left the stables, but she was still feeling his passionate touch. She was still spinning in her mind from the last deep full mouth kiss.

The canter of the horse rhythmically massaged her thighs, and she slowed the animal to enjoy it more. The little voice inside her told her it was not right, but the dominant voice, the one that had told her to find Oliver, laughed in delight. She had changed so much this day.

Oliver's hat bobbed on her head, not at all fitting, but she managed to keep it aside by keeping her head perfectly straight. Her neck would hurt later in the morning she told herself, because of the strain she was placing on it. But she had to keep the hat on; otherwise, her long auburn hair would fall out and flow down her back. Oliver's dark frock coat slumped at her shoulders where the man's body would have filled. She was much too small for the frock, but she hoped no one would notice.

Oliver's scent, his lovely aroma surrounded her because of the coat. Janet had been certain until today that people did not sense others by smell. It was a visual that brought dogs into her head, but now she knew different. She smelled people. Their scent remained with her forever. And Oliver's scent was the sweetest she had ever stored away.

Tickling her nose Oliver's scent joined with the other sensations brought on by the horse's gait, and Janet's memories. By the time she reached the academy building she was in full desire of having Oliver's arms wrapped around her again. She longed for his kiss and the touch of his hand on her breast.

She closed her eyes and allowed the horse to pace slowly on in the night. Her mind filled with visions. Her body filled with intense excitement she had first felt at the lake that afternoon. Her stomach twisted like the clock spring. Her heart beat faster, and her thighs grew moist and warm.

"Stop it!" Her little voice suddenly screamed out. "Stop it!" She opened her eyes and realized she had ridden too far. She turned the horse back along the main road and then halted it where the two had planned. Dismounting the animal, she tied its reins to a low branch of a nearby tree. She then removed Oliver's hat and coat. Bringing the latter to her face, she breathed deep. His aroma reached inside of her, and she allowed her head to spin in a desire for the man.

With a slight tear in her eyes, she placed the hat and coat next to the tree and then made her way quietly through the back-yards of the school's neighbors.

The academy was totally dark when she made her way through the back door. Cautiously she stepped each pace carefully positioned so that the board would not creak under her weight. Finally, she reached the sanctuary of her room. The four other roommates were snoring or breathing deep when she entered the bed. The youngest one was on her side, and Janet snuggled up against her. The teacher closed her eyes to visions of Oliver. The MaryEllen's fevered body added more warmth to Janet's dreams, and soon in her midnight world, she was sharing a kiss with her cavalier.

* * * * *

Oliver slipped through the dark streets of Litchfield, silently as only a seasoned soldier could. His mind recalling ever single second he had spent with Janet in his arms. The taste of her lips played on his.

The smell of her lavender perfume hung on his shirt, and he continued to enjoy it as he walked toward his horse.

Janet was to ride the animal just beyond the school and circle back through the back yards to the rear of the academy. She would hitch the horse to a tree near the road in a small hollow he knew from his morning rides. The hollow was far enough away from the road and other houses, that the horse would remain unnoticed. But hollow was also close enough that Janet should be able to walk effortlessly back to the school.

The lavender reached into his head, and he questioned. Janet could still have been with him. She could have been lying naked in the hay right now with him.

"No," he spoke to himself. "No, it was not right." He almost could not believe his own voice was saying that. It was the voice of a soldier, raised in the barracks where bragging was the chief occupation and soldiering the secondary skill. "No one then would have given up such a filly."

"I know, but this was different." He pictured Janet as the fifteen-year-old and then again as she was today. Her dark brown eyes pierced into his heart. And he knew he had been right.

"I love her." His voice trailed off unable to form any more necessary words. "There could be no more appropriate words for his feelings," His mind called back. "I truly love Janet." His lawyer's conviction came to his words as they formed crisp, precise angles in the night.

Things had changed so much in just one day, he thought. That morning he had been watching James Baldwin Mathers staring with puppy dog eyes at Janet from across the gallery of the Congregational Church. Now, in the middle of the night, it was he who was lovesick. It was he who was smiling uncontrollably and recalling passionate moments. How funny fate was, he thought and nearly laughed out loud.

Janet had been the vision in his heart all these years, but it was in a small town in western Connecticut that he had been able to find her again. This day had shown him that anything could be possible. His faith in good that he had lost on the battlefield came flooding back in. He shook with an excited shiver.

"God, I'm so happy," Oliver giggled. He actually giggled. "She will be there. Now and forever, she'll be there." He almost prayed to the divine, something he had not done since the ambush of his friends on the Raisin River. "So much has changed." He said out loud, as he reached his horse. "So much has changed." The excitement shook him again. Throughout the ride home, he fought with his emotions preventing him from shouting out loud how wonderful he felt.

* * * * *

Morning came too early for Oliver, but the neighing of Pegasus told him it was time for her morning ride. The horse had been with him for two years, and when he was near her, she would nudge him awake with either her nose or her voice. Oliver rolled over on the straw bed he had made the night before.

"Janet should be here." He whispered out loud looking at a vacant spot next to him. "Janet should be here now and forever." Sadness crept over him. It was sadness that his love had skillfully blocked all night long. It was the truth. Janet could not be there now or in the future unless she could find a means of breaking her contract.

Oliver sat up, not at all stiff from sleeping on the hard floor of the stables. In fact, he enjoyed it more than sleeping in the guest bed of the Wolcott House. He felt more natural sleeping in the hay and the wilderness. It was not natural for him to be in the civilization of the East. These thoughts joined in his scheming mind as it worked over the problem of Janet's contract.

"Tapping Reeve," The name of the founder of the law school left Oliver's mouth and filled the stables. "I could ask for his advice." He glanced at Pegasus. The horse responded to the look with affection, breathing hard and clumping the floor with her hoofs. "I know after our ride." He shook off the straw from his knee long shirt and began to dress. "But could Janet live in the hay?" He did not answer the question but just allowed it to mix with the other thoughts already mingling in his head.

The stables' Janis door opened and in walked Benjamin Arts. He was the governor's groomer, and his wife was the cook. He smiled bemused at the undressed student. "Studying with the horses again?" He asked, knowing full well that there were times when Oliver enjoyed the company of animals over that of men. Oliver nodded.

"I knew," the sixty-year-old man pulled a pot from behind his back, and the aroma of coffee filled the barn. "My wife noted that you had been in the kitchen last night, looking for a tin cup of this black gold." He smiled, several teeth missing from his grin. "There's nothing like it in the morning after a long night." He looked straight at Oliver, and the law student felt his soul revealing itself.

Benjamin had become a surrogate father while Oliver was a student. The older man had admired the ex-soldiers devotion to his horse as well as his isolation from the rest of the Litchfield society. Benjamin, in turn, had impressed Oliver with his pure nature and his love of animals. They had talked many times while grooming the governor's various steeds. Their conversations had covered almost every topic men could discuss while remaining narrowly focused on horses.

"For someone who has heard the music of the bullets, you seem to have forgotten how to muster for inspection." Oliver snapped to and finished dressing while the old man poured two cups of the delicious hot black coffee. The steam from the liquid floated in the air just above the cups, making the tin itself almost too hot to touch. The heat did not bother the older man. Benjamin reached out and snatched one cup in his big calloused right hand.

"We'll be parting company soon," Benjamin looked Oliver in the eyes, as the young man took his cup of coffee. "You'll be heading away, back to New York I recon while I'm taking my Mrs. to my son's home." The news came as a shock to the younger man.

"Traveling to your son's home, which one?" Oliver knew the man had three, each living in a different community.

"Matthew is being blessed." The old man smiled again. It was a deep heartfelt smile. "It seems that his wife is having a child, our first grandchild." A twinkle came to Benjamin's eyes, "An't that fine news."

He held his cup up in a mock toast.

"Indeed my friend." Oliver returned the salute with his own cup of coffee and then extended his hand. The two men shook hands.

"The Mrs. feels it is her place to go and help with the birth." Benjamin explained without being asked. "I'm heading her down there this weekend with the Governor's permission." He's even allowing me the use of a buggy or that new buckboard from Portland."

"Tell me the truth," Oliver leaned into the old man, mischievous in his tone. "You're just as excited to get there as your good wife."

"Well there is something about children," Benjamin mused. "They do bring about pride in a man, especially when your child has done well." Matthew Arts had done that. As a young boy, Matthew gained the attention of the second Governor Oliver Wolcott. His education came in the current younger Governor's factory and legal offices. He was allowed to attend Tapping Reeve's school and earned a name in the insurance field. After several years in Hartford, he had traveled to the coast to Groton where marine insurance was critical.

"But the first grandchild is always something more important than even financial success." Benjamin continued, "Especially if it is a male. There is something about knowing that your name will continue." He looked again into Oliver's eyes. "Remember that." He nodded his head to emphasize the fact. "Children can be wearing, but if you focus on the overall and not the just the moment, they will bring you joy." They drank their coffee in a silent salute to the future child.

Benjamin then refilled the two cups with what coffee was remaining in the pot. "Oliver," He spoke without raising his eyes to the young man. "You need to be a little more careful in the future."

"What?" Oliver stated puzzled.

"The young lady could have been seen." The meaning became clear. "So you know I kept the Mrs. busy in the house when I first noticed her coming. But warn her, reputations are not to be trifled with in this community."

"I will." Oliver thanked the man.

"Besides, if you sire a foal too soon, there will be doubt as to the pedigree." He laughed, as did Oliver, releasing some of the tension that had come over him. He did not want to look bad in the eyes of this man. He also did not want Janet to look bad in the eyes of Benjamin. It was one of the few times, Oliver could ever remember, caring enough about someone else to make sure their reputation was intact.

"We've not come that far." Oliver defended Janet's honor. The words came without thought. He had never been one to state his heart out loud, but with Benjamin, Oliver did not feel any embarrassment.

In fact, Oliver was not even surprised by his declaration. It just felt right.

"I believe you, but will others?" They caught each other eyes, as they walked to the stalls to brush and dress the horses for the day. "It is a sad thing but a true one that humans don't trust other humans outside of a church." The old man grinned. "If you were a minister, you could get away with seeing your young lady at any time of the night, but you're not a minister, just a humble human being."

"And I will not be able to rise from that state either by becoming a horse groomer." Oliver smiled at the older man. Benjamin laughed again.

"No, you have chosen the path of an attorney. There is no hope or redemption for you. You might as well do your penitence now." He threw the younger man a horse brush. "Manual labor is good for the sinner's soul."

"But I'm not a sinner, this time." He looked at the older man, and the horse groomer understood Oliver's meaning.

"So you care for this young lady. That's a pleasing sign to me and will be to my Mrs. Remember to let the young lady know as well."

"She does." Oliver confirmed. The old man nodded in approval.

"If you take the next step," His fatherly tone took over. "You need to remember to tell her, or show her every day. Even after years, you need to remember to show her in little ways." He smiled remembering his own wife. "Trust me on that. It keeps the home life content for both of you." He turned and busied himself with brushing the side of a horse.

The lesson was over, Oliver knew.

Benjamin's silence marked the completion of any lecture he might have fretted over all night long because he had seen Janet come to the stables. His country morality had been confirmed with the two facts that the young lady was still a young maiden in Oliver's eyes and that Oliver's heart was pure. They worked silently for the next few minutes, only breaking the silence when Oliver had saddled his mare and stood at the stable door.

"Enjoy the day." Benjamin looked up from his work. "I'll see to your wears so that they are returned to the attic."

"Thank you." Oliver politely responded, not at ease with servant treating him like he had treated his lieutenant in the army. Crossing to the old man, he reached out his hand. "Thank you for everything since I came here." The old man nodded, and they both could see the love in each other's eyes. Without another word, they hugged as if father and son.

* * * * *

Janet woke her head spinning and a sharp pain in her throat. She tried to swallow the pain away, but it only pierced more into her vocal cords. Like a knife or pinpricks, the pain stabbed into her with each swallow. Her tongue felt swollen as did her glands just under her jaw.

The pungent smell of vomit stung her nose, and she looked over at the sleeping child next to her. Sweat matted MaryEllen's hair against her face, where the fever had glued it. Vomit dribbled down the corners of the child's face and pooled on the front of her and Janet's nightdresses. A sandpaper-like rash made up of a series of tiny pinkish-red spots covered the neck of the young girl. Janet reached out to feel the forehead of the sleeping child, but the pain returned to her throat eliminating any desire she had for physical activity. It then traveled down to her abdomen cramping like a vise, squeezing her with pain.

"You have to get up," She told herself, unable to speak because of the pain. "You have to clean up this mess." Her voice called from within, but her eyes closed, uncaring. Her head spun out of control, as she closed her eyes. She fell. She fell into a darkness of consciousness as her body slumped back into the sweat soaked bed.

Dreams played in her head.

Endless falling dreams where she grabbed for tree branches and rocky cliffs that were just outside of her reach. Spinning downward and downward she raced, toward a fire, a hot flame that chilled her.

Confusing dreams where she was standing naked in the middle of Harmony, Ohio on the last day of school. "Now remember to take everything with you when you go home." Her voice told the parents of her students. The eyes of all the men stared at her, and she shook with a shiver that broke a sweat that covered her face with water.

Scary dreams where she was standing side by side with Oliver wading in a small pond. The water rose higher and higher as they walked toward the center of the lake. Soon it covered her whole body. Her clothing clinging to her, suffocated her, dragged her down and down into the cold, clammy reaches of death.

Death.

Death.

Is this death? She questioned herself.

* * * * *

For a moment she came to in the shared bedroom of Mrs. Pierces' Female Academy of Litchfield, Connecticut. A fever burned on her forehead. A knifing pain stabbed at her throat and the body of the little girl next to her was gone. Fresh lilac smells filled her nose, as did the pungent stench of lye soap.

Homemade soap she told her. She forced her mind to remember the steps she had done to prepare soap not only in Litchfield but also in Harmony.

"First, there was the collecting of ashes from the fireplace, and grease and fats from the cooking." Janet recalled, trying to force her mind to stay active. Trying to keep awake, for she sensed that if she fell back into the dream world, she would not come back to reality.

"Then when there is enough, you pull out the large soap barrel." Janet continued. Pictures of the large brown wooden barrel her father had constructed for her mother filled her head. "Water had to be added to the ashes. It will slowly trickle down and out of the special hole at the bottom of the barrel. This strange liquid was called lye." The smell came back to her head.

Was it a memory or the lye soap that had washed the bed around her, she could not tell? All she knew was that her throat still stabbed with pain, and her head was so heavy that she could not hold it upright. She slumped into the bed again, falling, falling into the unconscious world of dreams.

"No," she told herself. "Remember, focus on making soap. Where were you?"

"Oh yes, you've just made the lye. Yes the lye had to be added to the grease after it was heated in a large iron kettle. The black caldron her mother had in the barn, brought out every few months for just a job. The grease would be placed in the cauldron and heated to a boil. Then and only then was the lye added. Carefully you must watch it, as it slowly thickens into the yellow soap."

* * * * *

She opened her eyes.

The light hurt. Dizziness wrecked havoc in her mind as she tried to focus on the things around her. All she made out was that she was in bed, alone. Across the room in the high back wooden chair sat Abigail, her own eyes closed in a vain attempt to get some sleep. Janet opened her mouth, but no words would come out. Pain shot through her again, and her stomach twisted. Nausea ran through her, triggered by the dizziness in her head. Her ears ached, and she had to close her eyes.

A cough erupted from her throat shaking her whole body. Pain sailed throughout her body. A ringing resounded in her head, and a new sharper pain centered in her ears. Her nausea grew worse with time. All she could manage then was lying still in bed, begging for everything to stop: stop hurting, stop spinning, just stop period.

Darkness followed, and she found herself falling again, falling into the world of dreams.

Oliver's smile met her. His hand reached out and gently touched her fevered face. It was cold and comforting against her cheek. His blues eyes looked concerned, sad but not like when he recalled his fellow soldiers. This was a fear of the future not of the past. She wanted to reach back and touch him, but could not find the strength to do so. She wanted to talk to him, but could not force the words past the pain in her throat.

His eyes watered as she watched them. Then slowly, ever so slowly he removed his hand and bit his lower lip. "I love you."

He whispered close to her painful ears. His voice sounded as if it was coming through an ocean of water. "I love you. I know now how much you mean to me." He looked away toward Abigail still sitting in her seat. "I know how to make you free." He whispered and then slipped away before she could say anything in response.

Darkness came again. This time, she fell and fell fading in and out of consciousness until there was no sense of time, only the present. Memories, hallucinations, and reality all mixed together in a jumble of visions that were not comprehensible and frightening.

So she slept fever-flushed and fitful for a week, the victim of the many outbreaks of scarlet fever that killed too many people in the 1800s.

16

"I could have told you he would leave you." James Baldwin Mathers looked at Janet. A smile of relief came to his breaded face. It was almost an evil smile. He looked down at his brown woolen suit coat and picked off some small piece of lint or spring blossom. "It is his nature to disappoint. He finally realized that he just could not be one of us. He could not be one of our class." James sounded almost noble in his regard for the students around him.

Janet sat propped up in a high back spindle chair on the back porch of the academy. It was the first day that she had been able to see male visitors since her fever struck. The only one to come was James.

The endless illness caused sleepy dream world lasted not one day, as she first thought, but a few weeks. "It has been a couple of weeks," she thought, "since the night Oliver had kissed me just off of that porch." Panic filled her. "Now he's gone from Litchfield."

James broke the news almost immediately upon arriving. It was a fact that Abigail and the other girls had hidden from her over the weeks.

The loss ate a hole in her stomach. She felt nauseous and depressed. "Why had he left?" Her question left her mouth without her meaning to verbalize.

Her head did not want to believe what James was telling her. Her heart refused to listen and shut out all attempts to rationalize the words. But she continued to look at James, unwilling to let his words cause tears to appear. She did not want the man from Maryland to know how deeply she was hurting inside. She did not want him to know how deeply the knife of his words wounded her.

She could be strong. She had been strong in the past, when she lost Luella, for instance. Now she could be just as strong, strong enough at least not to show any pain, while James was there.

"I told you, he must have come to the realization that he was just inferior to the rest of us," James stated, not looking at Janet but surveying the backyard of the academy and its neighbors. "The last time I saw him was at the mock trial. He stood there as if distracted by someone in the audience. His eyes were constantly looking toward the door. He could not finish a sentence or even a thought without a glance toward that door as if he was waiting for someone to come."

"He was," Janet told herself. "He was waiting for me! She had promised. And she had not come." Tears blurred her eyes and she quickly looked down at her lap, clearing the tears.

"I couldn't come," she spoke in her mind as if she was arguing a case in front of Oliver. "I was sick in bed, unable to sit up let alone walk to the trial. I've disappointed him, like all the others in his life. I'm the reason he left."

She pictured the law school. It was a one room brown building with a raised platform in the front of the structure. Here the law professor sat and lectured. Here the student "judge" sat during the mock trial. She could see it all clearly in her head, but she had not been there when Oliver needed her to be. She had failed him just like all the others he had loved in the past had failed him. She was the cause.

"He then started his argument, some dribble about the slave being a human being, deserving his recognition as such. He brought in ancient Rome and the belief that this nation was founded without a class system. Can you imagine such non-sense? We clearly have a class system, and the slaves are the low end, never to be raised up over that boundary between chattel and human beings."

He had used her argument, she remembered. She had given him the words that should have carried the day. But her presence was missing. Her soul to reach out from the audience and provide a scaffold for him had been missing. She was the cause.

James scoffed. "His voice shook. I had never seen him so unprepared for anything. He was so nervous. I would have thought he was acting, but he didn't alter his approach. He just kept looking toward the door and stuttering more. His mind was clearly not on his case."

"No, it was on me," her heart called out. Tears burned at the corners of her eyes, but she refused to allow them to escape. "Oliver must have known that I was sick." Janet tried to rationalize. "Abigail or others must have told him that I had scarlet fever."

The name of the disease echoed in her head. Scarlet death it had been called in her lifetime. She had seen its effects. Oliver must have known as well, for little MaryEllen had died.

"Did he think I would?" Janet continued her mental argument, justifying Oliver's departure. "Could he have faced another loved one dying?" The tears pressed harder to escape, but she still held them back. "Poor Oliver," she bit her lower lip in thought. "The face of death once more confronted him. No wonder he had left. No wonder he had failed in the mock trial. His heart was crushed."

Janet bit her lip and forced herself to listen to James again.

"I, on the other hand, was perfect." James leaned back on his heels and swelled his chest up. "My words boomed forth with vigor. The musses were with me that day. All his would be points; I demolished behind the rhetoric I had practiced over and over." He looked into Janet's eyes.

"I turned to him, as I closed, his eyes locked on mine, and I could see his soul break as if God himself was ripping it from him. His whole world crashed down then. I could read it all in his eyes. He realized then that he was out of his place, and he stomped off." The evil smile returned to James' face. It was a smile of triumph.

"Do you really believe...?" Janet started to express what was spinning around inside her. But James raised his hand to silence her.

"Don't talk, just enjoy the sunshine." He walked to her side. "Are you comfortable?" His voice grew sweet, fooling Janet for a second. He kneeled down next to her as if to fluff the pillow behind her back. "I missed you." He breathed against her cheek. "I've spent the past two weeks thinking of only our kiss, and when we might share another."

He took a deep breath and began to recite a memorized piece. The teacher in Janet recognized the tone of voice.

"That sweet nectar on your lips tasted sweeter than any honey, enthralled more than any wine, and addicted me more than money, fame or reputation."

Janet looked into his hazel eyes. His excitement sparkled then. Janet's broken heart thumped and for the briefest of seconds, she recalled their kiss.

The world paused. "What are you doing?" her little voice asked.

"Security," The larger voice inside of Janet answered. "Everyone seeks security."

"But?" the question remained unasked.

"I wrote that for you." James' warm breath tickled her cheek again. "Knowing I would be able to recite it to your ears." He stood back up and caught her eyes. "I never doubted you would get better. I never, even when Miss MaryEllen died I didn't lose faith. I'll always be there for you." The pronouncement hung in mid-air.

"You had told Oliver that!" Both of Janet's inner voices shrieked inside of her. "You had said the exact same words!"

"But they were true!" She defended herself.

"But are they true now?" The voices asked back, and she looked into James' love struck hazel eyes.

Abigail Smith broke the moment by walking out the back door of the school. The same light summer dress Janet had borrowed two weeks before to visit Oliver, covered Abigail's figure.

The thought of Oliver and their night together knifed the woman from Ohio deep in the heart.

"Mrs. Pierce noted that it's getting late." Abigail said looking at James. The law student understood her implied meaning.

"Yes it is getting on, and you need your rest." He touched Janet's exposed hand, one of the few spots on her body that was not peeling from the effects of scarlet fever. Janet was covered from her neck to her toes in light cotton, hiding the dry peeling skin, while still hoping the rays of the sun would help her healing. "I must be going." He picked up the matching brown stove top hat that he had rested on the rails of the porch and placed it on his head. Tapping the brim he added. "May I come tomorrow?" Janet nodded.

James smiled delighted and bounced to the ground, his stride clearly showing his enchantment.

Suddenly he whirled on his heels and faced the two ladies. "It just came to me," exhilaration filled his voice, and he snapped his fingers. "It was so symbolic. Why didn't I see it before?" He pranced back to the ladies.

"Arthur told me about seeing Oliver on the Common." He unconsciously looked toward the center of town. "Shortly after the mock trial, Arthur was walking toward the Common, and there was Oliver, his bags tied to his mare, sitting astride that big chestnut. Arthur called to him, but he was too far away. He quickened his stride but didn't make it before Oliver rode off." He looked back at the ladies. "That's it." His excitement exploded from his eyes. "I see it now. It all makes sense." He stepped away from the porch so that he could act out what he meant.

"Arthur said Oliver sat there on his horse a moment in the center of the Common looking in all four directions and then rode off." He spoke with his hands in complete stimulation.

"So?" Abigail inquired for both of them.

"You see," James explained, moving in each direction as he spoke. "He looked first to the west, toward his ancestral home and knew he couldn't go there. His father had disowned him." James turned next to his left. "He looked then to the south, toward New York. But he couldn't go there either. He had ruined a young lady there his reputation would prevent him from returning." James then turned completely around. "He then looked to the north, toward the academy here. And he couldn't go this way either." He looked over his shoulder at Janet, "Because you were here. So he headed in the only direction he could," James turned to the right and pointed with his hand, "To the east. It is the only place he could start anew."

James shook his head and looked down at the ground in mock respect. "You know I almost feel sad for him." He looked again at Janet, suddenly remembering the sensation of Oliver's hand on his throat. Had he been planning to leave before the mock trial? James could not answer the question. All that he knew was that he was here; entertaining Janet Fellows and Oliver was not.

Janet's face looked tired and sad. "I've talked too much," James scolded himself and remembered he was leaving. "Well until tomorrow." He tipped his hat and walked off.

* * * * *

Depression can be like a fog. Rolling in from the ocean, depression blankets you, causing your vision and thoughts to be blurred from reality. You can stumble about, not truly able to see clearly for weeks, years, and even a lifetime. Or depression can be a hammer that slams down hard on your head blacking you out from reality, forcing you to crumble to the ground defeated, unwilling to go on.

For Janet, the tears came unchecked as the hammer hit dead center of her heart. James' words were the hammer blows, but somehow she had managed to keep the tears concealed until he had turned away. Abigail's comforting arms did not help her. They simply could not protect her from the hammer's solid metal head. Janet was devastated, absolutely devastated.

"Why?" She questioned. "Why did I get sick? Why had I failed Oliver? Why?" Her fantasy world crashed around her, to paraphrase James. But it was true about her. So much hope had sprung to life inside of her, because of their relationship. Now that hope, appeared gone, lost in time and her heart.

Sobs came over and over. She could not face the fact that hope could vanish.

"James could not have lied," her mind argued.

"But he had to have, otherwise what was left?" Janet's heart responded, between the sobs. Heartbreak reared its evil head, fogging all that she knew, as thoroughly as scarlet fever.

Tears continued to wet her cheeks as the reality of her world dawned. Two weeks of hallucinations, foggy visions, and fever-triggered dreams had left Janet unsure of the truth and fantasy. All that she knew for sure was that Oliver was not there with her.

Now sitting in the setting sun of Litchfield, she had heard the worst news of her life - Oliver was gone. And only Abigail's arms were there to comfort her.

"Could I have been fooled by Oliver?" A voice of doubt asked. It came from that cynical side of Janet that had ruled her life as an adult in Harmony. "Could he have only wanted to make love to her and then walk away?" The question hurt, physically hurt for it appeared to be too true.

Janet tried to cut through the weeks of illness to recall all of Oliver's words and actions that night in the stables. That would answer the horrible questions now festering in her heart. "Did Oliver really love her? Why did he leave? Was she the cause?"

* * * * *

Janet's eyes snapped open. The darkness of the night mixed with the glow of a three-quarter moon just outside the room's only window cast weird shadows. Janet's heart thumped with fear caused by its sudden ripping from the dream world to the present. She did not move, something in her head told her someone was watching her.

Panic played with her heart twisting it, tickling it to pump louder and faster. Her eyes darted around her, trying to take in as much of the room as she could see, without moving her body. If there was someone in the chamber, what were they doing there? Was it Abigail checking on her? Was it a teacher from the academy? Was it Oliver?

A week had gone by since her conversation with James on the back porch. In that time she had been sleeping several hours a day trying to regain her strength. Her room had been vacated except for her shortly after both Janet and MaryEllen had come down with scarlet fever. The other three had been lucky enough not to be infected. Janet knew from outbreaks in Harmony that scarlet fever was a picky killer. Three children in one house could all be exposed, but only one might get the fever. It was god's will; the ministers would say to the mother of the dead child.

Harmony had had an outbreak of scarlet fever just before she had left. She was well aware of its killing power. It had taken the lives of ten children in the town, ten of her students who had one day dreamed of being farmers, lawyers, and presidents. Now they were in the grave, attacked by a silent killer who seemed to strike perfectly healthy children overnight or within a day of a friend or family member taking ill.

She had seen the children's strep throats turn into a high fever and knew they would cause rheumatic fever, which affects the heart. She had observed the bodies showed the outward sign of the disease in the form of strawberry or pink rash patches all over the neck and chest. These spots dried out in a week or so like sunburn and peeled off if the victims lived.

They lived; if they were lucky enough not to have the disease attack other parts of their bodies. As lucky as she was, this time, she still suffered. The strep not only gave her the fever but also weakened her tonsils, causing them to become inflamed. The hallucinations, the dizziness, the weakness and the vomiting were all the result of this infection. She still felt some of these symptoms. No medicines were available that could stop the killer, only time.

"It's God's will," she heard the saying again. Janet did not believe that, but she was not in a position to allow her to speak up against the minister. She knew it had to do with something else, something weak inside the child, something the child did not have. That was her opinion.

She thought about MaryEllen and herself. The little child had been new to the school. She had come from an area totally different than Litchfield, just like herself. They shared the same bed, one on top of the other, and closer than they had been to the other girls. One or the other had the fever and gave it to the other.

The shadows moved again, and Janet's heart jumped. There was someone in the room! She was positive. Someone was there. The goose bumps crawled up her back. The new skin that had replaced the scarlet fever rash seemed more sensitive than her skin before the fever. She listened.

A low wind blew outside the building, scraping a branch against the clapboards. A distant door creaked back and forth with the wind. Maybe there was breathing, a quiet mouth breathing in her room.

"Do I move? Do I confront the visitor? What if it was a thief?"

The wind outside grew louder, pushing stronger against the walls. The school buffered the full force of the wind causing sharper wines and bumps among the shutters and windows. The branches scraped and clapped harder against the clapboard, and then stopped as the outside force slackened. Janet remained still, reaching out with her ears to hear anything new. A loud wind came again filling the academy with another burst of wines and scrapes. Still, Janet froze in bed, pretending to be asleep, listening.

The breathing vanished.

Janet waited an eternity in her mind, before slowly raising her head up. The room was dark, only slightly illuminated by the moon, but she could still see the chair and table across the floor from her. The shared dressers were in place, and her door stood slightly ajar, as she had left it. Nothing seemed out of place. She snickered to herself. "You're just scared of the dark." Her voice helped ease away some of her panic that had shot adrenaline through her body. "You're just lonely." She did miss having company in the room at night. But she was quarantined until the doctor felt any scarlet fever had dissipated from her system.

A new strong wind hit the academy, and a distant door,

most likely an outside door banged against a wall. The thud resounded throughout the school building, and again Janet jumped. A different wind slammed the door shut, and Janet could hear, or at least imagined, other bodies throughout the school waking, turning in their beds and listening.

It was then that she noticed the faint hint of lilacs on the air. The flowers had been blossoming in the neighborhood of the school, but the academy itself did not have any bushes in its yards. She sat up to smell the fragrance better. It always reminded her of spring in Ohio and her youth. The family farm had one small bush next to the house, but the school had a row of them alongside the building. How they had gotten there, no one knew. Why the town fathers had not dug them up, Janet did not venture to guess. She only knew they had been there when she was attending the school. Luella always brought a small bouquet of them into the building the second they came into bloom. Each day after that, it was the duty of one of the students to cut and place a new batch in the water bowl the teacher maintained at the front of the room.

Janet stretched to relieve the tension left over from being scared. In doing so, she looked again at the chair and a small table in the room. There in the middle of the table sat a blossom of lilacs propped up in a tin coffee cup.

Janet's eyes grew wide. She quickly scanned the whole room. The flowers had not been there when she had gone to sleep.

Where did they come from? She shook in fear. Someone had been in there. Someone had left the flowers.

"It had to have been Abigail." Janet spoke out loud, hoping her voice would reassure her. It did not. She stared at the tin cup and the flowers. The smell grew stronger in her mind. "No one else would have come here." She said. "No one would dare."

But deep in the back of her mind, two names bounced around, Oliver and Luella. These were two names that not connected, except in her fantasy world of the caviler. The caviler she had watched ride away over and over throughout her life.

She slipped out of bed and walked over to the flowers. The smell triggered a relaxing sensation throughout her body. Sitting down in the chair, she placed her face into the blossom. Memories stirred around in her heart and head. Pictures of her life, friends and family flashed back and forth bringing a twinge of every emotion from melancholy to euphoria.

"Who could have brought these here?" She asked herself again. "Abigail would have said something." Her voice filled the quiet room. "She would have, even if I was lying in bed. She would have checked to see if I was awake." Janet smelled the bouquet once more and closed her eyes in thought and delight.

"James." The name slipped from her lips. "James might have." Her eyes popped open and she tried to picture the law student sneaking into the Academy, but the vision would not come. Instead, only Oliver's face, only Oliver's frame appeared in her mind's eye.

She breathed in the fragrance once more, and Oliver's lips touched hers in memory. His taste, sweet with coffee or even salty tears lingered in her mind. His scent reached back from the past and tickled her nose. He would have snuck into the academy to bring her flowers. He would have.

Tears blurred the blossom from her sight. He was gone. She had caused him to leave. It was simply not destiny for her to have her cavalier.

She buried her face into the flower again; hoping the fragrance would eliminate the sorrow she was overwhelmed with.

"No," she sniffed away a tear. "No, you're too strong to allow that to happen." She sat back up away from the flower. "No, I'm a teacher." Her voice grew firm and clear. "I have a responsibility to Harmony. To the children of Harmony to learn the most I can here. And then to bring it back to them." Her heart beat loud once more, fighting back the sorrow and loneliness of which she had opened the door. "No." She stood up strong in her conviction again. "No. He is gone, and so is the dream." She threw her right hand out into the night as if she was physically throwing away the hopes and desires Oliver had sparked inside of her. "I have to go home."

Looking down at the flowers, she knew that James must have brought them. No one else would have been secretive. "I'm sorry James," She spoke to the flowers as if they were the young man. "But I can't. Each time I look at you, I see him. Each time I would kiss you, hold you, love you, it would be a shadow of him in my mind. I can't." She picked up the tin cup and flowers, smelled it one last time, and then deposited it outside the back door.

Her mind was made up. All hopes of ever living in her fantasy world were gone. She knew then and there that she was a teacher. She would go back to Harmony and live out the rest of her life, the matron lady, loved not by a young man from either Maryland or Connecticut, but all the children she had shown the path to academia.

Slipping back into bed she closed her eyes, and dreamed of her cavalier for the last time.

17

The animal sighed heavily as the chestnut mare crest the second of the two large hills located just east of the Litchfield common. It had been several months since it last climbed to the summit that formed the plateau known as Litchfield center. A hint of fall colors played in the air, and Oliver Block realized he had been away far too long. Nearly six months had transpired since he had fled the plateau after the mock trial, but it had taken time, too much time, for things to be worked out. There were too many memories to be overcome, too many emotions to be confronted, explained and conquered. But he had done all that.

Now he just hoped he had not missed his opportunity here in Litchfield by being gone too long. It was a fear that had accompanied him throughout the ride up the two hills along the turnpike road that came from Torrington, Connecticut. He knew that there was no curriculum to either the law school or the female academy. Students came and went after they had achieved the level of sophistication they wanted.

Six months had been bought and paid for by the town of Harmony, was he too late?

He scanned the Common, aware of a homecoming sensation within him. The façade of the Litchfield was as familiar as his clothing. There had been no changes over the summer months, not that he had expected any changes, but it felt good to discover that it was a reality.

The various familiar houses and shops still ringed the common. There remained only the four roads to the green area, north, south, east and west, a compass to the rest of the nation. And the steeple of the Congregational Church still reached toward heaven. It was pleasant to be home.

Oliver glanced behind him. Two rolling hills laid there streaked by East Road, a dirt pathway that led to the rest of Connecticut and beyond. He followed the brown ribbon up and over the far hill, Toll Gate Hill, in anticipation, but the coach was not in sight. "It will be soon." He said, and looked back to the village.

He had sat just like this nearly six months ago, he recalled. In the center of the green knowing that he had to change the world. Well at least change his world.

For days he had watched as Mrs. Pierce's Female Academy students performed their daily singing promenade along the common without Janet Fellows. Rumor had it that she was ill, deadly sick with fever. Then one of her roommates died. The blow came hard to the ex-soldier. He had brought his cursed life to yet another person. Faces from the past haunted him as he finished his preparations for the mock trial.

The words poured from him as they had never before. His inspiration was Janet. She had provided the spark he needed to make his whole argument and summation God sent. He would go beyond the law and venture into the rights of humanity. It was perfect. It was what made good lawyers stand out among the masses of law students. And it was all Janet's words.

Hope reigned in Oliver's head and heart that she would be in the audience when he used her words. It would be a sign from him that she would be everything to him. But she did not come. She could not come. His mind clouded over, and the words were hollow. He knew as he kept looking toward the doorway that he was nothing without the woman from Ohio.

Later as he sat on his horse, he came upon a bold plan. It was a plan he should have thought of sooner, but he had not seen the keys to it until they lined up that afternoon on the Common. The keys only became apparent as he watched Governor Wolcott's buckboard make its way up the dirt ribbon known as the East Road.

It was the same ribbon of a road that he was looking at now for the coach he knew was coming.

Six months before, he had needed money. The world ran on the gold standard, and he had none. His first thought was to return to his father's home, the triumphant son home from the war and with a skill of a lawyer. But that would not have brought him the cash he knew was needed to eliminate the contract with Harmony. So he turned his horse away from that direction. He then looked to New York. Would his patron support the financial freedom of a woman Oliver loved? His daughter originally was to be Oliver's soul mate, could the older man's generous heart be extended over to another non-family member.

The question dangled in Oliver's mind when suddenly the words Janet and Benjamin Arts said formed together, as if in a giant jigsaw puzzle. The resolution to all their problems became crystal clear in Oliver's mind. He spurred his horse to face the academy once, and whispered, "I love you," to his vision of a sleeping Janet. He then turned east and caught sight of the governor's wagon making its way to

Groton.

Tapping Pegasus' flanks, he began his odyssey. It was a long odyssey, one that took him first with Benjamin Arts and his wife to Groton for the birth of a grandchild. Then there was a hunt in Eastern Connecticut for another grandchild. Finally, he made a short jaunt to New York on the coastal packet, and now the long frantic return to Litchfield, racing time.

Again in Litchfield, Oliver dismounted the mare aware how exhausted was the animal. It had pulled through the numerous journeys without a complaint. It was an excellent horse. One, horse for sure, that his father would be proud to have bread. But it one Oliver had nurtured from a colt at the Premont horse stable just outside New York City.

The ex-soldier turned and slowly walked toward the Common, his thoughts on how to announce his return to Janet. He hoped that she had understood his coded message left on her table months before.

If she had understood, then she would be at the academy studying. If not, then everything was for nothing.

He looked down at his dust covered riding coat, breeches, and high black boots. He needed to spruce up, he cautioned, before seeing Janet again. Tapping his chest with his hand to brush off the dust, he heard the bells of the Congregational Church begin to sing.

Looking up Oliver noticed that several people were gathering around the church. Others dressed in Sunday clothes, passed by him, making their way to the structure. Oliver scanned his memory; no it was not a Sunday. He smiled; it had to be one of the countless weddings between the law and Academy students.

Just then two young ladies, apparently students at Mrs. Pierces scurried past him, deep in conversation. "Did you see James?" One asked the other.

"Indeed," one of the girls replied. "He looks so handsome today."

"Well, weddings have that effect on everyone." The first girl giggled. "Even you will look beautiful on your wedding day." Laughter pierced the fall afternoon greeting the joke. The pearls of the laughter, however, stabbed Oliver in the heart.

"James Baldwin Mathers." The name left Oliver's lips with contempt. "No!" Fear gripped his stomach twisting it into a knot. "No." He spoke and looked up at the church where his steps had unconsciously taken him. "NO!" His hand instinctively formed a fist, and for a second he recalled holding the southerner's throat in his grip.

"Oh God," Oliver chocked aware of what he had done. Oliver looked at the doors of the Congregational Church, slowly closing behind the last of the wedding goers. "Oh God, I gave him her!" Jealousy, rage, and complete despair took over the conscious of the ex-soldier.

He had come too late! His mind told him. He had spent too long away without telling her why. It was over; everything he had worked for was over. He looked at the closed doors thinking that were the perfect symbol of his life, love just behind them, untouchable.

"No! Damn it!" He caused himself. "You have come this far for her! You need to show her. You need to take her back. You can." Dropping Pegasus' reins, he darted up the small flight of wooden steps to the closed doorway. He might have come too late, but he had come back! With that, he kicked opened the doors and walked in.

* * * * *

Janet looked at her special dress and cooed with warmth. She and Abigail had been working on this one and one for Abigail these past two weeks. All their studies at the Academy had focused them on preparing for the wedding and the social obligations that would follow. Janet felt the fine linen with her fingers sore from the near constant sewing and smiled a sweet, heartfelt smile. It would be a beautiful wedding; Janet was sure.

She placed the dress over her shoulders and slipped it down to the ground. It showed her figure off with a modesty that she had to maintain as she marched down the central aisle of the church that afternoon. The smile burned at the corners of her mouth. How things had changed during the months she had spent in Litchfield, Connecticut.

Abigail bounced into the room, her dress loosely fitting over her shoulders. "Tie me?" She asked and the Ohio native nodded and walked over to tighten the fabric ties that secured the dress.

Suddenly her heart skipped a beat. "Tie me." The words brought back a memory of a stable, and the warm hands of a man long placed out of her mind. Tears blurred the bow Janet was tying.

"Oh come on," Abigail looked back at her friend. "I'm the one who should be crying, not you." Their eyes met, and laughter erupted from both of them. It shook them, eliminating the nervousness that had been building steadily for the past two weeks. "Remember, only smiles today." The younger woman sounded more in control of her emotions than her years would have hinted.

Janet nodded, not wanting to tell her friend why she had burst into tears. That was a part of her life she had put aside.

"Here let me do you." Abigail said and turned her friend around. "Do you recall that first day we met Arthur?" Abigail absentmindedly talked. "It was during one of those god awful promenades after church. Oliver made me walk with Arthur so he could walk with you." Abigail giggled.

"And you got drunk on the wine at the picnic." Janet shot back.

"And James rescued both of us." Abigail giggled again, reminiscent of her drunken laughter that first day.

"He does that well," Janet added. "Rescue people." She thought about the Maryland native. He had remained in the area for the summer months, working for Governor Wolcott in next town over, Torrington. His contract law background proved beneficial for the mills, and the governor was quite happy with his performance. But everyone in Litchfield knew full well why Mathers had not returned to his home in Maryland.

He was a constant companion of Janet, despite the woman's insistence that she could not ever love him. He continued to write poetry and even accepted the fact that Oliver Block was not his enemy.

Janet had told him it was Jon Coe who had tried to ruin his reputation. After an investigation by James, the two Southerners came to an understanding in a field one morning. Coe left town, his ego damaged.

These facts played in Janet's head as she stood there being tied by Abigail. The South Carolina girl had become close to Janet, closer than even Luella. Again the Ohio lady's heart skipped. That was the second name from her past that had passed through her mind on this day reserved for only future bliss.

Why?

"You are just afraid of the closing of the door." Janet's heart spoke to her mind. "When the wedding is over you see it as a door closing between you and Abigail." She looked over her shoulder at the younger girl. "But it won't happen if you don't let it happen."

Deep inside, however, the older of the two knew well that the two friends would be parting soon, each traveling to their own lives in different states. Travel was difficult, and the two would find it hard to gather together more than once a year if that.

"Please," Janet suddenly spoke from her heart. "Please promise me we'll never forget each other."

Abigail giggled and shook her head. "Silly, why would we?"

"Because we're heading off to different parts of the country," Janet stated the fact no one wanted expressed out loud.

"I don't know what's come over you-all." She looked at her friend in the eyes. "Is it the wedding? God, you-all know that Arthur and I will be right here in this little state. Anytime you-all want to visit just write, and the door will be open." She kissed her friend on the cheek and again Janet's heart stopped.

The last kiss she had received had been in a cold stable, warmed by the pounding of hearts and lustful thoughts. She blushed at the memory, and Abigail misunderstood. "Come on we need to be getting to the church soon."

Last minute adjustments to dresses and hair filled the girls' arrival at the church. They stood just to the right of the central doorway, giggling, laughing, and nervously crying. This moment was what Abigail and Janet had rehearsed for, dreamed of and hoped for all their lives: a wedding, a wedding of momentous importance.

"Are you ready?" They asked each other the excitement within choking the words in their throats. They knew that the whole community would be watching as they marched down the aisle, an aisle they had marched down in white dresses many times before as students. Today marked the end of that designation. They would no longer be students at the Mrs. Pierce Female Academy.

* * * * *

Unexpectedly the center door of the church burst open. The congregation, seated for the wedding turned in horror at the sound of the wood door slamming against the frame of the building shaking the panes in the various church windows. Meeting their wide opened eyes was a tall skinny man silhouetted against the mid-afternoon sunlight. Silence came over the church. The minister, the best man and the groom, standing at the altar looked down the aisle in shock. Instinctively the three stepped back as the apparition ambled into the tension filled structure.

Janet screamed as the door just to her left flew open. Abigail clung to her friend out of fear, and the other members of the wedding party fled up the staircase to the balcony of the church.

For a second nothing else happened and Janet convinced herself that the wind had blown the door in, but then he walked in. Janet's heart instantly recognized his tall frame. Tears of joy blurred his face and she stood shocked speechless by his miraculous appearance.

"Janet!" His voice barked and echoed through the silent church. "Janet Fellows!" it called again. "I have something to say to you before..." Oliver abruptly stopped as he looked from face to face down the central aisle. His eyes locked onto James Baldwin Mathers. The southerner dressed in a new blue suit, with perfect white breeches and waistcoat stepped forward of the party becoming visible.

"Oliver," The man spoke his hands coming up to indicate that the newcomer should step back. "You have the wrong idea." Block looked to the next man at the altar and recognized Arthur. It was the

Connecticut man's wedding not Mathers.

Embarrassment would have crumbled the ex-soldier, but Janet's arms suddenly wrapped around him, and her wet kisses smothered his face. He took her in his arms and hugged her, squeezed her, as if he would never let her go again. Then he tasted her lips, sweet, wet lips. Tears of joy erupted against his face, and he knew he had not come too late.

"I love you." She whispered in his ear.

He took her face in his hands and stared into her dark brown eyes. His clear blues eyes sparkled at her. All the emotions that had built up inside of them flowed into each other, and they could feel the pounding of each other's heart. Then loud as he could, he declared. "I love you." She was not embarrassed by the proclamation. It warmed her and comforted her. It was the one thing only Oliver Block could have given her. It made her whole.

"Miss Janet Fellows of Harmony, Ohio," he continued loud enough for the entire gathering to hear. "I want you to marry me." He stared into her brown eyes. The excitement jumped out and touched his heart again after all these months. He fought back the tears he was feeling and kissed her full on the lips. "Now, in front of this congregation, I pledge my heart to you."

She kissed him deep and passionately there in the sunlight of the open door. Their tongues found each other again and danced a brief second in ecstasy. She then folded her head into his warm longing chest. He blanketed her within his arms and smiled from deep in his heart.

"I love you." Her voice came full and warm. "I love you now and have for all the years that came before."

Just then a horn sounded announcing the arrival of the coach Oliver had so desperately looked for upon the ribbon of East Road. "I have a gift for you." He said pulling her toward the open door. Janet walked with him down the steps in time to catch the eye of the coach driver. The red vehicle, jammed with passengers, both within and on the top halted in a cloud of dust, as the ex-soldier waved his hand.

Many of the congregation joined Janet and Oliver filtering out of the church, driven on by curiosity. "I have a gift for you." Oliver said again, excitement getting the best of his voice. "Well, I have several gifts for you." He walked to the door of the coach and rested his hand on the handle. "First off," he pulled a paper from his frock coat inside pocket. "That is your contract."

Janet took the paper in surprise. "How did you do this?"

"I sold my soul." He mused and then added correctly. "I argued the best case I ever could for you, and someone listened." He opened the door, and an older gentleman dressed in a black three-piece woolen suit emerged. His tailor made outfit matched the finery of the students at the Litchfield schools. He clearly had wealth. "May I introduce you to Mr. Michael Premont the second."

"The lieutenant's father?" she asked.

"Yes," Oliver burst with joy. "Yes, the lieutenant's father." The gentleman laughed and took Janet's hand.

"Young lady I hear that you are an excellent teacher." He looked at Oliver. "You certainly have something magical about you, for you've captured the heart of this rogue. I know that is a hard thing to accomplish. My daughter tried, but I doubt she could ever have succeeded." He looked back at Janet and smiled. "But then it might be better that she failed."

He seemed sad for a second, and Janet remembered that Oliver's fiancé in New York had died. That girl must have been this man's daughter. She looked down at the ground ashamed that she had caused this man sorrow. A finger picked up her chin so that she was looking at the older man again in the eyes.

"Young lady, I have a proposition. I bought out your contract, on the condition that you will be the head teacher at a school I fund." His words spun in her head and Janet could not believe them. She looked at Oliver who had a smirk on his face. It was a smirk that was holding back an infectious laugh.

"You see," The ex-soldier glowed. "I argued that there could be only one person who could educate his grandson." He opened the coach door again and out stepped a young blond boy. But Janet did not see the boy; instead, her eyes were locked on the face of the woman still sitting inside the coach.

"Luella!!" Janet's voice called. "Luella!" The two jumped into each other arms and tears flowed.

There were tears from the two women, the men, and almost the whole congregation.

Several minutes passed before anyone could separate the lost friends from their embrace. Several more minutes passed before Oliver could regain enough control to hug Janet himself. And even more, minutes passed before Janet could find her voice again.

"How?" she asked Oliver, "Why?"

"A friend of mine, named Benjamin once said that children were lovely, but grandchildren make old men young again. I remembered you said that Luella Bates had returned to New London. Benjamin's son lived in Groton, the next town over. I figured that if I could find her than Mr. Premont might help me. I was surprised by how much he wanted to help me."

He looked puzzled at Janet. "I guess you didn't understand my message?"

"What message?" she questioned puzzled.

"The lilacs and coffee cup I left?"

"I remember them but what did they mean?"

"I didn't want to wake you, but I needed to let you know. The lilacs were to let you know I found Luella. The tin cup was to say it was from me and to let you know I loved you and had loved you since that first kiss by the campfire." Oliver blushed with emotion and looked over at Michael Premont. The older man was walking with the young boy across the Commons to look at the village. Beside him walked his adopted daughter-in-law. Janet followed his eyes and watched the family scene. "Mr. Premont wants you to run a school just outside the city if you want." He licked his lips nervously and looked into Janet's eyes, "If you'll marry me."

"God yes," she squalled and threw her arms around him again. They kissed.

Abigail stepped out of the crowd and tactfully cleared her throat. "Can I get married now?"

"If we can be married with you as well," Janet asked. The whole gathering shared the laugh that erupted from the lovers.

"Are you ready now to be married to me?" She looked at Oliver, and the ex-solder hugged her tight. They shared another long full mouth kiss. His tongue tickled her lips, and she allowed it to dance with hers. Her eyes closed, as she relaxed into his arms. A spinning came to her head as hot blood raced through her body and the cavalier never rode off again.